REALM OF FATE

KELLY N. JANE

18TH AVENUE PRESS

1

———

INGRID

Ingrid knew how to breathe once; a moment ago—a lifetime ago. Now, the air seared her lungs. Not with the stench of sulfur, as it should have, but with the cloying scent of wildflowers. A suffocating blanket.

Her heart pounded like a war drum, demanding and steady.

Ingrid attempted to bring her hand up to shade her eyes from the sun, but it snagged on the arm wrapped tightly around her waist. The warm body against her back crept into her awareness, and she tensed.

"Welcome to Alfheim, Ingrid," the dark elf whispered against her cheek.

Flinching from the warm breath, Ingrid pushed herself away from Jarrick. Her knees buckled, and she fell into the soft grass. Her back still echoed with the heat of dragon fire, the blistering inferno loosed from the skies because of Jarrick—the very creature standing before her.

Everyone she'd left in the courtyard on Midgard . . . was dead.

There was no way they could have escaped.

Bile rose as fear of what had become of those she cared for mixed with anger, overwhelming her body. Ingrid twisted and vomited into the turf. Her head spun. *How could this have happened? I shouldn't be alive if they aren't.*

Thoughts swirled in her head until she took slow even breaths, willing herself to calm and take in her surroundings. Jarrick had stepped back when she'd lost her stomach. She lifted her chin and welcomed even the tiniest addition to the distance between them. Ahead of her was a small grouping of tall bushes and beyond that, trees.

If she ran hard enough, perhaps she could get lost in the shrubbery. She had the advantage of her small size and could find a sliver of a space to hide. Then she could run farther. Get away and try a portal of her own. She'd never made one to travel between realms, and it was dangerous if she made a mistake, but what did it matter? The only person she'd hurt was herself. It was worth the effort.

Peeking over her shoulder to be sure Jarrick was looking away, she bolted. She stumbled as she rounded the edge of the first tall gorse-like bush, with its small yellow flowers and straggly branches. There were no footsteps behind her.

I got away! Ingrid slowed a half-step and twisted her neck to peer behind. *Why isn't he following me?*

Before she could turn her head forward again, she ran into a wall. A solid, yet warm and springy barrier. With an *oof*, she fell to her backside in the grass. She groaned a bit as she sat up and refocused her eyes.

In front of her, stood a pair of long, white, slender legs with tufts of hair fluttering above glistening black hooves. She followed the legs up to the majestic arc of an equine neck with a long, flowing white mane. As she continued, her eyes took in the beautiful head, and she gasped.

Between the attentive ears turned in her direction, was a glittery silver spire. It spiraled sharply into the air half the length of Ingrid's body and seemed to glow in the sunlight. The entire horse had an aura, like the sparkle of untouched snow on a sunny day.

Nowhere in her mind could Ingrid's imagination create such a being. She would have thought herself mad if she'd dreamed of something so spectacular.

The large dark eyes of the creature stared at Ingrid as a song-like voice, quiet and far away, played in the back of her mind. Almost imperceptible at first, it grew louder as she kept focused on the majestic unicorn.

Hello, Ingrid.

Ingrid cringed and slid her foot backward. She stared on, wide-eyed and unable to process the voice inside her head. Had she let her mental barriers fall? How did the creature speak to her?

Your barriers are solid and well-crafted, yet they are ineffective on my kind. Have no fear of me, child. It is rare that one from Midgard finds their way to our lands—especially one such as yourself. It is an honor to meet you.

"How do you know who I am?" Ingrid whispered though she wasn't sure if it was out loud or in her head.

For a millennium, the realms have watched the collapse of the spell safeguarding Midgard. It was foretold that Freya's descendant would rise to restore or destroy the protections. Your name has spread throughout all the realms.

A slight shift in the air brought a cinnamon scent, and the flick of the unicorn's gaze over Ingrid's shoulder let her know Jarrick had arrived.

Your strength will see you through with your task. Watch your surroundings and take care, honored one. We will speak again.

Wait! Who are you? Can you help me?

Curiosity dragged Ingrid out of her nervous panic, and she didn't want to miss her chance to understand the beautiful animal.

My name is Vimala. I am the fylgia of King Thelonius. I am at your service should you ever need me.

Can you get me out of here? Take me home?

No, I am afraid I cannot. As a fylgia, I am bonded to the king, and therefore, to Alfheim, but I will do what I can when the time comes. The king wishes you no harm and has concerns about his brother's state of mind.

You are not alone, as you believe, Ingrid. But take heart, you have the strength and ability to save yourself as much as you will others. The foretold events are unavoidable.

Vimala nodded her grand head slightly, careful of the glittering silver horn, then sauntered away. Her unhurried pace disappeared into the trees as Ingrid watched, stunned.

"Those carefully constructed mind barriers that Eir helped you create must not have kept Vimala out. You look as though you're ready to collapse," Jarrick said from behind her. His tone was smug as if he'd known Ingrid wouldn't get far when she ran.

There was also a hint of curiosity. His words seemed to imply she'd blocked him from her mind, at least.

Jorg could hear Ingrid's thoughts. They had believed it was because of their connection to each other. But when she'd trained with the goddess, Eir, Ingrid had learned that any immortal being with the desire to listen could hear her thoughts. After that, she'd studied the technique to palisade her mind.

Ingrid let out a slow breath and turned her focus to Jarrick.

"Shall we head to the palace, or would you like to stumble around in the wilderness for a while yet? You will surely come across others more dangerous than Vimala. Since that would cause trouble for both of us, I'd prefer you to come with me." Jarrick eased into a crooked grin while his eyes narrowed with a predatory gleam.

I'd rather fall on my dagger.

Tears pricked at her eyes as she remembered that she no longer had the knife Jorg had given her. The beautifully carved handle that fitted perfectly into her palm but hadn't helped her save his life. She'd lost that, too, along with everything else, in the courtyard's ash.

She would find time to mourn later. Right then, she needed to stay strong. The battlefield may have changed, but the fight continued.

Ingrid reached for her energies—the healing power she held deep within her core—to calm her nerves and strengthen her body, perhaps even guard against Jarrick. But they were missing.

Not so much gone as they were inaccessible—as if someone or some*thing* had locked them away. She could feel them flutter, but she couldn't use them. They were as much a prisoner as she was.

Ingrid and Jarrick stood on the top of a serene hillside, amid bright green grasses dotted with yellow, orange, and blue. Willowy clouds floated through a purple-tinted sky overhead.

In the distance, at the base of a towering mountain, sprawled a city with buildings of gleaming cream-colored stone. Flags of red and teal fluttered in the center where various multi-colored tents rose above one-story buildings. Above it all, nestled into the side of a snow-capped mountain, sat a castle sparkling like a gem.

It was an idyllic sight. Nausea rolled through Ingrid's stomach. Everything was wrong.

Her view should have been warriors—stretched to the horizon in gleaming battle gear, shrieking and slaying. Axes, maces, and swords flying with deadly accuracy. Berserkers preparing for Ragnarök on the fields of Valhalla.

That's where everyone else was. At least she hoped they were. Would Odin's valkyries choose a dwarf or a half-elf? Would they get a chance for glory in the afterlife? Ingrid had never considered an alternative. What was Alfheim's place for their dead? Was Jorg welcomed there if he wasn't in Valhalla?

There was no doubt in her mind that glory awaited Selby, and Bremen, too, most likely. But what of the others?

She wanted to scream, but instead, she clamped her mouth tight. Inhaling, she'd let the pretentious dark elf have his way for now. "Where are we going?" she asked between clenched teeth.

Jarrick gestured to the city in the distance. "I had thought we'd go into Lyallona, to acquaint you with your new home, but it appears you need time to adjust first. We'll go straight to the palace." He offered his hand to Ingrid, with a look that was clear she needed to accept.

There was a flash of light, and then they were in the middle of a wide, pebbled pathway in front of the main gates to the palace. Ingrid wobbled on her feet, and Jarrick braced her against himself.

"Careful now, you're still weak."

As much as she hated to accept his help, her legs felt like young saplings that couldn't withstand a simple breeze when he ushered her forward.

"Using a portal unexpectedly doesn't help, either," she mumbled. It occurred to her then that it was daytime. The moon had been rising over the embattled courtyard she'd left behind —before Jarrick had ripped her away. "How is it daylight? Twilight had fallen when we left."

"The solar cycle is different. Midgard moves at the hurried

pace of a petulant child. Alfheim has a more reasonable atmosphere for immortal life." Jarrick slipped her hand under his elbow as they headed toward the gates.

"Why didn't we portal inside?" Ingrid asked as she absorbed all the sights.

"There are wards that prevent portals within the palace grounds. Annoying more than anything, but they exist by the king's orders." A hint of disdain laced Jarrick's words.

As they walked through the gates and followed the wide path that curved upward to the glittering building sitting high above the city, Ingrid took special notice of the casual way the guards carried themselves. Unprepared for invasion, they appeared bored as if they were merely ornaments to complete the look of security.

I doubt they've ever had to defend the palace. That will work for me.

Jarrick didn't lead Ingrid to the front of the palace, but instead, they followed a smaller path around to the side. A different set of stairs greeted them, equal in splendor to those in the front, and they led to doors made of glass that shimmered like crystal.

Stone that shone like silver and seemed embedded with tiny diamonds formed the palace walls. Starburst pops of colorful light shimmered off the smooth surface from all directions. Ingrid had to arch her neck to see the top of the palace spires.

From the front, when they'd sauntered up the winding pathway, it had looked like the building was square, but as they stepped around to the side doors where they entered, another long wing extended toward the back. It was impossible to estimate how large the structure was. Ingrid lost count of how many longhouses would fit inside it and gave up trying.

The grand doors opened on their own as they approached.

Not three steps inside the marble-floored corridor, Dúngarr stood waiting.

Bile rose to her throat. The one who had terrorized her family and threatened to destroy her village stood within an arm's reach.

2

INGRID

Dúngarr should be dead, not standing there in front of her as if nothing was wrong. One way or another, she would make him pay for his crimes.

"Hello again, Ingrid. I'm sorry I missed you earlier," Dúngarr said. The implication of her village's demise twisted his lips upward in sinister glee.

Numb to any more pain, she accepted the confirmation of her destroyed family without an outward flinch. In her mind, it made little sense to her why she was left to suffer as the lone survivor. The responsibilities of her destiny required too much. Why did she need to be alone?

"Ingrid is here, as our guest. There will be no more talk of the past," Jarrick commanded. Dúngarr nodded, though it appeared to pain him. "Good, then what other news do you have for me?"

"Urkon has arrived and is waiting in your parlor. He has expressed that you should not delay, as he is busy with many tasks."

Jarrick chuffed with an amused look on his face. "Perhaps

one day he'll truly be as important to the realms as he *thinks* he is." Turning to Ingrid, he met her hardened gaze and glanced down at her fists held tight at her side. "There are rooms ready for you that I believe you will find quite comfortable. Dúngarr will escort you as I tend to my business."

Ingrid snapped her glare from the guard to Jarrick. Flames shooting from her eyes as she saw the hint of amusement in his. She held her breath. The cinnamon scent that surrounded Jarrick flared into a burning sensation in her nose and clawed at her throat. Without her powers, Ingrid had to accept that she was the weakest in the room.

"I'm sure I can find my own way," Ingrid offered. She tipped her chin up and held firm. The rush of blood screamed through her ears.

"As I said earlier, you are an honored guest here, Ingrid. You'll be treated with the utmost consideration."

So valuable that you killed everyone close to me without care.

Ingrid bristled—it might be a gilded cage, but she was no less a prisoner. In her peripheral vision, she saw the momentary curl to Dúngarr's lip. He didn't want to be near her any more than she did him.

An ironic pleasure passed through Ingrid. *Dandelion eater.* That's what Plintze had called the henchman when they'd first met. It made Ingrid smile at her friend's ability to stand against such a threat. She would do the same.

"Follow me," Dúngarr growled as he strode down the hall, not looking to see if Ingrid followed.

With one last glare at Jarrick, she sighed and shuffled after the guard. Deliberate to keep her steps slow, she bit her lip to keep from grinning as she watched Dúngarr slow, so he didn't get too far ahead.

"Keep up," he snapped over his shoulder when they were away from Jarrick.

Ingrid slowed.

She busied herself studying the gleaming cream-colored hallways with plush rugs and golden sconces. Before long, they all blended together, and Ingrid was sure she'd never find her way anywhere on her own. It seemed as though they might have walked in circles, but she couldn't be sure.

Finally, they stopped in front of a set of double doors that gleamed with flecks of gold against polished ebony wood. A circle of interwoven designs was split down the center where the doors met, and as Ingrid peered closer, the looped lines appeared to be some kind of writing.

A flicker in the back of her brain made her search her memories. Like a faint shadow of something she had known before, but it disappeared in the dark corners of her mind.

Just like my powers.

Dúngarr wiped his fingers on his trousers after he pushed Ingrid through the doors. With a hard swallow, she peeked down at herself. A lock of her hair fell across her face, and she brushed the golden strands aside, reminded that her appearance was as disorderly as her mood. The braid down her back had tugged free in spots during the earlier battle. A breeze coming through the open archways on the other side of the room lifted a smell from her body.

Afraid to leave smudges of blood and dirt in the pristine room, Ingrid took several tentative steps inside. From where the curtains fluttered, she could see a balcony and drifted toward the open air.

With a start, she realized Dúngarr was still there. She'd become mesmerized by the large open space. An oval dining table sat to her left with a silver candle holder with more than a half dozen candles. Not a bit of wax dripped down the edges though they'd clearly been lit before.

Beyond the table was a fireplace as tall as Ingrid with over-sized cushioned chairs on either side. Flames sparked to life as she watched, and screams tore at her memory. The smell of smoke and burning flesh searing through her.

"Stop! Put it out!" she screamed and spun to face Dúngarr. Confusion flashed over his features before one corner of his mouth tilted in mocking derision. Yet, he flicked his fingers toward the fire and snuffed it out. Wispy tendrils of smoke left abandoned, wavered until they dissipated.

Ingrid turned away from the guard and closed her eyes. The nauseous feeling rolled to a stop before she opened them again. She needed fresh air.

Ducking past the gauzy fabric as it lifted on its own with a breeze, Ingrid slipped outside. In the distance, she could see the hillside where she'd arrived on Alfheim. Lazy creatures that seemed to be large cats, but had twin horns spiraling from their brows, lounged among the fields of green from her new view. The breeze looped around her and brought more of the insuffer-able floral scent, making her dizzy.

Movement below on the grass surrounding the palace caught her attention. Jarrick spoke with another man as they strolled.

"Spying is a dangerous game, Ingrid." Dúngarr's gruff voice rasped against the back of her neck.

Why won't you leave? Or die? "Who is that?" If the guard planned to stay, he might as well provide her with some information.

Dúngarr raised the corners of his lips but stared with the eyes of a predator. "That's Urkon, the master of all seiðr magic. Once he destroys Freya's lineage, he can take back full control of the power that emanates from the Yggdrasil tree. He'll be unbound and the most powerful force in all the realms. Then all those haughty Asgardians will be reduced to slaves or dead." The tone of his words slipped from admiration to disgust in a blink.

Ingrid peered over the rail at the duo. Jarrick kept his hands held behind his back and stayed behind Urkon's shoulder as they walked. She'd seen many men show the same respect toward her father when they spoke with him.

A shiver made gooseflesh rise against Ingrid's tunic as she watched them. Where she stood seemed as high as the top of a dragon ship mast. She couldn't hear their words from the distance, but she could feel the darkness radiating from Urkon. He was shorter than Jarrick by a head and wore a dark cloak that trailed behind him as he strolled along. The hood laid against his back, lined in a deep crimson, the color of spilled blood.

As she watched, she wondered if Jarrick's plans to restore Vanaheim by overthrowing Asgard might not be his own. He'd said he wanted to bring back the proper leadership, to allow the Vanir their rightful home, and allow beauty and art to flourish again instead of the war-hungry ways of the Aesir. The man he bowed to oozed wickedness.

Ingrid reached out and gripped the rail as her magic shifted, coiling deeper and farther away from her. It was a stifling sensation that made it hard to breathe.

"If all he needs is to kill me, then why am I here?" *Perhaps you don't know as much as you think you do.*

Ingrid did her best to let a cold indifference slide across her face. Inside, she was a trembling mass of fear. Binding the spell wasn't just about protecting Midgard as she'd thought. It was a game between two of the most powerful beings in all the realms. Something about it made little sense.

Why would Jarrick tell her he wanted her to be the queen? Why would he keep her alive if his master needed her dead?

"Do you think I'm only the commander of Jarrick's guard? Information is the most valuable currency there is, and I am very rich."

There was a twitch in Dúngarr's cheek as he spoke. Ingrid stared at where it flashed. What did he gain by telling her so much? There was something else.

You're trying to get information from me. A slight grin tugged at Ingrid's mouth.

Fear slipped behind indignation as she stood tall. Robbed of her family, friends, and powers, she still had something Jarrick needed. Whatever it was, Dúngarr didn't know either, and that made him less of a threat. Ingrid had nothing to lose. That started with pushing the vile being in front of her into his rightful place—beneath her feet.

"You've delivered me to my rooms, now get out. In the future, don't enter without permission."

The twitch surfaced again in Dúngarr's cheek. It was all Ingrid could do to keep her features calm and neutral. After several long seconds, the elf flattened his lips to a thin line and spun away. His anger billowed more than the curtains he slapped aside.

When the door slammed closed, Ingrid sighed and leaned against the railing. As she did, a lump in her pouch pressed against her hip and all her strength melted away. She slipped her fingers around the two rune stones and pulled them out to view.

Both gray stones fit inside her palm though they were heavy for their size. The smooth ovals revealed the carved symbols on one side.

Thurisaz and Othala. Protection and home.

Ingrid slid down and pulled her knees to her chest. The smooth stones etched with her failed destiny broke her resolve. The weight of all that had happened and her grief overwhelmed her. Resting her head on her arms, tears flooded over her cheeks, and she did nothing to stop them.

3

JORG

The stench of sulfur lingered in the air for two days after the dragon attack. They'd dealt with most of the dead bodies and pushed the rubble to the sides, but Jorg's patience had worn thin. He needed to get away from the mess. Most of the food stores had burned, and it was all the excuse necessary.

He'd spent the day in the woods hunting with a handful of other warriors. It didn't take away the gnawing emptiness in his mind from Ingrid's absence, but it helped to calm his spirit.

I need to find you, Ingrid. This silence is killing me.

Bremen had stayed behind, busy organizing the departure of his people back to Ireland under Gavin's leadership. He walked up to Jorg after the hunters deposited their game. A deer carcass hung from a charred crossbeam, and women had already started to dress out a large pile of rabbits.

"It looks like you were successful," Bremen said.

"I don't know if it's enough for their journey across the sea. They'll have to ration." Jorg dipped his hands into a bucket of water and splashed it against his face as he rubbed the back of his neck. Slicking his hair back, exposing the pointed tips of his ears, he stood tall and faced Bremen.

"They'll be careful, and if they have favorable winds, they can make the journey in under ten days. There will be fish, too, and whatever dry goods we can send." Bremen watched the people hurrying about and nodded his head. "They'll be fine," he said, more to himself than Jorg.

"We'll need supplies as well," Jorg said. He wasn't sure how far it was to Svartalfheim, and he wanted to be ready to go as soon as Plintze returned.

"Of course. Gavin should have everyone on their way the morning after next. I'm eager to be on our way." Neither man looked at one another, the silence thick with their fears for both Ingrid and Galwain.

After Plintze had explained there might be a way into Alfheim through the dwarf realm, they'd all agreed to go there. Before they could leave, however, the dead needed to be cared for, which gave Plintze time to find and bury Lazuli. Somewhere in the forest, the little sprite's body lay where it fell after the dragon had plucked her wings. The dwarf had not yet returned, and Jorg was eager to get going.

Across the courtyard, Selby and Gavin's laughing and talking drew Jorg and Bremen's attention. The sound of joy was noticeable among the somber surroundings.

Bremen stiffened as he stared, and it took a good deal of effort on Jorg's part to keep a smile from forming. Selby had always been a shameless flirt around the village, and it amused him that she didn't understand the havoc she caused to his brother.

Brother, ha. We'll see.

The whirlwind of finding his mother and learning that the arrogant prince was his half-brother still hadn't settled within him. It didn't help that the dark elf who'd kidnapped Ingrid and his mother was also his father. Growing up not knowing his heritage, then having it all exposed at once, had been a lot to accept.

"Maybe with the extra food, they'll be on their way sooner," Bremen mumbled as he walked off toward the narthex.

While it might be a moment of amusement for Jorg, it quickly passed. The silence in his mind where he'd grown accustomed to hearing Ingrid's voice echoed his loneliness. The hunting had helped keep him busy but being back with little to do made him irritable. Guilt rode his shoulders like a hawk, and every minute they wasted before getting her away from his father pained him.

My father! What if that's the reason I feel so angry all the time? What if I'm just like him?

Jorg felt useless. They'd finished the hunting, there was no need to repair the damage to the palisade or buildings because no one would stay there, and his pack was ready to go. He kicked out a foot and mumbled to himself about wasting time, but in the dust that surrounded his toe, something else glistened in the afternoon light.

Instantly, he bent down and wrapped his fingers around a smooth object. When he wiped off the dust and grime, he gasped. It was the stone from Ingrid's necklace—her amber one. It must have fallen in the battle and gotten trampled into the dirt. This was the bead that glowed when she healed.

Hjarta, you need this! Don't you?

Squeezing his fingers tight, he let the cool stone mold into his palm as he closed his eyes. If he could only hear her voice, he'd know she was okay. He'd be able to think rationally. But she wasn't there. Only the dull, aching silence.

Standing alone in the middle of the courtyard wasn't the place for him to break down over missing Ingrid. He needed to go somewhere private. Space was at a premium now that most of the buildings were in ruins, which forced everyone to gather into the remaining smaller spaces. The forest was his only option to be alone.

As Jorg turned to head back into the cool shade of the trees beyond the broken gate, Selby's voice rang out to him. Pretending he hadn't heard her quickly crossed his mind, but that was easier said than done. Nearly everyone in the courtyard had heard her and turned their heads to the sound of her voice. Jorg sighed and waited for Ingrid's best friend as she strode closer.

"We need to talk," she said by way of greeting and then gave him no option but to listen. "I've already told Bremen that he needs to take care of this, but you need to help, too. Three of Wilbert's men have asked to speak with both of you. You should listen to what they have to say."

"Why?"

Selby rolled her eyes and put a hand on her hip. "Because they probably have insight we need. Not all the men were in the courtyard when the dragon loosed its fire. Some fled back into the woods. We need to know how many and if they'll continue looking for us. We certainly shouldn't arrive at the doorway to Svartalfheim with a bunch of magic haters following us to their front door."

"That's dramatic, even for you. Why would they bother with us? They fled because there was a dragon planning to char their hides. They have to believe that even if we are alive, it's only because we can somehow command such a creature."

"That's my point. If they're out there and believe they should carry on Wilbert's message, they could come back and outnumber us. We can't risk them trying to fight with us when we need to get to Ingrid and Galwain."

Jorg rubbed his hand over his face and blew out a long sigh into the air. She had a point. He wanted to get on the road and leave all of this rubble behind. Nothing would be right again until Ingrid was back. The amber still clutched in his palm helped to calm his spirit.

"What did Bremen say?" Maybe he could distract her and buy himself some time to get away.

"Turns out the two of you might be brothers after all. He's just as stubborn."

Jorg looked to the skies and tried to ignore her comment even though he wanted to grin. "Maybe he shouldn't worry so much about getting these people on the road. Just make them leave already, and we can deal with how to handle Wilbert's men."

"Yeah, well, some of them needed the extra time to heal." *Because Ingrid isn't here to heal anyone*, she'd left out, but they both knew what she meant. "There's something else that still needs to be done as well, now that you're back." Selby fidgeted with her hands and drew a circle in the ash with her toe. "Wilbert hasn't been buried. There's been a disagreement about whether to bury his body or use a pyre. I used your absence to buy some time, but something needs to happen."

"Why would you wait for me? I have no concern for that man's afterlife."

"I know, but he's your grandfather, too. Bremen has so much to deal with, and I thought it would help him know that he can rely on others."

"I'm sure he has a plan. He seems to feel the need to involve himself with everything. Are you sure he hasn't already taken care of the man?"

"Actually, Gavin had to move the body because it was causing a smell in the nave. I don't think Bremen wants to deal with it any more than you do." She sighed and stared at Jorg. "I think he's keeping so busy with the travel arrangements because he doesn't have to think about that. Would you talk to him?"

Jorg huffed and watched Bremen over Selby's shoulder as he spoke with the cook. It seemed odd that the man who needed to personally assist in every small detail would ignore the burial of his own grandfather. With no more conversation, Jorg stomped off to deal with the uncomfortable family issue.

4

INGRID

Ingrid sat, wedged between the railing and the potted plant until she was numb. Her tears had long since drained away, leaving a burning grit behind her eyes. She wasn't sure she could use her legs to stand if she wanted to.

It didn't matter. Whatever bravado she'd drudged up to use against Dúngarr disappeared. As she sat, her thoughts turned away from her family toward the origins of her pain. Freya had bound her family to a spell that had less to do with protecting Midgard than it did to prove herself the most powerful wielder of seiðr magic. It was nothing more than a game. A political move to establish herself over Urkon, maybe even Odin.

The fact that Ingrid was still alive made little sense to her. If Urkon could defeat Freya by destroying her descendants, then why didn't Jarrick kill her when he first found out who she was?

Ingrid huffed a laugh and pulled up the edge of her sleeve to view the jagged pink scar that ran down her forearm. *He did try.*

She'd survived a dragon attack—with the help of Plintze. The sticky essence Jarrick had shoved into her consciousness hadn't made her bow to him. She hadn't let him pull her away when he came to her in a vision. Maybe there was something she didn't know yet. Something he still needed.

The latch on the door to her rooms clicked open. Stiff and sore, she didn't move. Maybe whoever it was wouldn't see her and would leave.

An elegant hand held back one of the curtains, and a stunning female elf stepped forward to stare at Ingrid. She wore a velveteen gown in a deep purple that gathered at the shoulders with no sleeves. A belt of gold cinched around her slender waist, and her exposed arms were thin but showed the lines of tight, strong muscles. Her hair hung loose, long and straight in the same light blonde color of Jarrick's, and an air of dignity radiated as she approached.

"What are you doing?" Her voice was light and airy but held a tinge of power.

"Enjoying the hospitality of Alfheim." Ingrid chuckled under her breath at how it sounded more like something Selby would say. Her best friend would have been proud.

"Follow me," the woman said before turning to leave. Apparently, she was used to giving orders and wasn't someone sent to care for Ingrid.

Another spy to be my jailor, no doubt.

When Ingrid didn't move, the she-elf peeked around the curtain with narrow eyes before she stepped back onto the balcony.

"If you'd rather stay uncomfortable and hungry, that's fine by me."

Ingrid rolled her eyes and sighed, saying nothing.

"How long have you been sitting there?"

"A while," Ingrid answered with a small voice as she stared at her knees.

With a heavy sigh, the elf fixed her face with the expression one wears after they've eaten something sour. "Grab my hand."

Ingrid gazed at the long, slender fingers and luminescent skin that reached toward her. Then stared at her own hands crusted with dirt, her broken fingernails lined in black.

"Just take hold," the female ordered. Though she sounded irritated, her tone had softened a touch.

Ingrid clamped her jaw tight and latched onto the offered palm. She clenched her muscles, prepared for the effort it would take to stand after so long, but before she could do anything she was on her feet. Pain screamed through her legs. Unwilling to let the runes fall from her other hand, she fell onto her elbow against the railing with a muffled groan as her knees buckled.

"You're expected at dinner, but I think it might be best if you had a warm bath first. It will help your muscles return, and other . . . issues." The last part was more mumbled than spoken.

Ingrid only nodded as she accepted help to walk back inside. Little spikes jabbed into her legs as feeling returned to them. An exasperated groan made its way from her throat. Followed by an angry rumble from her stomach.

Neither woman said anything further as they shuffled through a doorway connected to the main room.

Walls washed in light blue surrounded a tiled floor in a mosaic pattern of white and blue swirls. In the center was a deep pool of steaming water. It was wide enough that Ingrid wouldn't be able to touch both sides at the same time and at least two body-lengths long. The end closest to where they stood had gradual steps leading down into the deep green water.

"If I let go, can you stand on your own?" The elf's voice snapped Ingrid's attention away from the bath.

Still mesmerized by the sights, she stared into the elf's eyes for a couple of seconds to process her words. The shooting jabs in her legs had eased. Ingrid pushed her weight into her feet and released her grip.

"Yes, I'm better now. What is your name?"

"Caelya." She turned away and removed items from a drawer across the room. "Your healing energies are suppressed. I can feel it though I don't know why."

Stunned, yet not surprised, Ingrid shook her head. It made sense, and it made her angry. It also made her question how Caelya would know such a thing.

"How do you know that I can heal?"

Caelya straightened, her arms laden with fabric and toiletries. She arched a brow at Ingrid as if her question made no sense. "Everyone here knows who you are."

Somehow, Ingrid had thought her imprisonment was a secret. That only Jarrick or Urkon would do such a thing to someone. Did that mean the king approved of such treatment? Vimala said he didn't wish her harm, but what did that mean? "How do I release my powers?" she asked between her teeth.

"I don't know, and I only offered the information so you'd understand why you might feel weaker. I haven't spent a significant amount of time with humans. Not in a long time."

Anger welled up in Ingrid. Of course, Jarrick made her weaker. He had all but radiated jealousy over of her time with Eir. *He's afraid of what I know, of what I can do.*

"I wouldn't go that far," Caelya said as she set down some folded fabric near the edge of the pool. "You have some impressive mind barriers, but when you forget to uphold them, it's as if you're shouting into my head."

Ingrid gasped. She'd let herself fall apart so completely that she'd forgotten about the barriers. Seconds later, using the skills Eir taught her, she formed the mental walls to block her thoughts.

"There is a cloth to scrub yourself with and one to dry when you finish. I've also laid out a shift on the bench. You'll find combs and other items to care for your hair and skin on the table."

Before Ingrid could ask questions, Caelya left the room. The hallway door clicked as it closed, and silence descended once more.

Another growl from Ingrid's stomach encouraged her to hurry out of her clothes and step into the fervid pool. She hissed between her teeth at first as she adjusted to the heat. Soon, she relaxed and melted against the side as she sat on an underwater ledge, letting the water lap at her chin.

Steam rose around Ingrid and melted away the tension in her shoulders. While she used the cloth to wash away the layers of dirt from her skin, she contemplated the reasons her magic might be subdued.

When she was in the courtyard battle, she'd unleashed a force against Jarrick that had brought him to his knees. It had been the strongest she'd felt yet. Unlike other times, she hadn't weakened with fatigue either. It was also the blow that destroyed Plintze. The image of his prone, motionless body laying in the dirt filled her mind.

No, I won't think of that. I need to concentrate. Their sacrifices will be in vain if I can't access my power.

Alfheim itself was a magical realm. The elves radiated with power, and it skittered through the air. Ingrid could feel it but couldn't catch it. Why? What was holding her back? She didn't think it was because she was human. Magic responded to magic, not race.

How was Jarrick able to control her? She was already weak from the transition to the new realm, but he had to have done something more. But what?

Reluctantly, she crawled out of the soothing water. Using the larger cloth, she dried herself and slipped into a shift made of a fabric Ingrid didn't recognize. It was softer than a lamb's ear and silky between her fingers. When she slipped it over her head, it hugged her body in a way that made her feel older—feminine.

After the bath, Ingrid realized how content she felt. How could she forget about everything because of a few comforts? What honor did it give to the memory of her loved ones by enjoying the hospitality of her enemy?

Ingrid paced around the room. Caelya had begrudgingly treated her with kindness, but maybe she could befriend her. *What am I thinking? No one is going to help me.*

She needed to find out what Jarrick had done to suppress her magic, but more than that, she needed to get away. If she was far away from Jarrick, perhaps it would break whatever connection he had on her.

The palace grounds were warded, but not beyond the walls. The skies had darkened somewhat. It seemed like as good a time as any to test those guards at the gates.

She had no clothes other than the crusty ones lying on the tiled floor next to the bath. To replace the light, silky underdress with those made her cringe. Perhaps she'd just take the runes and her boots. She'd leave her filthy leathers behind.

Rummaging through the items on the table in the bathing room, she found a small satchel with a long string containing herbs. Lavender, thyme, and one she couldn't determine wafted into the air when she opened it. After dumping the contents, she dropped in the runes and fastened the strings around her neck. The small pouch slid under the dress and warmed against her heart.

Boots tied, she stood in front of the door. Ingrid's heartbeat thrummed in her ears, and she took several deep breaths. Slowly, she opened the latch and the door swung open.

Ha! It's open! Did they really expect I would stay in here?

It was too easy, but she thought no more on it. She'd come from the right, so she sprinted in that direction as hard as she could. After several turns, there was no way to tell where she was. There had been no other corridors so she must be going the right way.

When she'd followed Dúngarr, she'd felt as though she was walking in circles, so perhaps she wasn't lost. It was the way the hallways worked—or so she hoped.

Stopping every so often to listen, she paused as she had several times but heard nothing. Inhaling deeply, she took off again and rounded a corner, smacking directly into the body of an elf. He was dressed in dark brown pants with a matching vest worn over a soft, flowing cream-colored tunic and a royal blue cloak fixed to the shoulders with jeweled epaulets. Darker hair, much the same color as Jorg's Ingrid noticed with a pinch to her heart, accentuated a clean jawline. Ears, tall and pointed, jutted out from his hair the same as all those Ingrid had met so far in Alfheim.

Strong and steady hands wrapped around Ingrid's shoulders and a pair of bright, light-green eyes stared down at her.

"Going somewhere?" he asked with a hint of a grin.

"I don't believe she has anywhere to be." Caelya stepped out from behind the tall elf's shoulder and stared at Ingrid with an arched brow. She smirked as she roved over the nightdress and boots.

No words came when Ingrid tried to speak. Her heart raced faster than a rabbit, and she couldn't think.

"Does she speak?"

Ingrid wasn't sure who the elf was, perhaps a guard or commander, but it didn't matter. She nodded even though she knew he hadn't spoken to her.

Caelya huffed. "Apparently, not at the moment. Let's get her back to her rooms."

"No!" Ingrid finally found her voice. "I . . . just want to look around."

The two elves shared a look, then stared at Ingrid again.

After several heartbeats, Ingrid slumped into the grip still on her shoulders. She knew her escape was once again thwarted.

The trio walked back the way Ingrid had come with no further comment. The halls blurred as she fought to keep the tears from falling, but she noticed they stood in front of her door after only two turns. She was positive she'd run much farther than that.

"Thank you for your kind escort, Kelvhan. I'll take her inside," Caelya said, breaking the silence and snapping Ingrid back to the moment.

"Are you sure you can handle this little wildcat all by yourself? She seems wily," Kelvhan said. The jest at her expense cleared Ingrid's questions about the corridors. She glared up at him.

Caelya opened the door with a roll of her eyes and tipped her head, gesturing Ingrid inside. "We'll talk more after my duties at court," she said to Kelvhan.

"Until then." Kelvhan bowed from the shoulders and strode away with a smile.

Once inside, Ingrid spun to face Caelya. "Why do you have duties at court?"

"It's my responsibility to be at Thelonius's side during certain times."

Thelonius was the king. Ingrid remembered Jarrick saying his name when he'd stolen Galwain. Was Caelya his wife?

"Why would you come to help me earlier? If you're the queen, don't you have slaves who do those duties for you?"

Caelya's eyes glittered as she glared at Ingrid. "First, we do *not* enslave others on Alfheim. That is a primitive and despicable practice."

They stared at each other. Within only a few short moments, Caelya appeared to get her flash of anger under control, and Ingrid absorbed the information.

Ingrid felt conflicted. She agreed with what Caelya had said. As chieftain of their village, her father had ruled against the practice of slavery. How was it that they could keep her against her will then?

"Second, Thelonius is my brother, not my mate. Why were you running? There is no way for you to get to your family."

Caelya's words brought reality crashing into Ingrid like a hammer. All fight left her, and she melted to the floor.

"I had to try." Her voice sounded small and defeated, even to her own ears.

Then Caelya's words echoed in her mind. Ingrid stared up at the elegant figure towering over her. The king was her brother, which made her Jarrick's sister as well—royalty still, yet a princess, not a queen.

But what had she meant? Of course, she couldn't get to her family. She shook her head as she tried to puzzle out why Caelya would have said it. "My family is dead. I just needed to get away."

"The village was empty when Dúngarr arrived. He razed it to the ground in anger, but he found no one." Caelya seemed to find that information amusing.

All air left the room. Sound ceased. A vision of her family, followed by a long line of others from her village, opened before her. They walked over the ridge of a mountain, and everyone carried heavy packs. Children and goats bounced alongside as they all trekked along the path. They had escaped. They were safe!

Ingrid smiled and rose to her feet. She was not alone. More than ever, she needed to bind the spell and protect Midgard. Not the way Jarrick intended, but how Eir had taught her. Nothing but death would stop her.

5

JORG

Bremen was in a conversation over the amount of salvageable dry goods available when Jorg walked up. Jorg remembered how angry the cook had been when Lazuli disrupted her very organized, well-run kitchen. Vevina didn't need Bremen's involvement—he was distracting himself.

"I'm sure the woman knows her business. There are other important matters to attend to that you're ignoring, or so I've been told," Jorg said by way of greeting.

Midway into his next sentence with Vevina, Bremen glared at Jorg. "There are many details to take care of. Each is important."

"I understand that you can't figure out how to dispose of that piece of trash we're both related to."

Bremen glanced at Jorg and then turned his attention back to the flustered looking woman before laying his hand on her shoulder. "Please do as much as you can and come to me if you need anything."

The woman nodded, visibly calmed, though she cast a disapproving glance at Jorg before she scurried away.

What is his problem? He tries to be so nice. It's ridiculous. Just get the work done and move on.

Bremen turned, his jaw set as if carved from stone, his eyes like daggers as he stared at Jorg. With slow steps, he closed the gap between himself and Jorg, who didn't move as he approached.

Standing within each other's personal space, they locked glares.

Each man stood a little over six feet tall, and both were broad-shouldered and determined. Unrelenting. Each was a warrior. They'd fought, they'd led men, they'd lost women they loved. Neither was willing to give an inch.

The air in the courtyard grew thick as silence crept over those standing around, and workers noticed the confrontation near the center of the courtyard. They were Bremen's people, and they watched their leader, wanting to see how he would handle the challenge by the foreigner.

Out of the corner of his eye, Jorg saw Selby looking around. She stepped closer to Bremen.

"Bremen, your people need to see you lead. You need to bury your grandfather, and we need to leave. Get everyone on their way and show them you're in charge." Bremen didn't listen as he continued to stare at Jorg. "Bremen." Selby's voice was more insistent this time, and she touched his arm.

"Selby, step back and mind your place," Bremen said.

Jorg noticed a distinct shift in the air, like a pebble dropped into a calm lake. Anger rippled from Selby.

If someone hadn't muffled a chuckle behind Jorg's shoulder, he'd have thought a bubble had been created around the three of them. Clearly, his brother had no idea what he'd just done. Bremen had said before that Irish women didn't fight alongside their men very often, and he obviously had no understanding of Norse women.

"Mind my place?" Selby said the words slowly as if confused at first. Then her eyes narrowed, and all her muscles tensed.

Bremen rolled his tongue over his bottom lip before he closed his eyes and slowly turned toward Selby. "Step aside. We'll talk later."

As Bremen started to turn and face Jorg once more, his head snapped to the side. His eyes flew open, and he roared as he spun to face Selby. She was massaging the knuckles of her right hand, the one that had just connected with Bremen's jaw.

Jorg had to bite his lip to keep from laughing out loud. He crossed his arms over his chest and smirked at Bremen. "I can wait to see what's left of you when she's finished."

Jorg slid his feet back three large steps, giving room for the new battle brewing in front of him. A second later, he caught a glimpse of Gavin sidling up next to him, the slight grin on his face matched Jorg's.

Bremen rubbed his jaw and stared at Selby.

"Don't you ever, *ever* speak to me like that again," Selby said. "I'm *every* bit a warrior as you, and I'll not be dismissed like a child."

"Never strike me," Bremen snapped back. He stepped closer to her, his fists bunched at his side.

No one worked anymore in the courtyard. In fact, they had crept closer, creating a circle around the two. Everyone wanted to watch the challenge.

It looks like they think this is a better show than the one with me would have been. They're smarter than I thought.

Selby didn't look like she had a care in the world. She didn't mind if everybody watched. Jorg let a chuckle escape even though he tried to stop it. Despite the circumstances, he would enjoy watching Selby defeat his newly met younger sibling.

"Are we taking bets," Gavin asked while keeping focused on the duo.

"Only a fool would bet against Selby."

"I'm inclined to agree with you. I think I'll just watch," Gavin said with a chuck to Jorg's shoulder.

In the center, Bremen and Selby still sized each other up. It looked as though Bremen expected her to back down, but Selby stood taller, settling herself into a wide stance. Her fists clenched and her shoulders back, yet relaxed. There was a reason she hadn't lost many fights when she trained. Only her sister could regularly best her, making them the two finest young shield-maidens in the village. Jorg doubted that Bremen had ever been challenged by a woman before. *This is going to be fun.*

"My argument is not with you, Selby," Bremen said in a low rumble that carried through the air.

"No? That's interesting because I thought you were struggling to remember how to lead and needed someone to teach you. I'm confident I heard you ask me."

Bremen rubbed his hand over his face and sucked in a deep breath. "I'm sorry if you didn't like the way I spoke. Just stand back, and we can discuss the situation later."

Jorg flicked his eyebrows while he glanced to the sky, stifling a laugh. He remembered how he and Ingrid had bantered once when they were training. She'd almost killed him, but he only thought of her fingers touching him when she healed his wounds. Choking his feelings before they overpowered him, he returned his focus to the present.

A few muffled chuckles came from a group of younger men across the circle from Selby. She kept her eyes trained on Bremen, but Jorg could see the white lining her knuckles and knew she was about to unleash her anger.

A shriek rang through the air, and Selby barreled her shoulder into Bremen, shoving him back into the waiting circle. Eager for the entertainment, the crowd bounced Bremen once again into the open area.

Hollers and cheers, some in support and some in jest, came from voices all around the circle. After the intensity of fighting dragons and dealing with so much death, it seemed that the men and women needed a diversion.

Bremen tried to sweep Selby's legs out from her, but she jumped into the air just in time. As she landed, she darted forward and struck a blow to the back of Bremen's shoulder. He spun and lashed out with his arm, connecting to Selby's side and caused her to stumble backward.

Neither of them had weapons, which gave Jorg a surge of relief. He didn't mind letting Selby beat up the smug mongrel, but he didn't want anyone to get killed either. There had been enough death to those he loved lately.

Not that I love him—or her, for that matter. What is wrong with me? Pay attention. Jorg didn't know what came over him. There were too many emotions to process; that was all. It had to be.

Bremen and Selby circled each other again. It was clear that Bremen didn't intend to attack. He might defend himself and land a blow or two, but he had a look on his face that said he enjoyed the sparring.

Several of the comments that came from the crowd seemed to indicate they thought it wasn't going to end in bloodshed either. A woman yelled a particularly crude suggestion to Selby about how to distract Bremen that made Jorg snort and shake his head. Apparently, this fight had turned into a sporting event, at least to everyone except Selby. She was angry and getting more so the longer the battle went on.

Lunging for an attack and then retreating, her form was excellent. She was a bit slow, Jorg thought, and he decided to work with her when they finally started on their journey to find Ingrid.

Selby was plenty skilled in the straight forward tactics of brute force, but she could use a little finesse. That's one of those things Jorg's dad used to grumble about. How he could move so fast and slide in and around others, so they lost track of him. When he was growing up, he thought it was just because he was fast or too clever for his opponent. Now, he knew it was his elven blood.

Selby tried to tackle Bremen once more, and he managed to sweep her over his shoulder so she landed on her back in the dirt behind him. Someone, a woman Jorg suspected, tossed a spear to the ground near Selby.

That was not a good idea. She bounded to her feet and tossed the spear from hand to hand with a smile on her face. Evidently, she'd forgotten all about any feelings she might have had for Bremen. It was a fight, and she intended to win. The playful smirk Bremen had worn through most of their sparring disappeared.

Bremen held up his hands. "Selby, this has been fun, but let's not get out of hand. Put the spear down, and I'll concede," Bremen called out to her. His tone was such that he sounded as if he were speaking to a child, but partially to a wild animal—and that part was far more accurate.

"You need to apologize," she answered.

"For what? You attacked me."

"Then I guess you still don't understand. You must not yet know where my *place* is." Selby stopped playing with the spear and readied it in her hand for an attack. Her posture telegraphed that she would soon charge. Jorg added that to the list for training later.

"I do understand. Please forgive my lack of tact in thinking you an ordinary woman."

"Ha!" a woman from the crowd cried out.

"Take him down, Selby," a different female voice hollered.

Several other feminine, and masculine, voices rang out. Jorg scratched behind his ear and shifted his feet. His brother would not come out of this well. If he overpowered Selby, the women would grumble and complain, and they might *forget* to make the next few meals. However, if he let her win, he might just be in jeopardy of losing the trust of some of his men. From the looks on several of their faces, they had started to believe in Ingrid's best friend.

The two circled each other again, and it seemed as though Bremen was contemplating the same thoughts as Jorg. When Selby made her next charge, she feigned right and before Bremen could counter, she swung the spear from the left. It was a good move, and Jorg might have fallen for that one, too.

Bremen's feet flew out from under him, and he landed in the dusty ash with a thud. A whoosh of air expelled from him, and Selby let the tip of the spear hover an inch from his throat.

"Yield," she said.

Bremen lay in what looked like a daze while he caught his breath. Selby waited patiently, her eyes focused on his face and her spear held steady. There was not a bit of remorse or regret in her expression.

When Bremen finally moved, he slowly brought his hands up as if to surrender. That's when Jorg saw the twitch in Bremen's foot. Selby stood with one foot on either side of Bremen's leg. Before Jorg could call out to Selby, Bremen slammed his legs together. He grabbed the spear and pulled with his arms as his legs pushed Selby in the other direction. She let go of the spear to catch herself as she landed on her side. Half of her face buried into the dirt.

From a sheath that Jorg thought must have been under Bremen's shirt and between his shoulder blades, he pulled out a foot-long dagger. He'd had the weapon the entire time. Now he pinned Selby to the ground and lay the blade flat against her throat, keeping the sharp edges away from her skin.

"I won't yield, but I will offer a truce," he said just loud enough for the quieted crowd to hear. Then he leaned in and said something else. Jorg was sure that he, with his extra keen hearing, was the only one who could hear the proposition Bremen made.

Selby relaxed and nodded. Bremen stood and offered her a hand up, which she took and easily jumped to her feet.

"A fine warrior and my match in every way," Bremen said with a smile and a bow.

Cheers, laughter, and a few grumbles erupted from the crowd as it began to disperse. Bremen replaced his dagger, and Selby rubbed her face against her shoulder. Dirt and ash still covered both of them, and the scent of stirred-up sulfur lurked in the air. The spark that lingered between them when they looked at each other, however, created an ache that threatened to tear Jorg's chest apart.

6

INGRID

Ingrid's family was alive. The idea battled for position in her mind. Could it really be true? Were they able to escape, or had she only envisioned what she wanted to see?

The possibility was all she needed to believe. It was reason enough to get back home. If her family might have a chance at a new life, she was their only hope. Wherever it was they settled again, they would need Midgard to be safe from invasion by the other realms.

Ingrid wandered to one of the chairs before the cold fireplace. She ran her fingers over the expertly woven fabric.

Whatever her mission took, she'd see it through. She'd follow the destiny set out by the Norns for her life and bind the spell. It would give her family a better life and defeat Jarrick at the same time. The perfect revenge.

Though, she wasn't sure how to do it anymore. Eir had trained her to use the well at the base of the Yggdrasil tree in Asgard. It also required her bead.

Ingrid's hand rose to her chest. Where the amber used to rest before Greer had ripped away as she fought him in the court-yard. The runes lay heavy against her skin instead.

"Did you not know that?" Caelya asked, causing Ingrid to startle.

So lost in her thoughts, Ingrid had ignored the princess. "No," she whispered and turned away. Her stomach turned on itself, and it became harder to breathe. Her family might be alive, but she would never see them again.

"Then perhaps that gives you a little encouragement to help Jarrick in his plans to protect Midgard." A vase of flowers sat on a table near the door. Caelya fussed with several blooms, perking up the arrangement.

Ingrid scoffed. "Jarrick wants to enslave humanity, not safeguard them. He wants the veil to drop and allow other realms to invade." Whoever Caelya thought her brother was didn't match what Ingrid knew of him.

Because of Jarrick, Jorg and Selby had died. Because of Jarrick, she'd accidentally killed Plintze. Because of Jarrick, her life was torn apart.

"I don't believe you have all the facts—which are not mine to share. My brother may be overzealous in his methods, but he would never enslave anyone." She kept focused on the flowers as she spoke, tipping her head as she eyed their placement.

Stunned, Ingrid shook her head slightly. "You should ask him. Find out what he truly wants for the future of the realms and see how that matches up with your Alfheim ideals." *Everyone treats me as if* I'm *naive.*

"Thelonius is aware of the situation and monitoring it closely. Urkon is an honored Vanir and must be given full respect and privileges on Alfheim. The king knows that his influence on Jarrick has become an issue. It's why you're here instead of Montibeo."

Was it the king, not Jarrick, keeping her locked in her rooms?

Ingrid clenched her hands tight at her side. "What does that mean—an honored Vanir? Does the king know he's risking a new war between the gods?"

"That's absurd. The elves and the Vanir are related, cousins so to speak. Our duty to them has never disappeared. Many fled Vanaheim and came to settle here. The old ones, who wanted to preserve their independent heritage, live in Allanar. They are allowed sanctuary, and Thelonius won't disrupt the peace we've shared." Caelya faced Ingrid, finally satisfied with the flowers.

My father would never allow such things. He'd have protected his people long before, not turned a blind eye.

"Your king is weak if he'd rather allow other realms to suffer so he can avoid his own discomfort." Ignoring Jarrick and Urkon's use of the dark arts without check seemed like too high a price to Ingrid.

Caelya glared, her mouth tight. A flicker of fear skittered through Ingrid. Perhaps she'd said too much. She steadied herself and decided she hadn't. The truth was the truth whether anyone liked it or not.

"It is not a matter of avoiding anything." Caelya sneered between clenched teeth. "Thelonius understands that we must choose our battles wisely. Rushing forward with rash behavior only leads to disaster."

The elves only considered themselves, that was clear. The king didn't want to disrupt his own realm for the sake of the others. That meant he wouldn't help stop Jarrick or Urkon. If humanity suffered, that was just a reasonable casualty.

Not to me! I'll have to find a way to defeat Jarrick myself.

Ingrid stepped closer to the princess. Something else Caelya had said pierced through her thoughts. "Where is Montibeo?"

"It's Jarrick's personal residence. He's been more sullen and angry over the last decade, staying up in that cold, dark place. It used to be his favorite place to go for time alone to think and have space away from court. I spent many happy times there, myself." Caelya's expression softened as she looked lost in a memory. Then she stiffened, and her features hardened. "Now, it's where he practices the more questionable aspects of the seiðr magic he learns from Urkon."

Why would the king turn a blind eye to such a thing? "And that's where he would have taken me, except the king said to trap me here instead?"

"You're not trapped. Don't be so dramatic." Caelya fidgeted with a bracelet on her wrist. "You're a guest, one that will dine with the king at this evening's meal, in fact. Having you stay here was just a precautionary measure to ensure your safety. I'm sure that Jarrick has no plans to hurt you, though Voxx might not agree." Caelya flashed a wry smile.

Ingrid huffed. She *really* didn't know her brother as well as she thought. "Who is Voxx?"

Caelya tipped her head to the side and eyed Ingrid as if she contemplated what to say. "Jarrick's fylgia. Do you understand what that means?"

Ingrid shrugged. "I met Vimala earlier. She told me she was bonded to the king and Alfheim, but I wasn't sure what that meant."

"A fylgia is an animal that chooses another to share a special bond. One that integrates their souls. They become interconnected and communicate spiritually. If the bond is severed, the fylgia dies, which is why they are so careful with whom they choose. Only royalty can be considered for a bond, and not everyone is granted the privilege."

"Is Voxx a unicorn also?"

Caelya chuckled quietly under her breath. "No, certainly not. Voxx is a dragon."

The air took on a sudden chill. Pebbles rose on Ingrid's skin, and the scar on her arm ached. She thought of the time she'd come face to face with the gigantic dragon who'd given it to her. How Jarrick had used it to speak to her. The realization hit her that the glittering black creature scorching the courtyard had been the same one.

"Is she large and as dark as the sky at winter solstice?" Ingrid asked as she stared into space watching the memories play in her mind.

"Yes. She is the largest of all. The dragons keep their nests in the mountains near Montibeo, and she chose Jarrick when she was little more than a hatchling before it should have been possible. Their bond is especially close."

I killed the wrong dragon. "Does it work the other way? What happens if the fylgia dies?" Could that have stopped all the death and destruction in the courtyard? If she'd known, she could have saved everyone.

"No, not in the literal sense. The spirit of the fylgia merges into their chosen partner. The death of a fylgia is said to be like the severing of all emotion. It causes madness and mental clarity deficits, but not death. It has only happened once, long ago."

Of course, it wouldn't have killed Jarrick. That would have been too easy. Was there any way Ingrid could rid herself of his hold on her? Everything that had gone wrong was because of the dark elf. To defeat him, she had to find out how he could stifle her magic. She needed the power she'd drawn upon in the courtyard. Then she could stop him and avenge the death of her friends.

"Thankfully, Voxx is not allowed to roam near Lyallona, so you won't see her here. Besides, I think both she and Jarrick have been happier lately since his wife's return."

Ingrid snapped her attention to Caelya. "His wife is here? Are you speaking of Galwain? She's here in the palace? I need to speak with her!"

Of course, Jarrick would have brought Galwain to Alfheim

when he stole her away. It was also when he'd found out Jorg was his son. He'd said he wanted them to be a family again. Did she know he'd lied and instead came back to kill their son?

Caelya whirled around and towered over Ingrid, pinning her with a narrowed glare. "How do you know Galwain?"

7

INGRID

Ingrid saw no reason to hide her connection to the queen, but she internally recoiled at discussing her relationship with Galwain's son. "We met a few days before Jarrick stole her. I know . . ." The thought made her throat swell and her eyes sting. Pain tore at her heart, and she couldn't continue.

"Galwain has stayed away from her homeland for many years. How is it that within days of her return, Jarrick finds her and brings her back here? What connection is there with you?" Caelya spoke with a measured and direct tone, leaning closer to Ingrid.

"I was friends with her son." Ingrid forced the words past the lump in her throat.

"Which one?"

Silence echoed off the stone walls as Ingrid stared. She'd been deliberate in inferring a single son, yet Caelya knew there were two. Jarrick hadn't known that.

"What . . . what do you mean?" Ingrid tried for nonchalance even as she stuttered.

The princess closed her eyes and drew in a deep breath before letting it out. "When I first met Galwain, I hadn't yet reached my age of maturity. We became fast friends and spent much time together. Our mutual carefree youthfulness made for many fun adventures whenever Jarrick would travel." She looked over Ingrid's head into the air, and her eyes shone with softness as she spoke. Then as she hesitated, her expression cooled.

"As I neared my confinement, Galwain found out she was pregnant. She was near her term when I left for Sodell . . ." Caelya's words trailed off, and she smoothed nonexistent wrinkles from her skirt. "She broke her promise to Jarrick and Alfheim. That's all that matters now."

Caelya started for the door, but Ingrid hurried to step in front of her. Determination and strength lined her face.

"He killed him. Has he told you that?"

"What are you talking about?" She was irritated, either at Ingrid's presence in her path or the conversation, it wasn't clear.

"Jorg—Alberich, as you might know him. Jarrick killed his own son."

The luminous features of Caelya's skin paled. Her chest rose and fell harder, and she slid her foot backward. "That's not true. If he found his son . . . He would do anything to have a relationship with him. You're mistaken."

Ingrid stood firm and kept her features steady as she let her silence confirm the information she'd shared.

"Why would he do that? Does Galwain know?"

"Galwain left before it happened, so I doubt that she does. She had another son—as it seems you're aware—born later after she fled from Jarrick. He is dead, too."

"Why?" The elf's voice was impatient and sharp.

"He wanted me and what he thinks I can do for him. Nothing else seems to matter. He called two dragons upon us. I killed one," Ingrid huffed at the wry satisfaction it gave her, "but the other, Voxx, was unleashing her fire as Jarrick snatched me here."

Neither woman said anything. The air heavy with grief.

Turmoil churned within Ingrid as she thought about facing the queen. One part of her ached for their shared loss, but another still burned with anger at how Galwain had abandoned Jorg. Ironically, had she let him grow up with Jarrick, he would still be here, safe and alive. Did that mean his death was Galwain's fault or Ingrid's?

No! She squared her shoulders and glared.

Jorg was dead because of Jarrick and his obsession with restoring Vanaheim. His belief in Ingrid's powers to help him overthrow Asgard and the part he wanted her to play in his new regime. Galwain was as much a victim of Jarrick as Ingrid. Perhaps, they could work together to destroy him.

"Can you arrange for me to see Galwain? I'd like to be the one to tell her."

A knock on the door startled Ingrid, and she noticed Caelya shudder before she called out for whoever it was to enter. The air chilled when the door opened.

"Aguane." Caelya nodded a greeting. "Help Ingrid dress and try to make her presentable." Ingrid saw the eye roll she offered the newcomer. "She is expected at court, so please work quickly."

Caelya strode through the door without looking at Ingrid again. She'd avoided answering whether she would help Ingrid meet with Galwain. Why?

There wasn't any more time to contemplate an answer as Ingrid realized the new stranger was definitely not an elf.

Ingrid swallowed hard and tried not to stare. The female didn't concern herself with Ingrid's worries, however. She glided to a gown draped over the back of a chair and separated out the pieces it required.

She was tall, slender, and wore a flowing gown that looked more like mist than fabric. The way Aguane moved made Ingrid wonder if she had actual feet or was floating. She could have been using the transparent, shimmering wings attached to the back of her shoulders, but they remained folded tight against her back.

Long hair of snowy-white matched her skin, and her gown flowed over her shoulders like icy tendrils. But it was her crystalline eyes, so light blue they almost glowed, that made Ingrid suck in her breath.

She'd never heard of a being like the one before her, except possibly a valkyrie, but Eir held that title. This woman had to be something different. While Ingrid gaped, Aguane arranged the clothing Caelya had left during her earlier visit. She turned, radiating an essence that wrapped around Ingrid. Before she'd consciously decided—or maybe she had—Ingrid stepped forward to get changed.

When the woman finished, Ingrid wore a gown of turquoise that matched her eyes and hugged her newly realized curves as it opened into a v-shape down her chest. A belt of silver threads, woven with tiny jewels of sapphire, garnet, and amethyst, circled her waist. Long sleeves, ending at a point on the back of Ingrid's hands, were snug but not restrictive.

Beckoning Ingrid to follow her, Aguane glided toward the bathroom. She had Ingrid sit on a bench and brushed her hair. Unlike the painful effort it took Moirin to arrange her hair when she stayed in Bremen's camp, Aguane worked with deft, gentle fingers.

While her hair was guided into place, Ingrid allowed herself to think once again about Galwain. Ingrid may not ever see her own mother again. Neither would Jorg. Galwain had lost Jorg when she gave him up as a baby to keep him safe from Jarrick. Now Ingrid had lost him too because of the dark elf.

It was time for him to suffer. Jorg had told Ingrid about how he couldn't hear her voice in his head anymore when she'd gone away to Asgard. The silence had nearly driven him mad. Eighteen years of that had to have affected Jarrick.

If Ingrid could talk to Galwain, she could teach the queen how to block her mind. That might make Jarrick vulnerable, then he'd lose his grip on Ingrid's powers. She and Galwain could escape together, and Ingrid could find a way to the Yggdrasil tree and bind the spell. Everything would be made right.

Aguane applied kohl to Ingrid's eyes, then held a hand mirror out for her to view the results. No longer in braids, Ingrid's blonde hair cascaded over her shoulders in waves with some pulled back from her face to fasten at the back of her head with a golden clasp. It was hardly a practical style for battle, but Ingrid sat up a little taller and pulled her shoulders back. A woman, not a girl, reflected at her. Confident, prepared, and capable.

Caelya had said she would go to court. As if she wasn't a prisoner held against her will. So many people had underestimated her throughout her life. She stared at herself once more. Perhaps it would be easy to lull Jarrick into believing he controlled her. If he wanted her to become queen of his new regime, she'd play along. Her family was alive, and Galwain was nearby. Hope dared to prick at her heart.

If she couldn't defeat Jarrick in battle, she'd pull him down from within his own palace.

8

———

JORG

With Selby and Bremen distracted by the need to clean up from their fight, and probably have a word or two over it, Jorg slipped away. He hadn't wanted to talk to Bremen, anyway. Selby could help deal with the Wilbert issue. As far as Jorg was concerned, the man was not his relation.

He'd not gone five strides, however, when a familiar lumbering dwarf climbed over the embankment. With the gate destroyed, the only option to get in or out of the courtyard was to climb down and back up the steep grassy slope of the ditch outside the broken palisade wall. Jorg stopped and waited for Plintze.

So much for some time to myself. It's not like he minded being around Plintze. If anyone knew how to keep their words to a minimum, it was the dwarf. Besides, being back meant that he'd found and buried Lazuli. That had to be hard, and he'd done it alone. Jorg hoped he would never personally find out exactly how hard a job that was.

They nodded at each other without exchanging words. Plintze tilted sideways and peered behind Jorg at where Selby and Bremen stood. Jorg didn't bother to look over his shoulder; he knew what was happening. He thought sometimes that if he could stop himself from having exceptional hearing, he definitely would. They had apologized to each other and now found the fight amusing.

"Do I need to know what that's about?" Plintze asked.

"Probably not, but you did miss the chance to see a decent fight. I've made a mental note to teach Selby a few things while we're on our way to Swartaflheim. She almost had him there for a while."

"Humph. I'd have bet on her." Crinkles showed around the edges of Plintze's eyes.

Jorg had not expected him to be capable of smiling for a long time. The little sprite had been fickle and challenging, but it was good to think he'd heal from the loss of his friend.

Now that they were all back together, they needed to push Bremen to get going. Gavin was capable of doing the last of the preparations to get everyone on the boats back to Ireland.

"I'm surprised everyone is still here. Why is it taking so long for them to leave?" Plintze asked.

"Dwarves don't hear others' thoughts, do they?" Jorg chuckled under his breath, but he was only half joking.

It wasn't a thought he'd considered and didn't know how comfortable he was with anyone reading his mind. Except for Ingrid. He'd have gladly let her into his head. Their connection, however, was only a one-way conversation, and the void of silence she'd left behind created a constant throb that pounded against his skull.

"The delay is what started the whole storm between those two, actually. I was going to push Bremen to get moving faster when he decided to insult Selby."

"I don't want to wait around. If they aren't ready to go, they can try to catch up to us."

"Well said." Jorg hadn't dared let himself believe that Plintze would agree to leave without the other two. It felt like a flower bloomed in his chest, and he was ready to head out that moment. "Let's go tell them now . . . or maybe not."

When Plintze furrowed his brows with a questioning look, Jorg pointed with a nod of his head toward where the gates once stood. Striding toward them with elegant steps, was Eir.

A guttural growl came from Plintze's chest, and Jorg couldn't agree more. Where was the goddess earlier, before Jarrick had ripped Ingrid away?

Why didn't you show up to help?

"I couldn't interfere," Eir said without a greeting when she arrived next to the duo.

Jorg narrowed his eyes and studied the woman. This time, he fully believed his thoughts had been heard.

Eir met his stare and didn't flinch. "I taught Ingrid how to guard her thoughts. I can see I'll have to do the same for you."

"You should have taught her how to return from being pulled through a portal," Jorg said.

With a shake of her head, Eir clasped her hands together and rested them in front of her. "We did work on how to make portals, and she's quite good when it is within the same realm. Moving between realms is a skill that is not easily mastered. A simple mistake and she'd be lost forever in the gap between the realms. Not only would that be disastrous—but also irreversible. I have come because I have a plan that may get her back."

Jorg's heart squeezed. If the goddess had a way to get Ingrid, perhaps it was better than going into the dwarven tunnels. The thought of which was unsettling if he was honest with himself.

"There is a door to Alfheim from Svartalfheim," Plintze said.

"And if you use that, not only will you endanger yourselves to the point that you may never make it to Alfheim, you would also alert all the realms to Midgard's weakened position. The giants would find that information very interesting. You know that your fellow countrymen will sell anything, including information if they can make a profit." Eir cocked her brow at Plintze, and he nodded.

There was no use trying to deny it. It was the biggest reason no one trusted the dwarves. They would double-cross anyone for the best profit. Everything had a price to them, and the highest bidder was the best type of friend.

"Let's go speak to those two." Eir twisted her mouth in obvious distaste for either the appearance of Selby and Bremen, or the fact that they were now lost in their own world as they sat off to the side talking. Jorg guessed for the latter.

The three approached the couple and stood just out of arm's length without notice. Finally, Plintze made his customary grunt, and Selby turned in their direction.

"Thank you, Plintze. If you two are quite finished ignoring everything around you, we need to discuss a plan to retrieve Ingrid," Eir said with undisguised irritation in her voice.

Bremen rose to his feet, offering a hand to Selby as he did. "We would be happy to hear your plans, and I hope they include the rescue of my mother as well."

"If that's possible, of course. But Ingrid has to be the primary focus, or nothing else in *any* realm will matter."

The look on Bremen's face was a mixture of frustration, respect, and concession. Jorg had already thought about what might happen if it came down to a choice between Ingrid or his mother. For him, the choice was obvious, though difficult. He understood Bremen's emotional turmoil.

The council chamber they'd used for meetings was destroyed in the dragon attack, as was most of the monastery, but a small room near the kitchen was still intact, and Bremen commandeered that for them to speak in private.

The small room had a single bed, a small side table with a

candle, and one hard-backed chair. With the five of them in the space, it became immediately claustrophobic to Jorg. He'd been on his way out to the forest when Plintze arrived. The small space was the opposite of what his nerves could handle.

Selby and Bremen sat on the edge of the bed, leaving just enough room for Plintze as well. Jorg leaned against the wall, giving the chair to Eir. Before she sat, she turned to face him.

"Can I see it?" She held her hand out to Jorg with a sad smile.

He stared for a minute trying to decide if he would acknowledge that he knew what she wanted. Finally, he opened his palm, exposing the amber bead he still held.

Gently, Eir took it from his hand and held it in the air between them. Jorg's palm felt instantly cold and empty, like his heart.

"When I gave this to Ingrid, I had imbued it so I could stay connected to her. I needed to know when her abilities began to manifest in order to train her." Eir cupped both her hands around the bead and closed her eyes. She mumbled a few incoherent words and then brought her hands to her lips.

Jorg couldn't tell if she blew into her hands or sucked the air out, but he couldn't move. He was transfixed on what happened before him. His heart pounded, his breath shallow as he watched. When Eir looked up, she met his gaze and stepped uncomfortably close to him. He leaned into the wall as far as he could, but then she blew into his face.

Unable to move or blink, he felt the warm air wash over him. A fine mist formed and swirled around his vision. With a sudden gasp, the mist shot up his nose and into his mouth, temporarily choking him before dissolving into his body. A tingle spread throughout his chest, and he heaved several hard breaths before settling back into an easy rhythm.

An empty space in his mind still existed where Ingrid's voice had resided, but he no longer felt the pain. The throbbing headache faded away, and it almost made him dizzy with relief.

"The bead will respond to you now. It will guide you in the direction you need to go to find her," Eir said as she placed the bead back into Jorg's palm.

He couldn't speak. His knees felt weak, and he had to blink back the sting of tears. Jorg could only nod, grateful for the wall at his back to keep him upright. Eir smiled and seemed to understand.

When she turned to face the others, he realized the strength of her presence. She'd been Ingrid's guide, and he'd forgotten to think of her as a goddess of Asgard. The power she wielded in the small quarters was palpable. From the wide eyes and motionless rigid spines of the other three, they'd felt it, too.

"Now that's out of the way. Let's talk about why you should *not* go to Svartalfheim," Eir said with a pointed stare at Plintze.

9

INGRID

Caelya returned and sullenly escorted Ingrid down several hallways made of cream-colored marble stone. It was impossible to memorize an escape route. She wanted to ask more questions about Jarrick's castle and Galwain, but the princess seemed intent to hurry in silence.

It took Ingrid two strides to match each of Caelya's graceful steps as they sped through the halls. Caelya wore a flowing gown in the same style as Ingrid's, but hers was deep green like the forest. It was regal and shimmered when she walked. The silver crown embedded with jewels that adorned her head created a total vision of elegance and royalty. Spirals of vines and leaves wove around and created small peaks with the largest centered at the front. Rubies, sapphires, emeralds, and diamonds nestled among the vines like beautiful thorns.

Though Ingrid was sure they'd turned a different direction than they'd gone before, the halls all looked alike. Each had the same smooth stone, plush rugs, and occasional side table with decor that seemed familiar yet foreign at the same time. It was as if the halls themselves could disguise their appearance.

When they finally made it to a door at the end of a hall,

Caelya hesitated and appeared like she wanted to say something but changed her mind. Instead, she just flung open the door and ushered Ingrid through.

They arrived in a large open area with a ceiling that soared overhead with golden arches forming a domed center. Golden sconces lined the walls of the circular room and silver torches were placed among lush potted greenery. The walls shimmered in the light, and the floor tiles shined like glass.

Even with the soft, silken slippers on her feet, Ingrid was afraid to step through the sparkling chamber. In order to squelch her rising nerves, she asked about something that had been bothering her.

"Have you stayed in contact with Galwain? Is that how you know she's been in hiding—and about Bremen?" Ingrid's curiosity burst out. She needed to know how the princess knew so much about Galwain's life.

"I have not heard from her in many years." Caelya glanced over her shoulder as she walked in front of Ingrid. "But—I have spoken with her since her return."

Ingrid nodded. That made sense. More than the concern she had that Caelya was somehow a spy for Jarrick.

"Come, this way," Caelya coaxed in a low voice. "We should arrive before the others."

Ingrid followed in a daze as she gawked at all the beauty. Even though everything had been unfamiliar since she'd arrived, it was the first time she'd truly felt like she was in a different realm. She scoffed at herself because after all she'd seen, the room before her was what surprised her? She'd been surrounded by new sights, beings, and even the air was different. Yet, somehow, this room made it all real to her. She was on Alfheim—probably forever.

They left the grand hall and entered a smaller room. There were many softly cushioned chairs set around. Some looked to be for one person, and some were built for several to sit on in groups. There were even a couple small tables that had game boards on them, at the ready to play. As with every other room, a large fireplace took the space of one wall, with ornately carved stone surrounding it.

Ingrid shivered though the room was at a perfectly comfortable temperature. There were no flames, but the sight of it still forced her to shove away the memories of dragon fire.

She turned away quickly, looking anywhere other than the fireplace, and noticed there were no tables for dining. As she took in the sights, two creatures—she didn't know how else to think of them—entered the room through a simple side door.

Each wore a white tunic covered by a long black jacket that split in the back to reveal the tail of a deer. Ingrid's gaze trailed down two slender legs covered in tawny fur that ended with delicate cloven hooves, yet each held a silver tray with arms and hands of a man. Their faces were also that of a man, but with a small cleft in their upper lips that blended into their nose. Finally, poking through their hair were soft, deer-like ears that stood alert.

"Fauns, my dear," Caelya whispered next to Ingrid's ear, snapping her attention to the floor. "They would prefer you didn't stare but would be happy to offer you something to drink."

Ingrid glanced up at Caelya who clearly enjoyed Ingrid's discomfort. "I'm not thirsty, thank you." She used her most polite voice and smiled. The opulent surroundings had mesmerized her, but she needed to remember why she was there. She was a prisoner, being used in a game by those who thought she was weak and controllable.

"No one will poison you. Everything is safe."

"And *you* are the one I'm to trust? The one who helps make sure I stay caged for Jarrick?"

Caelya moved her gaze to the ceiling and exhaled sharply. It gave Ingrid momentary satisfaction.

"I'm impressed at your bravado, however, your distrust of me is unfounded. At least, for tonight." Caelya's mouth twitched as she fought a grin.

There was something in the gleam of her eye that made Ingrid accept her words as truth. Caelya could work with Jarrick, but she wasn't lying. At least, it didn't seem so. Perhaps some food and drink would help her stay strong and keep her wits.

When a faun approached her with a tray of slender chalices, she accepted one with a smile. The faun nodded back and winked. She stared as it—he, she?—tip-toed away with quick steps. The chalice was half filled with a bubbly rose-colored liquid that had a subtle floral scent.

Hesitantly, she lifted it to her lips and took a tiny sip. The bubbles tingled on her tongue, and the sweet apple-like flavor practically evaporated before she could swallow. It was delicious, but she waited to drink any more until she let it settle to see what happened.

As she and Caelya waited in the room, it filled with more elegantly attired elves. Both male and female who drank freely from the faun's trays and chatted politely among themselves. No one approached Ingrid though she'd caught all of them sneak peeks in her direction. No matter, she didn't want to know them either. Galwain was the only person she wanted to see. Hopefully, she'd arrive soon.

Ingrid wandered to the edge of the room. Several rows of books sat on shelves next to one of the game tables. She roved over the titles, somewhat amused at how many appeared to be stories of romance. Then one simply titled, *Herian*, snagged her attention. It was one of the numerous identities of Odin. Curious what the elves might say about the god of Asgard, Ingrid started to reach for the tome but stopped herself. A sensation of being watched skittered across the back of her neck.

Peeking over her shoulder, she found Caelya watching her with a curious expression. Perhaps she should wait for another time to read. Caught in the midst of her indecision, she gasped and forgot everything when she spied the next individual to arrive.

A man strode through the doorway. The one she'd seen speaking with Jarrick. Urkon—the dark arts master who wanted her dead!

10

JORG

Plintze squirmed as Eir stared at him. It made little sense to Jorg why she focused on the dwarf. It wasn't like he was leading any of them to his homeland without a clear understanding of the dangers. She acted like he had a hidden motive.

"We need to get to Alfheim, and that's the best way we've heard. Do you have any other ideas?" Jorg said. He expected it would draw Eir's stare to him, but she stayed focused on the dwarf.

"Have you told them everything?" Eir asked.

"Not yet. I had something to do first," Plintze said. His words growled out like a quern stone.

"We can discuss that later, but you know the dangers of the tunnels. It is unwise to believe you can make it through, let alone those with human blood."

"What are you talking about?" Bremen asked, standing up and forcing Eir to face him. It annoyed Jorg that he'd been able to draw her focus.

"The dwarves are merchants. They buy and sell anything that will make them a profit. Their clients are whoever is willing to pay. The giants want Midgard. Their lust for the human realm is what the final battle will be all about. Call it ragnarök, doomsday, the end times, whatever you want—it is when the giants invade Midgard to enslave humanity."

"What does that have to do with us? We just need to get through the tunnels so we can get to the door to Alfheim. Perhaps we can make it through unnoticed," Jorg argued.

"A single human is worth more to the giants than anything. You walk into those tunnels with two and a half of them," Eir glared at Jorg, "and you will be found before you can take two breaths. Which you may not be able to do, anyway. The air down there is stifling hot and far denser than it is here."

"I know my way around. I used to sneak in and out of the tunnels all the time. There is a place that we can hide for a few hours until they adjust."

"You haven't been home in a long time, Plintze. Those tunnels change all the time with all the mining. Besides, if you get caught, you will set off an alert to all the realms that Midgard is vulnerable."

"What are you suggesting? We can't just sit here and do nothing," Selby said. She was the only one at the moment that seemed calm, which made Jorg nervous. If Selby was the voice of reason, they might not be thinking clearly.

That thought sounded like something Ingrid would say. Maybe her voice wasn't completely gone. He peeked down at the stone in his hand. Was it helping him to feel her again? Did that mean she wasn't as far away as they thought?

"I'm suggesting you wait. Let me contact Thelonius, the king of Alfheim, and tell him the situation. I don't believe that Jarrick has kept his brother appraised of all his plans. If he is endangering the serenity of the elves, they will not abide by that. They enjoy their peace away from the warring of the other realms."

"I won't just sit and wait for you to have some dinner party with a king while Ingrid and Galwain are trapped. Who knows what Jarrick is doing to them?" Bremen clenched his jaw as he spoke through his teeth, and for the first time, he looked as angry as Jorg felt.

"Jarrick has not worked this hard for his plans to just hand them back if his brother asks nicely," Selby added.

"Let me contact Thelonius before you all go charging into danger. Then we can move forward from there. You have to agree to wait for me, or it will only cause Thelonius to ward all the entrances to Alfheim and protect his own realm. Then we'll have no options to get to them."

"How sure are you that you can speak with the king?" Bremen asked.

Eir rolled her eyes at his insistent and irreverent tone. Jorg could tell the goddess's patience was wearing thin having to deal with all of them.

"He is an old friend. I'm positive he'll speak with me."

"Then we'll wait."

"You don't know how long this could take. I won't agree to that!" Jorg growled the words between his teeth louder and faster than he meant to, but he didn't regret it. There was no way he would follow Bremen's leadership in this, and he had no right to agree to any plan without them.

"Give me two of your days, and I will be back with word," Eir said, directing her words to Jorg directly. "Can you accept that?"

Jorg stared at her, unmoving and unblinking.

"We will all accept that," Bremen answered. "It will give us the time we need to get my people away as well."

Eir closed her eyes and tilted her face toward the ceiling. When she faced the group again, she stared into each of their eyes. Saving Jorg for last.

Don't make me regret this.

The words startled him, and his eyes sprung open wide. The goddess shook her head and smirked.

Eir turned to Selby. "Come with me. I have a task just for you."

Bremen stood as Selby did, but Eir stopped him with an open palm. "Just Selby." She ignored his protest and glided out the door.

"It'll be fine," Selby said with a shrug, then hurried away, leaving the room in silence.

THE NEXT DAY was a frenzy of getting supplies loaded and groups formed so all the Irish could head out. The people built a new, temporary bridge to allow the wagons to leave the courtyard and follow the road toward the sea where the boat would meet them.

Jorg kept himself busy with the most physically demanding tasks. By the end of the day, his muscles ached, and he was covered in sweat and mud, but he'd been able to keep his mind clear while he worked. It was the nights, and the times he was alone with his thoughts, that he dreaded.

After Eir had left the day before, everyone had gone off to different tasks, avoiding more conversation. It seemed that none of them wanted to question the decision to wait for Eir. What-ever the goddess told Selby, she'd kept to herself.

Now with all the tasks finished, the people would leave first thing in the morning, and there was nothing left to do but think. Jorg pulled the cord he'd strung Ingrid's bead onto out from under his tunic. It lay still and cool in his hand. He remembered Ingrid wrapping her hands around it before she would insist on a direction as they searched for Eir.

Perhaps that's what he needed to do. Concentrate on her, let the bead give him a sign of which direction they should go in to find her. He held it tight, his knuckles turning white—but there was nothing. It didn't even warm in his palm. Frustrated, he dropped the bead back under his tunic. Waiting another day would *not* work for him.

Spits of meat had been roasting over several fires all afternoon, and the smell made his stomach rumble. He'd eat first, and then after the others went to sleep, he'd slip away. Maybe the bead would show him the way, maybe it wouldn't, but he needed to start the search.

"It is a bad place to get through," Plintze whispered before he bit off another large bite of roasted mutton. "Eir was right about that."

Jorg had sat next to Plintze because he didn't want to talk to anyone, and there had been no other open spaces. Not only had he been surprised by Plintze striking up a conversation, what he said stunned him more.

"Impossible?"

"No."

They sat in silence for a bit after that, eating, thinking, and watching the surrounding people. There was a buzz of excitement that coursed through the courtyard. Everyone was eager to get on with their journey because, for them, they were going home. The awful attack that left a third of their friends and family dead could be put behind them. Memories would be left in this terrible country when they stepped onto the boat.

Though Jorg knew they missed their dead as much as he did his own family, they seemed willing to put the experience behind them and move on. He wished he could do the same. His village was destroyed and everyone he cared about with it. Everyone but Ingrid, and she was out there somewhere alone, in danger. The others looked forward to the future with excitement for the possibilities it held. He searched for a way to keep what he had.

"What will we face?" He knew he would go to Svartalfheim no matter what answer Plintze gave, but it would be good to have an idea. He also didn't worry that the dwarf wouldn't agree to go with him.

"Any dwarf that finds us will turn us in for a reward from the council. The council will then sell you to the highest bidder. They will most likely send me to go mine with the goblins, that is, until they rip me apart for their dinner."

Jorg held the next bite of meat in the air halfway to his mouth. He looked at Plintze out of his peripheral. "And if we don't get caught?"

"The tunnel to Alfheim only still exists because it is beyond the goblins. No one dares to go ward it closed."

"So, goblins either way." Jorg nodded to himself as he put the bite of juicy roast into his mouth. "Sounds like a good challenge."

"The air stinks, the ceilings are low, and we'll have to avoid the forges, so it'll be ice cold."

Before Jorg could answer, Selby and Bremen walked up and sat on the other side of Plintze. Many of those around the fires started to make their way to a place to sleep. Bremen greeted the only other two sitting at their fire and then no one spoke. A few minutes later the two men got up and left, headed in different directions. The spit was empty, and the fire burned low, indicating it was time for everyone to leave.

Since Plintze and Jorg hadn't finalized their plan, they sat content to wait.

"When are you leaving?" Selby asked.

"I was thinking of making a trip into the woods any time now and then finding a place to rest under the stars. If you want privacy, there are other fires with no one sitting near them. We were here first." Jorg smirked and gave her a wink.

Ignoring his diversionary comments, she smiled. "I'm impressed that you two waited until dark. We've had our packs ready to go all day."

Bremen poked the fire and nudged the flames a little higher, so they glowed against his face. "I came here to negotiate a treaty with the king of Mercia, and I know how those meetings go. They are slow with everyone posturing to get what they want for themselves. Jarrick will finish whatever plans he has before Eir and the king can come to any sort of agreement."

"If you think that, why did you agree to Eir's plan?" Jorg didn't hold back the sneer in his tone.

"As I said, I've been privy to many negotiations. She needed us to agree, or she would have moved to the next step which would have been forcing us to agree. This way, it moved things along quicker." He pulled Selby's hand into his own and rubbed it with his thumb. "I doubt she believed that we'd wait when she made the suggestion."

"So, you don't believe she's going to talk with the king?" Plintze asked.

"I think she is. In fact, I think she's distracting him to buy us time, so that we can get into Alfheim. Why else would she tell us the elves might ward off their entrances? She's a goddess, right? She'd know that."

Jorg snorted and shook his head. Of course, Eir knew. She'd told him as much when she spoke into his mind as she left. As much as he hated to admit it, his little brother had a point. He might not be as useless in helping as Jorg had thought.

11

INGRID

Unable to will her body to respond, Ingrid froze. She gaped at the stranger who had closed the door gently behind him and now met her stare. A sinister smile crept across his face.

The surrounding air radiated a peppery unpleasantness. A heaviness pressed into the room as if the light had been squeezed into a dark container. No one else seemed affected by Urkon's presence.

Ingrid's heartbeat hammered at her chest. When a faun entered and called out that it was time to "move through," she remained still. Caelya reappeared at Ingrid's side after having spent her time chatting and laughing with the other elves.

"He can't hurt you here. Ignore him and come with me," Caelya said in a voice so low Ingrid almost couldn't hear her through the thrumming in her ears. When she felt a light touch at her elbow, she finally shook her paralysis and followed.

They stepped through a set of double doors together into a grand dining hall.

One long table of polished dark wood sat in the center, and the edges of the room were lined with more fauns in the same white shirts and black jackets. They all faced the table and looked straight ahead. It was unnerving to Ingrid, but no one else seemed to even notice their presence.

At the far end of the table sat a single, grand chair with velvet cushions in a buttery yellow. The king's place, no doubt. Flanking the table on either side of the larger throne were two equally ornate, yet slightly smaller chairs. Ingrid followed Caelya forward. She stopped at the chair to the king's right and gestured to the chair next to hers for Ingrid.

Without the need to glance, Ingrid knew that Urkon had slithered his way to her other side. The heated pepper scent bore straight into her senses and caused a headache to take shape between her brows.

Suddenly, everyone silenced and stopped shuffling into their places. Startled that something was amiss, Ingrid peered around the room.

She instantly realized what the commotion was all about. Jarrick grinned at her as he entered the room from a different doorway, following another male who could only be Thelonius.

The king had the same white blonde hair as Jarrick and light green eyes that immediately latched onto Ingrid's. She stared, awestruck. He was captivating and beautiful. An aura seemed to glow around him as he moved. He wore a light green tunic that flowed past his knees and was embroidered with golden thread in an intricate leaf and vines pattern.

When he arrived at the head chair, he broke his gaze with Ingrid and nodded to the rest of the room as he sat. As one, the others lowered into their chairs. Caelya tugged on Ingrid's sleeve to make her sit, which she did with more of a plop than an elegant motion like everyone else.

Jarrick sat across from Caelya at Thelonius' left side. He wore a crown as well. It was similar to Caelya's and equally dazzling. After he settled into his chair, he rubbed the back of his neck in a similar way that Jorg did so often. Ingrid's eyes stung, but she settled herself quickly. She would not—could not—show any weakness. The king's crown was also in silver but solid rather than the more delicate openness of the other two. It peaked higher in the front with a single pointed leaf. Smaller leaves made the other points around the circle, and each was adorned with a jewel the size of Ingrid's thumb. The center stone was a single sapphire even larger than the rest.

"Thank you for joining us this evening, Ingrid. I've been eager to meet you," Thelonius said, his eyes once more intensely concentrated on her.

"Thank you for having me. I've looked forward to our meeting as well." Ingrid tried to remember how her mother would behave when other chieftains visited the village. Always polite, offering the best of the food stores and giving deference to the guest. Even when sometimes, as Ingrid knew, the guest was more of an enemy than a friend to her father's position. Her mother would have fit in here. Ingrid would try to make her proud.

"Are you adjusting to Alfheim well? I hear it can be a struggle in the beginning." The king spoke as though she had come of her own free will, yet he knew differently. She'd play along and see where the conversation headed.

"It was difficult at first, but I believe I'm well now." She wanted to ask about Galwain, to find out why she wasn't there, too, but she decided to let the king be the one to give information. She'd listen and learn.

The fauns moved around the room, placing gilded platters of roasted vegetables in front of each guest. There were also spicy sauces in yellows and reds that slightly burned the nose and glasses filled with sparkling wine. It differed from the rose-scented drink she'd had in the other room and decided on caution. Though she appeared to drink, she only held the glass to her lips so as not to draw attention to her decision.

"Hello, Ingrid. It's nice to finally meet in person." Urkon leaned near her as he spoke quietly. His voice rasped with the brittleness of dry leaves, death and destruction from where life used to flow.

Ingrid didn't answer. She couldn't. Something about the man . . . was he a man? . . . told her to respect the power radiating off of him. He scared her in a way that Jarrick never had. Even though the first time she'd met him, he had possessed Voxx on the moors.

With a hard swallow, Ingrid sat rigidly. Peeking a glance across the table, she found Jarrick watching her. Expectantly. What was that about? Was he waiting to see how she reacted to his mentor? Something clicked inside Ingrid.

Slowly, she turned her head and fixed her stare on Urkon.

Ingrid picked up her glass, more for something to do with her hands, and tipped her chin to Urkon in greeting as she brought it to her lips. Tongue-tied she couldn't bring herself to make small talk.

"There is much I can teach you that Eir could not. She has no idea the true power you hold." Urkon bore through Ingrid with an intensity that would have made her knees buckle had she not been sitting. Power radiated from him, and she swallowed hard, taking a quick drink to try to cover it.

"I was trained well, thank you. I'm sure I don't need any more help." Her voice slipped through with more confidence than she expected as if part of her mind took control over the weakness in her body. Whatever it was, she was grateful and sat a little taller.

Urkon's eyes glittered, and his nostrils flared slightly. "You only think so because you don't know better. You have more raw talent than you understand. Eir was afraid to test you, but I was not."

What did that mean? Ingrid pinched her brows and peeked at those sitting around her. Everyone was engaged in their own conversations and didn't notice how close Urkon had leaned toward her. Leaning back in her chair, Ingrid tried to create more distance between them. It made no difference. She wanted to turn away. Talk to Caelya. Stare at her plate. Anything other than engaging with the evilness next to her.

"A tremor rumbled through the realms the day you were born. I felt it and was drawn to Midgard to find you. When I did, your essence was light. I needed to be sure I was correct."

The air shifted around Ingrid. From the corner of her eye, she noticed how the room seemed to still. No one moved. The fauns froze in place with trays hovering midair. Glasses were held to lips that didn't drink.

"What are you doing? How is this possible?" Ingrid tried to keep the bravado she'd possessed moments before, but she couldn't. Urkon's powers were too strong. She dared a peek at Jarrick, and even he sat frozen.

"You should be at Montibeo where you can be free to learn what I can teach you. Then you would understand how easy it is to control those with weaker minds."

Ingrid caught the small movement of Jarrick's fingers from her peripheral vision. Afraid to move, she clamped her mouth tight and sat tall. Whatever Urkon wanted, she'd try to resist.

"I should have taken you there the day I'd tested your skills. But, as a compassionate individual, I allowed you to stay with your family. Raising a human child would have only tortured me. Then Eir came along and warded you with that bead. Thankfully, we no longer have that between us."

Her bead had kept her protected? It suddenly made sense. Eir had told her it was a way to keep track of her magic. To know when she was ready to train, but that wasn't all—it also kept others away from her. Conflicted and confused, Ingrid didn't know how to process that. A surge of anger welled in her knowing it was one more way she'd been lied to.

"Surprisingly, you almost healed your sister, even though you were no more than a child yourself. I'd tried a few smaller incidents to entice you to unlock your powers, but the stronger boost of emotional motivation finally worked."

"What?" Ingrid whispered the question but didn't need an answer.

The vision of how she'd tried to heal her sister after she'd been impaled by a fishing spear slammed into her thoughts. Blood had covered her hands from the effort, but her sister had died anyway. They'd both been so little at the time. Ingrid had blocked the memory of it until she was caught in the middle of a battle in Jorvik. She'd healed so many men without thinking about it and then her mind had opened to the memory.

It hadn't been an accident. It had been a test . . . orchestrated by Urkon? Ingrid couldn't breathe. She'd been a pawn her entire life. First by Freya who'd connected her to the spell, then by Urkon who'd used her poor sister as a test. She'd only been a toddler! Eir had even kept information from her about her bead.

What power did she have of her own?

She needed to leave, not just the dining hall, but Alfheim. There had to be a way. How was she ever supposed to separate who she was from who everyone wanted her to become?

"I can help you unlock your full potential. Come with me, and I'll show you," Urkon said, disrupting her panic.

"Not ever," Ingrid hissed. "I will never go with you."

"You will." Urkon snatched Ingrid's wrist. She shivered as a wave of cold air washed over her. Her vision blurred and then cleared an instant later.

Ingrid stood in the center of a large throne room. Polished

obsidian stone glittered on the floors and the walls from ensconced torches that hung every few feet. Dark columns rose five fathoms into the air that held up beams that arched to a point at the center of the massive space. The columns formed a walkway through the center of the room to a high dais five steps above the floor. In the center of the austere platform was a single throne. So tall and grand Ingrid was sure she'd not be able to reach the seat without a stool.

Despite the amount of open space, the atmosphere caved in upon Ingrid. It was as if the sticky essence Jarrick had one once shoved into her mind floated through the air. Squeezing the vitality—the life—out of everything.

Something stirred in the shadows, and Ingrid moved only her eyes to spy what it was. It was a goblin, she guessed, based on the stories her brother Hagen had told her to scare her when they were younger. Then she realized it wasn't one goblin, but many, teeming along the walls and hiding in the dark. No, they weren't hiding; they were chained.

A scream caught in Ingrid's throat, clawing to get out. She couldn't move. Couldn't make a sound. *Where is this?*

Boot steps echoed off the smooth dark stone, and Ingrid slid her attention to whoever approached from behind her. Using only enough movement to see out the corner of her eye, she watched as Jarrick strode through the room. Seeming to ignore her, he continued to the front.

Chains rattled behind, and Ingrid turned to see a grotesque creature that appeared half-elf, half-goblin. It walked upright with a hunch to its shoulders and a limping gait as it pulled a chain attached to a collar around Galwain's neck. The queen was filthy and wore a shapeless gown of rough-spun linen as she stumbled along. Tripping up the steps, she fell to her knees in front of the throne. The elf-goblin shoved her until she lay on the ground beside where Jarrick sat.

A chill washed over Ingrid again, and when her vision cleared, she sat once more at the dining table.

Activity resumed all around her. The others acted as if nothing had happened. Ingrid grabbed her glass and swallowed the entire contents. How was she ever supposed to defeat the beast sitting next to her?

12

JORG

Following Plintze's lead, the group had traveled only at night, sticking to paths in the forest rather than the roads. It might not make a difference to be so secretive since Eir probably knew what they were doing, but it made them feel as though they had a chance for success. Even if the goddess knew what they were up to, they might still surprise the dwarves and Jarrick.

The fresh air, game trails, and silent tracking soothed Jorg's nerves. Combined with taking action, he was invigorated. To their credit, Selby and Bremen were all business and seemed as eager as he was for the activity. So far, the bead hadn't been helpful in any way except to help Jorg calm his nerves. He pulled it out from his shirt and held it in his palm whenever they would stop to rest. In that way, he supposed, it was a comfort. Perhaps that's what Eir meant.

Two days after they'd left, Plintze halted at the edge of the trees.

"See that group of boulders over to the right?" He pointed at an outcrop in the hillside that looked the same as many others they'd passed as they worked their way through the fells.

"What of them?" Jorg asked.

"That's the closest entrance. It'll take us a little closer to a forge than I'd like, but it's also where we'll get to the outer tunnels that aren't in use anymore."

"How do we get through them? There doesn't seem to be any gaps big enough to crawl through," Selby said.

Plintze sighed. He looked uneasy and agitated.

"Are they sealed in a way we can't see? Do you need to do something to make the entrance clear to our eyes?" Jorg asked, dropping his hand to the dwarf's shoulder.

"Humph." Plintze nodded.

"Ingrid told me about how she first met you. That you made her turn around when you showed her your home for the first time, and again when you were both inside. She said you didn't want to let her see your dwarven magic. You can trust us, Plintze. Just like you trusted her," Selby said.

Jorg's heart clenched. Selby sounded so kind and concerned. Things had changed so much since they'd left the village so many months ago after the dragons first appeared.

"Ach, come on," Plintze grumbled and strode toward the boulders.

When they reached the pile, each stone was as big as two men and so close together they would be impossible to move. Jorg, Selby, and Bremen stared at Plintze without a word, waiting to see what he had planned.

"After we go inside, there will be a barrier to cross. It separates the realms. I don't know how it will affect all of you." Plintze shifted his feet and adjusted his wide-brimmed hat.

"We knew the risks before we came. Whatever we face, we face together," Jorg said and then looked at the others for confirmation.

Bremen nodded and reached his hand out to Plintze. When Plintze returned the gesture and their hands clasped, there was a shift in the surrounding air. Not in the literal sense, but Jorg could tell that the deal was final, there would be no turning back and no regrets by any of them.

When Plintze turned to face the boulders, Jorg slipped Selby's hand into his and squeezed quickly before releasing it again. He saw the tight smile she gave, but he also saw the single tear that tracked down her cheek. Failure was not an option. They *would* rescue Ingrid, nothing would stop him from that. But he would also make sure his friends came home, too.

Plintze raised his hands and waved his staff high into the air while he said some words in a language Jorg had never heard. A slight breeze picked up and rustled the grasses around their feet. Jorg blinked, then blinked again. The air seemed to waver in front of him, and the boulders swayed like grass.

Soon, they shifted apart, and the opening to a tunnel appeared.

Impressive. "Let's go then," Jorg said. The dangers they would face faded away from his mind as excitement bubbled within him.

Plintze wasted no more time and strode into the dark with Jorg close behind. Bremen followed Selby.

After about fifty steps in, the low light from the moon disappeared, and the darkness was so complete Jorg couldn't see Plintze in front of him. He could hear his footsteps and those of the others behind him. It was like no other darkness he'd experienced. He had felt no barrier like Plintze had mentioned, but there was something different about the tunnel for sure.

The slope of the ground descended, and Selby took ahold of the back of Jorg's tunic. *I was afraid you'd be too stubborn for that.*

Not long after, Plintze came to a stop. Because Jorg had kept track of the sounds, he knew to stop as well. "What is it?" he whispered.

"The barrier is just up ahead. Can any of you feel it yet?"

There was a pressure to the air. Jorg had thought it was just because they'd gone downhill. He opened his mouth and wiggled his jaw to pop his ears.

"It's like when a storm is approaching. The air feels heavy," Selby said from behind him.

"Yeah, that's just the edge. Whatever you do, don't stop. Hurry and get through as quick as you can, understand?"

No one could see Plintze's face, but his words carried urgency enough to make them all agree.

"Keep together. Don't let go of each other just in case anyone needs help," Jorg said and reached around to take hold of Selby's hand. He could feel her do the same behind her with Bremen. "Okay, Plintze. Let's go."

The scratching sound of loose dirt mixed with small pebbles from the path indicated that Plintze had started walking again. This time though, he wasn't going at a slow, careful pace. He charged forward, gaining speed. Jorg followed suit, and within a few steps, they moved in unison at a jogging pace.

The barrier slammed against Jorg as if he'd fallen from a cliff into a lake. It bent and gave into the shape of his body, but not without a toll. From the tips of his ears to the bottom of his feet, the force of a shield wall pounded against him over and over. Jorg grit his teeth and tightened his grip on Selby as he leaned into the pain.

He shoved forward, willing his feet to keep moving. No sound came to his ears though he knew a growl escaped his throat. The pressure threatened to crush his chest. His legs were as heavy as lead and burned with every step. *Don't stop!*

With a burst of the last amount of effort he could summon, he shoved forward. Then tumbled forward when all the pressure suddenly released. Unable to stop his momentum, he flew to the ground, sprawling into the dirt and sliding to a stop against the side of the tunnel.

Grunts and a couple curses later, Selby and Bremen were dumped to the ground next to him with as much grace.

The air was thick and heavy. Jorg rolled to a sitting position and leaned his back against the wall. The others did the same, except Plintze who stood before them watching.

"Are ya all right?"

"I'm in one piece if that's what you want to know. Give me a minute to know if anything's broken." Selby straightened her tunic and spat as she wiped dirt from her face.

"Take a few sips of water from your flasks, but we don't have too much time to rest. You'll have to adjust quickly," Plintze said. His voice was stern, but also held a tinge of concern.

He's nervous, not worried. "We need to get going," Jorg said.

The tunnel was warm, bordering on hot. Plintze had said the tunnels would be cold because they needed to stay away from the forges. That didn't bode well for where they might be.

"Stick close to me and stay silent. Your scent will be bad enough to draw attention." Plintze reached a hand out to Jorg to help him stand while Bremen and Selby helped each other. "Let's move."

The ground continued to slope downward as they moved with cautious steps. Every crunch under their feet made Jorg's heart race. It was hard to breathe in the thick air, and he didn't know how well he'd do in a fight. He'd seen Plintze in battle and knew the dwarf had good skills. In his home realm, he was probably better. That meant any others they'd face would be, too, if they were caught.

At least the darkness had become less intense. They could see each other now. It was no more than a dark night in the woods after getting adjusted to it.

Plintze held up his hand for them to halt. The tunnel led to a set of stairs going down at a steep angle. Jorg expected Plintze to turn and go down like a ladder, but he moved forward and took each step with ease.

After a quick peek over his shoulder, Jorg followed. He nearly had to sit on the steps as he worked his way down. How the dwarf had navigated them so nimbly, he didn't know. Selby kicked his head more than once as she struggled behind him—or above him, as it were.

When they finally reached the bottom, Plintze stared at them with anger boiling in his eyes. Obviously, he didn't understand their trouble, and he huffed as he turned and strode away. Jorg steadied himself and took as deep of a breath as he could before he hurried after, hunching slightly because the ceilings were lower in this section.

The tunnel made a curve ahead of them, and Jorg picked up the pace to make sure he didn't lose track of Plintze. He saw no other tunnels where they might get lost, but he didn't want to take any chances.

A point of a spear jabbed into his midsection as he rounded the corner. Selby gasped and Bremen grunted as they, too, were met with iron.

Laughter, gruff and gravely, bounced off the walls. The tunnel was only wide enough for two bodies if they squeezed together, and when Jorg looked around, he counted six dwarves ahead of them, and two had somehow managed to get behind them. Plintze was ahead of them, restrained with a dagger to his throat.

The dwarf holding his spear against Jorg's stomach backed up a step and cocked his head sideways to get a better view of Jorg's ears. He let out a loud guffaw and turned his head to speak over his shoulder.

"Plintze you have not returned for so long. It was wise to bring such gifts with you. Though we'll still have to see what the council thinks of your offering. An elf was a good choice. If it doesn't bring a high enough price, it will at least be good entertainment for the goblins."

13

INGRID

Everyone at the table ate, drank, and spoke in complete oblivion to the fact that they'd been trapped by Urkon. What kind of power did it take to hold a roomful of elves static and unaware? Except, not *everyone* had been unaware. Anger radiated from Jarrick. He said nothing for some time though he kept darting glances toward Urkon. For his part, Urkon appeared to be a complete gentleman. Having left Ingrid to contemplate what he'd said and shown her, he'd begun a conversation with the elf on his other side.

They spoke of a new café that opened recently in the marketplace and the wonders of the dishes it offered. Ingrid couldn't eat, couldn't even lift her utensils. While she sat amid polite conversation and soft laughter, Galwain was chained and tortured. She was her last connection to Jorg. There was no way Ingrid could let her stay in those conditions.

"I'm sorry to see that Galwain couldn't join us again this evening, Jarrick. I'd hoped she had recovered by now." Thelonius' words snatched Ingrid's attention.

Where did the king think his sister-in-law was? And what did he think kept her from the dining table?

"She is better each day. I'm sure she'll be able to join us soon." Jarrick smiled at his brother and then settled his gaze on Ingrid, a warning laced within an acknowledgment.

He knew what Urkon showed her. That's why he was so angry. What was it though? Was it that Ingrid knew how he was treating Galwain? Or was it that Urkon had controlled him while he did it? It was hard to believe that Jarrick would care what Ingrid thought.

"Is she ill?" Whatever game this was, Ingrid needed more information.

"There's nothing to worry about. Even though Galwain lived here many years ago, she wasn't as lucky as you to recover so quickly to the lighter atmosphere. She is tired and weak, but stronger each day," Jarrick answered.

"I would love to pay her a visit. We have so much to catch up on," Ingrid said.

She noticed that Thelonius, Caelya, and Urkon all sat still waiting for Jarrick's response. *They all know where she is and what is happening to her.* Despite how hard she tried, Ingrid could feel her heartbeat gaining speed. Her chest ached as she willed herself to take slow, steady breaths.

"She is looking forward to visiting with you. As soon as she recovers," Jarrick said with a tone that froze the air.

Ingrid nodded so she didn't have to speak.

"Perhaps Ingrid's abilities to heal would give Galwain the boost she needs?" Caelya said with a smile though it didn't reach her eyes and confused Ingrid.

What did she want in all of this? Was this her way of helping Jarrick chain Ingrid, too?

"Ingrid has other duties where she will need to use her strength," Urkon chimed in.

A flutter in her belly and a tingle throughout her body gave her a shiver. For the first time since she'd arrived, her magic stirred as if it were awakening. Ingrid sat up taller. She tried to pick at her food to cover her surprise and excitement.

Thelonius' attention was diverted to an elf down the table who'd asked a question, but, Jarrick continued to stare at Ingrid. Another pulse, deep within her middle, flashed through her. The air soon felt as though it were closing in and squeezing Ingrid. She glanced at Caelya who spoke quietly to one of the fauns. Pain gripped Ingrid's chest, and her breath caught.

She met Jarrick's gaze, and a slight curl formed on his lips. Ingrid pressed her hand against her chest. She didn't want to draw attention or give in to whatever was happening. Could she stop herself from being dragged into another vision?

As hard as she tried to push it away, the pain grew worse. Then she slammed her eyes closed as a voice rumbled through her mind.

In the same way it happened in the courtyard, Jarrick's voice pounded against her temples. The ache that had started from Urkon grew until she nearly collapsed from the pressure. With measured breaths and sheer will, she managed to lower her mental barriers just enough that she could hear Jarrick without so much force.

"You don't understand what's going on, Ingrid," Jarrick said into her mind.

"What's there to understand? You have Galwain on a chain, at Montibeo, where you practice dark magic. It seems pretty obvious to me."

The ability to speak to Jarrick in her mind gave Ingrid pause. She'd never been able to do that with Jorg. It squeezed her heart, but she couldn't let herself be distracted.

"Galwain is my wife, and she is not under duress. Urkon wants you to believe that so he can control you."

"And you don't?"

"I need you for the purposes I've explained to you. Urkon needs you for his. You don't know the dangers of what he asks."

Ingrid looked around at the table. Nobody else seemed to notice their internal conversation. They went about their business as if nothing was happening between her and the dark elf. How was that possible? The new world of being able to speak into someone's mind—having a conversation that no one else knew about right in the middle of a crowded dinner table—made Ingrid nervous.

"So, what is it he wants from me?"

"He needs the thread Freya stole, the one that binds you to the spell."

"I can't give that to him. Can I?"

"It's woven within the essence of your being. In order to retrieve it, he must sacrifice you at the base of the Yggdrasil tree. When you die it will release."

Ingrid swallowed hard. She looked in her glass, recently filled by a silent faun, but she dared not take another drink. Her throat was dry, her mind swirling. She'd known Urkon wanted her dead. Dúngarr had told her that, but what did the thread give him?

"What will that cause?" Even in her mind, her voice sounded small.

"Urkon's powers are bound to the spell. Freya managed to ensnare him to ensure that she possessed the power of the seiðr alone. If that thread remains, even though the spell falls, Urkon will stay bound. The only way his power can be restored is to destroy the thread and reverse the spell completely. Then he would once again be the most powerful seiðr magic user in all the realms."

"So, you want me to let the spell fall but leave my essence in place so that Urkon stays bound. Why?" It made no sense. They were working together. Urkon was the dark arts master, Jarrick's mentor. Why would he tell her that information?

Then it hit her like lightning. Jarrick didn't need a mentor. Jarrick needed to rule. If Urkon's powers were released, he could control Jarrick as much as anyone else.

Ingrid was no more than a mouse caught between two cats. That never worked well for the mouse.

"What if I don't help either of you? What if I bind the spell and keep the protections around Midgard safe? Neither of you will win. Asgard will stay in control, there will be no war between the gods, and humanity will stay safe. Like the Norns fated."

"You're no longer in a position to negotiate. You are a means to an end. That spell will fall. Whether you want any say in how that happens is your only choice at this point."

They stared at each other across the table, neither saying anything, neither backing down. Ingrid pushed her barriers closed, the pain secondary to the information he'd shared. If she helped Jarrick, he would defeat Urkon. If not, she was dead. Perhaps it was a time to choose her battles. If she sided with Jarrick, she would at least have more time to stop the change in power.

Her father had saved the village despite Jarrick's efforts. He'd gotten everyone out because he didn't sit around and wait. It was time for Ingrid to do the same. She had to get Galwain away from Jarrick, but stopping Urkon had to come first. He'd killed her sister as a test.

Rage welled up inside her. She'd do whatever it took to stop Urkon—even if that meant joining Jarrick.

14

JORG

Bars dug into Jorg's back, and he tried to find a more comfortable position. They'd been herded through the tunnels, drawing a growing crowd while the ceilings closed in lower and lower.

Everyone except Plintze had to hunch over to keep from hitting their heads. The dwarves had knocked Bremen and Jorg to their knees and dragged them into a cage. While Selby had screamed as they hauled her through the crowd. The clink of an iron door slammed shut had confirmed she had her own cage across the room. Plintze remained free but under guard while everyone waited for the council members to arrive. The room had a large central fire, and it was stifling hot when they'd entered. With so many bodies pressed inside, wanting a glimpse of the captives, the air grew thicker.

Loud chatter buzzed, adding to the dizzying experience as everyone vied for position to see the humans. An elf was rare enough, but no human had ever been in the tunnels. The excitement level crushed against Jorg.

Who knew I could be happy to be behind bars? At least it keeps them back.

The idea of having so many bodies pressed close to him or worse, clawing at him, made Jorg claustrophobic. He yanked at his tunic and couldn't stop twitching his foot. The sulfur-like smell of the forges burned his throat and seared a headache into his brain far worse than he had from Ingrid's missing voice.

Bremen squirmed, no doubt just as uncomfortable. "We need to get out of here before we can't breathe anymore," he whispered. "Have any ideas?"

He'd tried to come up with a plan since he'd first felt the spear tip in his abdomen. Now with Selby across the room and Plintze under guard, the options were slim. "We can't do anything behind these bars. They're too well-crafted to break. Maybe when the council comes, we can persuade them to let us go."

Neither man harbored any belief in the sentiment, nor could they offer any other suggestion. Plintze would not look in their direction, so they had to wait.

A commotion by Selby's cage drew their attention, and Bremen popped to his feet. Crouched because of the small space, he grabbed the bars and tried to shake them. "Leave her alone!"

Raucous laughter broke out at his pleas. Selby had backed herself as far away as she could, but the dwarves grew emboldened. They reached through the bars to touch her arms or hair.

Even though their weapons were stripped, Jorg knew Selby was as good with her fists as she was with a blade. Bremen knew it, too, but Jorg couldn't fault his brother for his anger.

While Bremen tried to grab a dwarf who taunted him, the room rippled into silence. Bodies shuffled back from the central fire, allowing open space for three dwarves who filed in to face Plintze.

No one stood behind them, and the fire cast their shadows on the wall as if they were giants.

"Plintzelgermir, it has been many a year since you remembered your homeland. We're told you brought us an offering to pay the debt of your absence?"

The dwarf in the middle was the tallest of the three though the difference between them was only about a hand. None of them would pass Jorg's waist if he could stand to his full height. They all had long dark beards trailing to their knees that were given a fiery tint by the glow of the flame. Their sleeveless tunics highlighted the impressively honed muscles of their arms. Blackened soot glistened with moisture in the oppressive heat and added to their threatening appearance.

"I've brought you nothing, Eitri. I have negotiated safe passage through our tunnels for these travelers, and this detainment goes against the merchant code. I demand free passage at once."

Jorg focused on the fierce council as they listened to Plintze's bluff.

"I see. However, another matter nullifies your claim. You see, the merchant code is enforceable only if there has been full payment, *and* if a more profitable deal is not presented. You know the rules, or has all that sunlight damaged your memory?"

"I have your portion in my pouch. We were on our way to pay when these fools attacked and wouldn't listen to reason."

"Well, that's another matter then. Let's see the payment."

Something wasn't right. The tone in the leader's voice held a hint of amusement, and the other two were outright smiling. Jorg stared at Plintze, trying to figure out his plan.

"He shouldn't give up any payment," Bremen whispered. "Not until we're free."

Jorg agreed. He cleared his throat, hoping to convey the message discreetly to Plintze.

"I have the payment," Selby called out. "It's in my pouch not with Plintze. That was a lie to protect me."

"Selby! What are you doing?" Bremen yelled and shoved himself against the front bars as close to her as he could get.

"Is that so?" Eitri laughed, and most of the room joined him. After a couple of minutes, he held up his hand for silence. "You gave your payment to a *woman* to hold?"

"It would be the last place any dwarf would think to look. It made good business sense." Plintze shoved the guards in front of him aside, stepping closer to the council. "I will not allow her to give it to you until we are on our way."

The dwarf on the leader's right scoffed. "Why would we do that? You don't pay attention very well."

"Now, now, Nabbi, let's not give Plintze a hard time. He looks as though he's grown soft while he's been away. Maybe his brain has gone as pudgy as his body?"

Another round of laughter ricocheted off the walls. Even the fire surged, making the shadows on the wall dance like fiends.

Plintze stood his ground and glared at the council. He must have come to the same conclusion as Jorg—they weren't going to negotiate their way out of this.

"It doesn't matter if the woman holds your payment or not. We'll find it later."

Bremen growled and grabbed the bars harder. Jorg scooted forward and put a hand on his brother's shoulder. They needed to listen and figure out the dwarves' demands.

"You see, a more profitable arrangement has already been made."

"Negotiations have just begun. What is this offer? I will beat it," Plintze said.

Eitri smiled a sinister, knowing smile. "While granting humans passage through our realm may be forgivable, bringing the other one is treasonous. Elves have been our enemy since they declared their craftsmanship equal to ours. You'd remember that if you'd bothered to remain loyal to your own. At least your love for the pathetic humans has created an opportunity we could not pass up."

"You know nothing. Listen to me!" Plintze shouted. Jorg itched to stand next to his friend and battle the whole room if necessary.

"Silence him." Eitri gestured to one of the guards who grabbed Plintze and held his arms behind his back while another placed a gag in his mouth.

All three of the council members turned toward the wall and stared at it. Bremen and Jorg glanced quickly at each other. The air began to shimmer, and the shape of a large oval appeared on the flickering stone.

"It's a portal," Jorg said between his teeth.

After only a few heartbeats, the oval cleared, and a large face appeared on the wall. A man with chiseled cheekbones, a cleft chin, and perfectly styled black hair stared into the cavern. Behind him, the sky was blinding and bright as snow swirled in circling gusts. The man had a fur-rimmed tunic but didn't look as though he cared about the wintery conditions around him.

"I think that's a Jötun," Jorg said.

"I thought giants would be ugly, and . . . dumb-looking," Bremen mumbled back.

Jorg caught him glancing toward Selby, no doubt wanting to see her reaction to the handsome figure looming over the room.

"How kind of you to take the time to speak with us directly, Beolach," Eitri said. "As you have predicted, the wards around Midgard are falling. We offer you first opportunity to bid on the grand prize of two apprehended humans."

"Your kindness is appreciated, Eitri. A vulnerable Midgard is valuable information indeed. I will pay for *that* and consider the humans a bonus. Though, one doesn't look human." Beolach stared at Jorg, his brow pinched.

"That's true—one is an elf, though he is not for sale. We are going to ransom him to Alfheim, but you are welcome to make a bid if you'd like."

"As I said, the information is what I value. However, the elf might prove worthy in another negotiation. Where is the other human?"

The council turned and growled at the crowd. They waved their hands to make a path exposing Selby.

"Ah, have the two males brought to the Jötun entrance. I will have my emissaries ready with whatever payment you require as the highest bid. The female is of no use to me."

"Your generosity is most appreciated. Thank you and know that we will cooperate with the giant realm in whatever you may need when Midgard falls."

"I'm counting on that, Eitri." The portal blinked closed, and darkness descended on the room again, more oppressive than before.

"Plintze, it is your lucky day. A profitable deal has put me in a fine mood. I will allow you to go free. The treasure you have brought us will be a fine down payment on the debt you owe for betraying your homeland." Eitri then turned away from Plintze. "Guards, take the female to the kitchens and have her prepared for service. Deliver the others to the giants' border immediately."

Chaos erupted when Plintze charged to the front of Selby's cage. Bremen roared and grabbed a dwarf who'd moved too close to the bars. Jorg followed his lead, and they both tried to wrestle away weapons. Suddenly, a shooting pain hit Jorg in the shoulder, and he fell to the ground. His entire body twitched uncontrollably.

As he tried to fight off the sensation, he saw Bremen in the same condition on the ground next to him.

The cage bars rattled, and several dwarves entered. They drug them by their arms out of the room and into the tunnels.

Another shock wave coursed through Jorg before he could regain his senses. In the back of his mind, he heard Selby shrieking as she fought, but the sounds were getting farther away as he scraped along in the dark.

A commotion drew the guards' attention, and they dropped Jorg, his head hitting a hard stone as he came to a stop. The effects of the last shock had waned, and his senses returned.

Whatever, or whoever, created the distraction behind them, gave enough time for Jorg's head to clear. He rolled his head to the side and met Bremen's gaze. His brother gave the slightest of nods. A tight set to his mouth indicated he, too, had regained some strength. Before their guards could realize they were coherent, both men jumped to their feet and attacked.

They dispatched the guards quickly, but heard more footsteps hurrying in their direction. Crouched in a ready position under the low ceiling, they stood shoulder to shoulder in the tight quarters.

Three bodies rushed around the corner, and they tensed. Jorg dug his toes into the dirt and leaned forward, but then pulled back. Even with the darkness, he recognized Plintze. Another dwarf skidded to a stop with him as Selby threw herself into Bremen.

INGRID

Ingrid sat through the remainder of dinner in numbed silence. Simple inconsequential chatter filtered into her awareness, but she engaged in none of it.

With Urkon on her right and Jarrick across from her, she found it hard to breathe as she contemplated her escape from both power-hungry men. She couldn't allow herself to be used as a game piece on a tafl board.

If she stayed close to Jarrick, she might be able to rescue Galwain, but he'd killed his own son to ensure he could use Ingrid. After he held all the power, why would he allow her to live any more than Urkon?

Urkon had killed her sister just to test her abilities. The few bites of food Ingrid managed to swallow churned in her stomach.

No matter how she spun it, or who ended up in control, Midgard would fall. It seemed that even if she did as Eir had trained her to do, she'd still end up helping with the destruction.

Another option crept into her thoughts. The more she considered it, the more she realized it might be the only way she could save herself—or help anyone else. She had to end them first. A huffed laugh escaped under her breath. It had only been a few months ago that she was forbidden to train as a shield-maiden. Now she was contemplating ways to destroy two of the most powerful beings in all the realms.

"You've been so stoic, Ingrid. I was concerned. Have you enjoyed your evening after all?" Thelonius asked. Silence crowded into the room. It seemed as though all conversation halted while everyone waited for her answer.

Ingrid's heart hammered against her chest, and warmth bloomed over her cheeks. "Your hospitality has been lovely, and the conversation enlightening." She nodded to the king in deference, trying her best to remember her mother's behavior during tense dinners with so-called allies. She'd always held herself with grace and dignity, yet made sure that her dagger was as accessible as her smile.

I need a dagger.

The king smiled, but his stare burrowed into Ingrid. She sat taller and softened her features. The war raging through her insides was kept contained within a silk wrapper.

"Vimala is not easily impressed, yet she liked you. She could feel your strength. Now that we've met, I agree with her." Thelonius held Ingrid's gaze without wavering as he seemed to contemplate his next words. "Remember who you are. Others don't always truly see us, but it's far worse if we don't see ourselves."

The facade slipped from Ingrid's face.

The king broke the connection and stood. When the rest of the guests rose, Ingrid's body reacted without her, bringing her to her feet. She'd been too engrossed in Thelonius' comment. Had he meant he knew why she was in Alfheim? That he knew of her destiny? Would he help her?

"I'm sure Ingrid is tired. Caelya, will you please escort her back to her rooms?" Jarrick's voice broke through Ingrid's thoughts.

Don't be a fool, Ingrid. No one is going to help you. That's what the king meant. He wanted me to remember that I'm alone and whatever needs doing, I have to do it myself.

"It was nice speaking with you, Ingrid. I'm sure we'll have another opportunity soon," Urkon whispered. He'd leaned forward as Ingrid turned to step away from her chair and pinned her in place. Subtle and quick, but the gesture was clear. She was trapped.

At least, that was what he'd wanted it to mean, but there was a stirring inside of Ingrid. She may not have her powers, yet she could act. She was Norse. Regardless of anything else, she had the blood of her mother and father flowing through her veins. If her magic never returned, she wasn't helpless.

"Aguane will be here shortly to help you out of your dress," Caelya said as she opened the door.

Ingrid hesitated before she walked into her rooms. "What is she, exactly?" Thoughts of being alone again with the floating woman sent a shiver up her spine.

Caelya rolled her eyes and huffed. She strode through the door ahead of Ingrid and turned to wait. Once inside, with the door shut, the two stood face to face.

"Aguane is a sylph. She's a cenobite, a holy woman, from Sodell. When elves near their age of maturity, it is a stressful experience—physically and emotionally. Sodell is a sanctuary of confinement within the frozen peaks of the Oirthear Mountain range. Sylphs are normally solitary beings. I had a particularly difficult time, and Aguane saw me through it. The experience touched her as much as it did me. When my transformation to adulthood was complete, she chose to stay with me."

"Is she a spirit?"

"No. They are living beings, only rather than flesh and blood, they are the embodiment of air—the fabric of all its elements. Aguane confines her true self to live here for my sake. Do not underestimate her, however. Though she appears as fine as mist, she is stronger than a hundred elven warriors."

Ingrid shivered. "How do you communicate with her? She doesn't speak to me."

"Are you sure? Her voice is as much the gentle whiff of a butterfly's wings as it is the gale forcing waves against jagged cliffs during a storm. Perhaps you should learn to listen better."

Caelya chuckled and left. Alone, Ingrid wrapped her arms around herself. The night air coming in from the balcony was balmy, yet her skin pebbled. How would she ever learn to navigate within Alfheim? Every direction held someone, or something, that she didn't understand.

As she contemplated her new surroundings, the temperature shifted. Ingrid dug her fingers harder into her arms and spun toward the door.

Once again, Aguane seemed to float barely off the ground. Tendrils of her gown shifted about the floor as if they drifted in water.

Ingrid's tongue grew thick inside her mouth. As hard as she tried to form words, she could only stare. The sylph reached out her hand toward the fireplace with her head cocked to the side.

"No, please don't light it," Ingrid managed to squeak out in a hurry. "I . . . I can't stand it."

Aguane gave a slight nod, then narrowed her eyes. Her stare pierced through Ingrid with startling accuracy.

What does she want?

The sylph stepped closer. Ingrid remained rooted to the

ground. Inside, she screamed at herself to run, but outwardly, she froze. Aguane reached her hand toward Ingrid's temple. A feathery touch fluttered against her skin. The bedchamber faded, and light surrounded Ingrid. She was in the air, floating as if she was part of the breeze itself.

Then, from behind her right shoulder, came a gust of wind. Something leathery yet sharp as glass grazed her shoulder. Unable to scream in her dreamlike state, Ingrid held her breath as the dragon flew overhead, inches from where she hovered. Scales black as midnight shimmered with a hint of blue or green as the serpentine body moved. Wings, wide enough to encompass a longhouse, stretched thin enough to see the delicate bones that held them together.

"No! I can't do this, take me back!" Ingrid screamed.

Suddenly, she was inside a mountain-sized dark cavern. The orange glow of flames flickered on the walls, illuminating dozens of smaller alcoves. Far below, fire swirled and sputtered like boiling water. The stifling heat seared Ingrid's lungs. Sweat dripped down her face and into her eyes. She swiped away the salty burn and swallowed down the fear scratching its way up her throat.

Inside each alcove was a nest, large enough that Ingrid wouldn't be able to touch the sides if she sat in the center. Many were empty, but those that were occupied held dragons. Sleeping dragons, with their bodies curled around objects that appeared to be large, oval stones, speckled in various colors. Not stones, Ingrid realized, but eggs.

Slowly, she twisted around. In the distance, she could see a point of light, the opening to the cavern. Awestruck, she continued to view the numerous sleeping beasts as she turned. Then she spotted an area that, at first, looked like another alcove but without a nest. Only, it wasn't. It was the opening to a tunnel —a pathway deeper inside the mountain.

Once again, the scenery changed. Cold mountain air dried the sweat on her body and caused her to shiver uncontrollably. A castle nestled into the side of the mountain rose into the air. Tall spires peaked several round towers surrounding a central building. Stone of glittering black contrasted against the snowy landscape.

Montibeo. The name impressed into Ingrid's thoughts. This was Jarrick's castle. As she watched, a figure appeared out of the clouds in the distance. Small and shadowed, it grew larger as it approached. The black dragon from the courtyard—Voxx, Jarrick's fylgia—flew toward the castle. Ingrid watched as she angled her wings to fly lower, then tucked them to her side and disappeared into an opening below the castle.

Bright light flashed, and an instant peace washed over Ingrid. Soft and gentle singing settled her mind. When the light cleared, she once again stood in her room. With legs too shaky to stand, she crumpled to the floor.

Whether or not she joined Jarrick, she had more dragons to face. The smell of smoke and flame, which reminded her of her loss, was the least of her worries. The dangers in her path grew beyond reason. Who was she to think she could defeat Jarrick or rescue Galwain?

I am a descendant of Freya and chosen to protect Midgard.

Ingrid pushed herself to her feet. She wouldn't give up before she'd tried. Jarrick and Urkon would destroy everything, and she was the only one to stop them. A snarl twitched her lips as she clamped her mouth tight.

Defiance simmered in her blood. "Thank you," she said to Aguane. The sylph nodded, and her crystalline eyes flashed brighter.

The next thing Ingrid knew, her dress was removed, and a night dress slipped over her head. It was so gentle and effortless she barely felt either motion. Moments later, she was alone. Her hair had been brushed, and she found herself propped up against the wooden headboard under the soft, warm comfort of her bedding.

As she sat in the silence, rays of silvery light from the moon peeked into the room. Something glittered on one of the chairs near the dark fireplace. It was the gilded edge of a book.

Odd. Where did that come from?

Ingrid was sure she had seen nothing sitting there before, but she wasn't in the mood to investigate. She had a rebellion to plan.

Neither Urkon, nor Jarrick could succeed. If that meant Ingrid had to become an assassin rather than a savior, so be it.

16

INGRID

Ingrid watched as the morning's lavender rays peeked over the balcony. She hadn't slept, and what little she managed hadn't been peaceful at all. The entire night, she'd contemplated how she would overthrow the two powerful elves. Jarrick had a connection with her. At least, it seemed like that whenever he spoke to her. It was kind of fatherly at times, which she found odd.

That would be what she used against him. She'd use that bond, that closeness, and find a way to defeat his plans.

It was Urkon who had her confused. The dark arts master was a mystery. From the way his eyes pierced through hers to the way he seemed to know what she was thinking. A scowl came through with every word he spoke. Thinking about him made her skin inch.

Urkon had no need for Ingrid that she could use. She was a means to an end for him. No matter which angle she examined it, Ingrid couldn't find a weakness to exploit.

She hopped out of bed and stretched, letting the kinks work out as she rolled her neck from side to side and swung her arms back and forth. There was a solution—she just needed to think harder.

Fresh air will do me some good.

She strode toward the balcony, and something caught her eye that made her stop. The book that had appeared in her room the night before still sat untouched. She wanted to read it but didn't have the desire right then.

Even still, she didn't want to lose track of the book. Somehow, it had showed up in her room, and that made her curious. Was someone trying to tell her something? Did the book have information that she might need?

Maybe so—she'd have to find out later. Right then, she needed to find a safe place to stash it where no one would find it. She picked up the heavy tome and clutched it to her chest as she peered around the room. The mattress! It was the only place someone might not check. She shoved the book under the heavy padding, pushing as far as her arms could reach toward the center.

There, now it'll stay safe until I have time.

Returning to her feet, she continued her path to the balcony. Fresh air washed over her when she stepped outside. The skies were clear and calm . . . *peaceful.*

What she wouldn't give for gray clouds, a drizzle of rain, and a bit of mud. She missed her village. She missed her family. Then she remembered her village no longer existed. Dúngarr had made sure of that, but her family *had* escaped. Wherever they'd gone, they were safe. Now she needed to make sure all of Midgard had the same opportunity. The Norns fated her to protect humanity—she wouldn't fail them.

She heard the door open and spun around. When the breeze lifted the curtain, Ingrid saw Caelya standing in her room. She headed inside to find out what the princess wanted.

"Are you going to get dressed for the day, or would you like to come with me dressed like that?" Caelya asked as a greeting.

"I wasn't aware I had anywhere to be."

"I thought you might like out of your rooms for a while. Though, if I was wrong, it won't bother me." Caelya turned to leave.

"Wait, where are you going?"

The elf faced Ingrid once again. "I'm going with Kelvhan to the marketplace this morning."

"Jarrick has allowed that?"

"Jarrick doesn't make all the rules," Caelya said. "If you want to go, you have to get ready now. I won't wait for you."

Ingrid said nothing more and rushed to the bathing room. She found her turquoise dress, the one she could fasten by herself, and hurried into it, adjusting her rune pouch to hide within the fabric. She quickly plaited her hair into a single braid and rushed back into the other room, hopping as she fitted the dainty slippers onto her feet. When she made it to Caelya, she closed her eyes for a heartbeat, then pulled her shoulders back, brushed down her skirts, and folded her hands.

"I'm ready. Was that fast enough?" Blood pounded through her ears, and she struggled to breathe steadily, but she maintained her composure.

The corner of Caelya's lips twitched, and mirth lit her eyes, but she said nothing. Turning on her heels, she opened the door and strode away as Ingrid hurried after her.

"How does that work? Why is it that I can go through the door with you, but on my own, these hallways turn against me?"

Caelya glanced down at Ingrid and then returned her gaze to the front. "There's a spell on the door."

"That much I guessed. Does it only work on me?" It was one of the other things Ingrid had thought of throughout the night.

To stop Jarrick, she'd first have to get out of the palace. If Caelya had that information, she was one step closer to a plan.

"I didn't do the spell. I don't know how it works. But yes, it's connected to you."

Hmm. Ingrid would think on that more. There had to be a solution. It was personal, something that Jarrick must have designed only for her. She decided to leave that thought alone and concentrate on where they were going. "Who is Kelvhan anyway?"

"Are you going to talk the *entire* time?" The princess sighed, then spoke into the air. "This is my punishment for being nice."

"I won't talk the whole time. You should meet my friend Selby. She never takes a breath." Ingrid smiled as she thought of her friend. Growing up, Ingrid never had to carry a conversation. In fact, with such little practice, it surprised her that she could. Then pain stabbed her chest when she remembered she'd never hear Selby's voice again.

"Kelvhan is a member of the king's guard . . . and my friend."

"Friend, huh? What kind of friend?"

"The kind that can put you in the dungeon instead of a fancy room."

Ingrid grinned. "The palace has a dungeon?"

She caught the annoyed glance that Caelya darted at her, but she kept her eyes forward. A member of the king's guard would be a good friend to have. Someone who knew their way around. Someone allied to the king rather than Jarrick. Caelya's companion he might be, but his loyalties would be to the king. A good friend to have, indeed.

When they made it through the doors and down the stairs to the gravel path, Ingrid felt the weight on her shoulders lighten slightly. The expanse of space, the wide path, and the fresh smell of greenery invigorated her.

Other details didn't escape her notice either. Like all the shrubbery next to the stone palisade wall. *Good places to hide.*

No one milled about. It was quiet ... deserted.

They really aren't worried about keeping prisoners around here.

If she could get out those doors alone, she would be free.

When they passed the guard booth at the gate, both males stood tall and nodded to Caelya. They'd barely glanced at Jarrick when they'd walked through the first time. The princess was beautiful; maybe that was it. She was regal and had an air of confidence around her. Ingrid couldn't help but admire her as well.

The path split as they approached the marketplace. The smaller path veered to the left while the wider path continued to the right.

"Where does that lead?" Ingrid asked, tipping her head to the narrow track.

"That's the servant area, those who work for the market owners and prepare their wares for sale."

Ingrid nodded, making a note to herself.

Elves filled the market. Everywhere Ingrid looked there were groups talking and pondering their purchases. Unlike in Jorvik, no one shouted or haggled here. Everything was so civilized. The elves spoke to each other with lowered voices in calm tones. While no one screamed, yelled, or got into a fistfight in the middle of the street, no one laughed either.

They were all so stoic, not angry or excited. They smiled and nodded. A few seemed like they might laugh, but if they did, it wasn't noticeable. There weren't any extreme emotions either way. The elves held themselves with dignity and composure at all times. Ingrid didn't understand it. Where was the passion? She'd take a longhouse full of rowdy warriors singing songs, spilling mead, and enjoying life over this serene but boring bunch any day.

As they strode through the streets, they came to a section that was even more crowded. Ingrid became unnerved as the crowd thickened and she couldn't see over or around anyone. Being short worked against her. Although ... maybe it didn't.

No one paid any attention to her. She could slip right through the crowd and no one would notice. Right then, Caelya reached over and took Ingrid by the arm with gentle fingers.

"Kelvhan's over here, this way."

Ingrid followed along closely, and when the crowd parted, she saw the guard standing by a booth, talking casually with another male. She supposed he was handsome; all the elves were. Kelvhan had the same brown hair as Jorg. With a wry grin, she realized she constantly compared all the males to Jorg, and no one ever matched up. A sting blurred her eyes that she blinked several times to thwart.

"Kelvhan, you remember Ingrid," Caelya said with a nod toward Ingrid as she smiled at Kelvhan.

"Of course. It's nice to see you again." Kelvhan gave a slight bow. There was a mischievous twinkle in his eye.

Ingrid instantly liked him, despite the circumstances. Becoming friends with him would be easy, but she wouldn't let herself become attached.

"Is it always this crowded?" Ingrid asked, lurching forward when someone bumped into her back. She scoffed at the apology that wafted into the air.

"Not always," Kelvhan said. "But the king's birthday is coming up. The whole city celebrates, and everyone's getting ready."

"The king's birthday?" *Interesting.*

"Thelonius hates it, but many years ago, we deemed his birthday a feast day. Now the celebration lasts an entire week. This is only the beginning. Festivities won't be in full swing until several days from now."

"Will I be able to attend?" Ingrid tried to keep the excitement out of her voice. An event like that would keep everyone distracted.

Caelya and Ingrid stared at each other. Ingrid knew it wasn't Caelya's decision to make, and the princess seemed to know Ingrid was up to something.

"She's feisty," Kelvhan said with a chuckle. "I'm starving. Let's go find something to eat. Then you two can continue whatever is going on here."

Caelya pursed her lips and gave a slight nod, turning away from Ingrid. Kelvhan led the way as they squeezed through the crowd.

You'd think a king's guard and a princess could command more space. Ingrid pursed her lips. It wasn't the outing she thought it would be. She'd grown hot and irritable while crowded between bodies with no breeze.

A merchant stopped Kelvhan and started a conversation. While she and Caelya waited, the crowd thinned out for a moment. Ingrid noticed a path just across the road. It looked like a cart path between buildings that was more than likely used for supplies.

Ingrid peeked at Caelya and Kelvhan. Neither paid attention to her.

I can't waste this opportunity.

Another quick glance, then she darted into the street, and the crowd absorbed her. Wiggling her way through unnoticed, she made it to the other side of the road. When she reached the cart path, she sprinted as hard as her legs would move.

She passed the first row of market booths and made it to a section of simple sheds used for storage. Darting between two of them, she stopped to listen. No footsteps or rattling armour followed her. A peek around the corner proved the path was empty. It had been easier than she thought.

She jogged away, staying between the buildings. Her victory

was short lived because only three steps later, rough hands clamped over her mouth and around her waist.

"What do we have here?" a low, male voice rumbled against Ingrid's back.

17

———

JORG

Jorg kept his fists up, wary of the dwarf standing behind Plintze's shoulder.

"We should keep going. There is a small alcove up ahead where we can hide," the newcomer offered.

The two dwarves hurried away, with Jorg left to follow reluctantly. Bremen and Selby were only a half-step behind. When they reached the nook, they ducked in and crouched down on their heels. Voices rumbled through the tunnels, but no one ran as far as where they hid—yet. It was only a matter of time before the bodies of the guards were discovered. In the silence that followed, they held their breath. Exhaling, Selby plopped down onto the ground.

"We should give it longer," the new dwarf scolded.

Jorg stared in the voice's direction, the darkness shielding him from having a clear view of the speaker. It was an oddly familiar sound.

"I think we are safe for now, Mimum," Plintze said.

"'*Safe*' is not how I would describe it," Selby answered. "We still have to get through these tunnels without getting caught. I can't even see across this alcove."

"I know where we are. You don't need to worry," Plintze said.

What is happening? He almost sounded . . . happy. "Are you all right? Did they hit you with one of those sticks they used on Bremen and me?"

"Ach, no. They'd never use a goblin breaker on another dwarf. We probably should have taken one of those with us though. Do you think we should go back for one, Mimum?"

"It's too risky now. You'll have to make do," Mimum said.

"Plintze, you need to introduce us to your friend before we take advice from someone who just tried to sell Jorg and me to a giant," Bremen whispered. Jorg heard his feet crunch against the dirt, ready to lunge and fight if necessary.

"This is my mother, Lynheid," Plintze said.

"Were you waiting in the tunnels for us?" Selby asked.

"No, I was there in the room, near you. Plintzelgermir let me know to protect you so I had shifted closer to you before they drug the others away."

"You had to notice her. She was the most beautiful female in the chamber," Plintze said with complete sincerity and oblivion toward Selby.

"Oh, yes . . . that's who you were." Selby had a hint of amusement in her voice, and Bremen made a little noise that sounded distinctly like a muffled chuckle.

Even Jorg let a grin twitch at his lips. He hadn't observed any female looking dwarfs, not that he was searching for them, but it did seem as though he'd have noticed.

"Why have you come home now, my son? It is such a time of upheaval with the giants and the prince. You shouldn't have brought humans down here," Lynheid said.

"What prince?" Jorg asked before Plintze had a chance to answer.

"The elven prince, Jarrick. Our council has been negotiating a deal to become the sole weapons provider for Midgard when the wards drop. The giants are eager to begin amassing large quantities as soon as the deal is sealed." Lynheid then whispered something to Plintze, in a language Jorg didn't understand.

"Jorg has always lived on Midgard, Mimum. He is safe," Plintze answered.

Safe . . . Right. As long as she doesn't know who my father is.

"When do they expect the wards to fall?" Bremen asked.

"The talk is soon, but no one knows for sure. There are rumors, too. Might any of you know of those?"

Jorg didn't believe that Plintze's mother would sell them out like any of the other dwarves surely would but giving her any information would be a risk. He said nothing and waited to see how Plintze would handle it. *Please don't risk Ingrid, friend.*

"In Midgard, there isn't much talk of the other realms. Some humans don't even believe they exist. I'm afraid we don't have any information," Plintze said and shifted on his feet.

"These humans are different? You haven't answered me about why any of you are here."

No one spoke for several heartbeats. "I'm only half-elf, and I've recently learned who my true mother is. She's in Alfheim, and I need to find her," Jorg said. He figured since none of it was a lie—*technically*—it would work as a good reason.

"You aren't expecting to get to Alfheim from here? Those tunnels haven't been used for travel in centuries. They aren't safe. You'll have to go back and find another way."

"We don't have time to find another way, Mimum. We *must* use the tunnels."

"Plintzelgermir, you have been away far too long if you don't remember the dangers. Nothing survives through the goblins. I could not bear to know you were lost. It is hard enough for me to know you are living in such a harsh, exposed realm. Won't you stay? Let your friends go back to their home and find another path. Stay with me where you'll be safe."

"I couldn't do that. Besides, you know I'm different now. I'd never be accepted."

"That's not true! I've never told anyone how you have the ability to walk in the sun. They don't know. Don't you want to come home? No one carves the filigree molds like you. Your skills will be valued now more than ever."

In the time they'd sat in the alcove, Jorg's eyesight had adjusted to the darkness. He could see Lynheid as she stroked Plintze's cheek when she spoke. He wanted to force the dwarf to stay behind and not abandon his mother, but he knew better than to interfere. Plintze's situation was not the same as his with Galwain. Their separation was for different reasons and not Jorg's to judge.

He could also see how Selby had melted into Bremen's side. How his brother held her close to him. The bead hadn't indicated they'd traveled any closer to Ingrid. The wasted time they spent talking in the dark only kept her from him. They needed to be on their way.

"Mimum, I can't stay. I have my own reasons for finding Ing —Jorg's mother. I miss you every day, but I must go. And we must risk the goblins. There is no faster way into Alfheim."

"You are such a brave boy. The bravest of all dwarves. Do not move from this spot until I return." With surprising speed Lynheid darted away into the tunnels, leaving the rest of them stunned.

"Where did she go," Selby whispered, and Bremen chuckled. Selby would never master the art of a quiet voice.

"I don't know, but Plintze, if you know how to get us to the correct tunnel, we need to go," Jorg said. Thinking of Ingrid had made him too antsy to sit still and hide any longer.

Footsteps in the tunnels made them all shift back and wait,

hoping it was Lynheid, but prepared to fight if it wasn't. Uneasiness spiked through Jorg. Would Lynheid turn them in to keep her son from leaving? To keep him from the goblins?

When she arrived again, alone, Jorg relaxed and chided himself for his thoughts. In her hand was a stick the length of a club but the circumference of a spear. One end had a silver tip, and there was a slight hum in the surrounding air.

"If you have to go, take this with you. I could only find one, so you'll have to make it count."

"What is that?" Jorg asked.

"It's a goblin breaker. One of the weapons they used on you in the tunnel. It can render a goblin immobile and spastic."

"Yeah, we're familiar with that part," Bremen said.

Plintze took the dangerous club and handed it to Bremen. Jorg bristled, but Bremen was closest.

"Thank you, Mimum. I have something for you, too." Plintze pulled off his pack and reached into it. He withdrew what looked like a wooden box with carvings all around it. His mother gasped when she saw it.

"You still have it. And you carried it all this way?" Lynheid's voice hitched as she reached for the box.

"I'd hoped I would see you. I want you to have it back—if it won't get you into trouble. No one can know you helped us in the tunnels," Plintze said in a quiet tone. He sounded like a small child confessing to his misdeeds.

"Plintzelgermir, I will display it proudly and challenge anyone to take it away from me. My son is the best woodcarver in all Svartalfheim, and it's time everyone remembers that." She took the box away from Plintze and held it close to her heart with one hand while she drew him in for a hug with the other. He threw his arms around her.

Jorg wondered if they should all leave to give them a moment. Before he could suggest it, Lynheid pushed herself away from Plintze. "Go now. There's no more time. The council will send out scouts when you don't arrive at the Jötunheim entrance."

Selby and Bremen hurried to rise to their feet as fast as Jorg. The group shuffled out into the tunnels, thanking Lynheid for her help. They moved a few steps away as Plintze said goodbye one more time to his mother.

"This way then, and make sure you keep up," Plintze said as he squeezed by them. They all hurried after him, not wasting any more than a quick glance to acknowledge that Lynheid had rushed off the other way.

"No problem, *Plintzelgermir*," Selby said.

A growled "Humph" returned from the darkness.

Speeding through the darkness in a hunched position had Jorg's legs burning. It had to be affecting the others, too, but no one complained. Bremen still carried the goblin breaker, but Jorg didn't want to ask for it and sound afraid.

He also didn't like that Plintze had given it to his brother. Not long after they'd left Lynheid, he'd seen Bremen squeeze Plintze's shoulder, too. It shouldn't affect him that a friendship had grown, but it did. He felt more alone than ever.

Just then, Jorg's chest hitched and rattled as if his heart had fluttered in a spontaneous pattern. He reached up to rub at the feeling only to realize the bead had started to hum. When he pressed his hand against it, the heat it produced seared into his chest. It was hot enough that he wanted to yell out, but he didn't dare. The bead worked! This was the right direction, and he was closer to Ingrid. In the midst of his joy, a sound broke through the air and grabbed his attention.

An odd clicking noise in the distance made Jorg reach out and tap Plintze's shoulder. He came to a halt and turned.

"What's that noise?" Jorg whispered.

"We're close then," Plintze mumbled, understanding what

Jorg's keen hearing had detected. "That would be the creatures warning the goblins that we're here. If you heard them, then they heard us." Plintze shuddered. "A Myrmex is like a cross between a giant spider and an ant. Avoid the stinger on the point of their hind end and you'll be fine. It'll hurt if they bite you, but the stinger has the venom. Once released, it signals the others, and they swarm to the spot."

"Good to know," Bremen said and pulled Selby close. Even in the darkness, Jorg could tell that her face had drained of color.

The bead hummed stronger against Jorg's chest. "Ingrid is in Alfheim, and there's a bunch of dead myrmex and goblins in my way." He growled and jogged forward. By the crunch of the path behind him, the others followed.

and wanted to know. "They were so different from everyone else."

"Kelvhan has taken them to the dungeons to find out," Caelya said. "I'm sorry for what happened. I know you feel trapped here, but you're not alone. Many are on your side."

Ingrid continued to stare at the fireplace. *How am I supposed to believe that? What has she done except help Jarrick keep me as a hostage? No one is here for me.*

Images of Galwain flashed through her mind. An abused dirty queen, in worse shape than Ingrid. Both of them placed there by Urkon. Who would rescue her?

"You tell me I have friends, that you're one of them," Ingrid flashed a glance at Caelya. "But Galwain is trapped at Montibeo, and nobody cares about her. How am I supposed to believe it'll ever be different for me?"

Caelya released a long breath and let silence creep over them before she finally spoke. "Galwain is not in as much comfort as you, that's true, but she's not abused. I just saw her yesterday."

"What? You visit with Galwain?"

"Of course. She was my best friend, before she betrayed my brother. She took his son away, and I don't think he'd struggle like he does today if he'd had his family. There's a bond that's created between an elf and their true mate. They communicate with each other's minds. It's more intense than just speaking. It's an emotional and spiritual connection that bonds them closer than a fylgia. If that goes away, the pain is unbearable. Jarrick's has lived like that for almost twenty years because of Galwain."

Ingrid understood better than Caelya knew. Jorg had explained it to her the first time she left for Asgard and he couldn't hear her anymore. He'd said he thought his head would crack open because the pain was so intense. Should she consider it a blessing? That while she was in Alfheim and waiting to do the bidding of dark elves, she didn't have to worry about Jorg's pain?

"So is Jarrick better now that Galwain has returned?"

Caelya stared into her mug and fidgeted her fingers against the pottery's smooth side. "He has not discussed it with me."

Ingrid scrunched her brows together. "But the pains are gone? He can hear her again?"

"I don't know." Caelya sat her mug on a side table and leaned back into the cushioned chair. "Galwain says he hasn't tried. They've only spoken once since she's been back, and that was briefly when she first arrived."

Ingrid sipped her wine. "Why is that? When he took her, he said he wanted to put their family back together. Why won't he speak to her now?" Ingrid stood and paced closer to the fireplace. She put her hand on the mantle and stared into the dark cavern.

"I can only guess. If he connects to Galwain again, then he opens himself up to being hurt by her. By keeping their connection from forming, he is protecting himself."

Ingrid rubbed her temples. Why would he do that? Why would he choose to stay in pain?

Perhaps forgiveness would interfere with his plans.

"Galwain and Jarrick fell in love at first sight. They had no worries, no troubles when they met together in secret. It was youthful and easy. Jarrick is different now. He wants to prove himself a great leader, to have his own realm and not waste away as second to Thelonius," Caelya added.

Ingrid faced her. "So, you think Jarrick should be allowed to lead, regardless of what he does or what he wants to do with that leadership?"

"Thelonius is a good king. I have no issues with his leadership, nor do I want him to do anything different. But Jarrick's a good leader, too. He deserves to be king."

"You think that's what he wants? To become the king of Vanaheim? How do you see that working out? Odin, Thor, Tyr, and all the gods are going to step aside and let Jarrick rule? Jarrick wants to usurp Odin. He wants to become a god himself."

"No! That's not true. At least, not from Jarrick. Who knows Urkon wants?"

Ingrid paced to her chair and back. Caelya defended Jarrick, but he was her brother. She did, however, seem to have a sense of caution concerning Urkon. He'd threatened Ingrid more than once using subtlety and implied threats. Maybe if they could work together and get Jarrick to connect with Galwain again, Urkon would lose his hold.

"Take me to Galwain. I need to speak to her directly. She's the only one with a chance to persuade Jarrick to leave Urkon. They want to use me to start a war. It won't just destroy Midgard, but all the realms."

"You're being overly dramatic. Urkon wants power, I'll admit. But no one is stupid enough to start a war with Odin. I don't know where you got that information."

Caelya stood up stared off into space after she finished speaking. A pinched expression belied the confidence she projected.

"Do you understand why they want me?" Ingrid asked. "Has Jarrick explained to you what I can do?"

Before Caelya could answer, a knock sounded at the door. "Come," the princess called out with visible relief crossing her features.

Kelvhan poked his head in before entering. "I'm sorry to disturb you, but I thought you should know what I've learned right away."

19

INGRID

Ingrid raced through the halls, following Kelvhan and Caelya. They'd tried to leave her behind, but she'd insisted on coming. The men who attacked Ingrid were currently in the dungeons only because no one had informed Jarrick, but Kelvhan was sure someone would move them soon. They had to hurry. He wanted Caelya to hear their information for herself, and Ingrid refused to wait alone until they'd returned.

When they reached the grand rotunda, instead of heading to the right as Ingrid had before, Kelvhan rushed them through a small door hidden behind a potted tree and down a darkened corridor. Sparsely placed torches tucked into rings secured into the stone walls illuminated patches of darkness. A slim wooden door, aged by time and use, blocked the end of the passage.

Kelvhan glanced at Ingrid, then focused on Caelya when his hand covered the handle. The princess gave a quick nod. Grabbing a torch, he led the women through the doorway and down a set of stairs that spiraled like the inside of a snail shell.

Cool air mixed with the darkness as it grew damper the farther they descended. Ingrid kept her arms out, bracing her hands against each wall so she didn't slip on the narrow steps. They had to be inside one of the towers she'd seen when she'd first arrived. From that view on the hillside, everything was light and airy. Nothing spoke of an eerie underground and dungeons.

They reached the bottom, and Ingrid hugged herself. Rubbing her arms as she fell into line between the tall elves.

I don't need their protection.

But as much as she tried to rally her spirit, it was no use. The attack had left her shaken. Surrounded by those stronger and faster made her feel safe—if that was possible in a dark tunnel with walls so narrow they nearly brushed each side of Kelvhan's shoulders.

The musty smell of standing water and mud permeated the air, and the only sounds were their footsteps against the stone floor.

The walkway reached an open area with more torches positioned along the walls, giving the most light since they'd left the rotunda above. Several hallways branched off the central space. A distant rattling of chains echoed from one of them.

"Last chance. Are you sure you want to face them, Ingrid?" Kelvhan asked.

Ingrid swallowed and rolled her lip between her teeth. Did she? Was she brave enough?

"Yes, lead the way," she said, standing taller and meeting Kelvhan's gaze.

The hint of a smile sparkled in his eyes before he headed toward the metallic rattles.

With just a few long strides from the king's guard, each side of the hallway turned into a series of arches with wide columns in between. Under the arches, iron bars formed the front wall of the small rooms. Each cell was empty, but the arches stretched far into the darkness, and the sounds grew louder as they walked.

"I didn't think Alfheim used iron," Ingrid stated out loud as she peered into the next darkened space. Stone walls, stone floors, and nothing else graced the cells.

"It's necessary down here," Caelya answered. "This part of the palace was built before the ancient war of the gods."

"Do each of the halls contain this many rooms?" Ingrid couldn't imagine the need to hold so many prisoners.

"Yes, though only a few have ever been used," Kelvhan answered then halted before the first occupied cell. He held the torch close to the bars to illuminate the elf inside. Ingrid recognized Beril, the leader of the duo who'd captured her.

She slammed her eyes closed, then caught herself. With eyes open and shoulders back, she glared at the prisoner. He was trapped, and she was safe.

He wore the same grimy clothing as she remembered, but a few welts appeared on his face that hadn't been there before. Elves healed quickly, and she wondered what—or who—could have caused enough damage to linger that long. She peeked at Kelvhan standing tall and confident. A grin twitched at the corner of her mouth. Yes, she was safe.

"So, what is this information I need to hear?" Caelya asked. Her hand rested on her hip as if she was bored.

"Take these off, and I'll tell you anything you want to know, princess." Beril's gruff voice tried to sound alluring; the absurdity was nearly comical. He was chained to the far wall with a shackle around each ankle.

Caelya inspected her nails and sighed.

Ingrid would have given anything at that moment for a spear. Beril had wanted to ransom her. She would love to feel the sharp point as it pierced his flesh in perfect vengeance.

"I stopped here to show Ingrid what a coward looks like," Kelvhan said. "The one with the information is farther down."

Beril's eyes widened before he growled and lunged toward

the bars. Ingrid flinched slightly and clenched her teeth. She would not give such a filthy creature power over her ever again.

"Don't say anything!" Beril screeched into the air. Slamming his fist against the stone wall. He was pathetic. Ingrid smiled.

"Are you ready to continue, Ingrid?" Kelvhan asked, ignoring the outburst.

She nodded and faced the guard. This time, she truly meant it.

They passed many more empty cells before they reached the next prisoner. This time, Ingrid didn't recognize his face, but as he screamed out curses, she knew his voice. Quarn, the one who'd held her, *touched* her. Her eyes fluttered as she fought for control of her stomach. Then she stood tall.

"Explain who you are and where you've come from. Though I'm sure my friends would find it entertaining if you wish to proceed as before?" Kelvhan said with authority. This elf also had welts and a few cuts on his cheek and jaw.

"I would, for sure," Ingrid said.

"I won't say it again. I'm done talking," Quarn growled.

Standing there, staring at one who'd overpowered her, Ingrid clenched her fists. Inside, her magic rumbled and flashed. Startled by the feeling, she gasped, and everything settled far away from her again.

Pounding her thighs, Ingrid released a frustrated growl.

Kelvhan handed the torch to Caelya and stepped into the shadows. "I don't think it's Jarrick restricting your magic," Caelya said with a glance to Ingrid.

Well, someone is, and I want it to stop. Ingrid swiped away a loose pebble with her toe.

When Kelvhan returned, Quarn's eyes bulged, and he waved his hands. "No, no, no! I'll tell them."

"What is that?" Ingrid asked, staring at the club-length stick in Kelvhan's hand and dismissing her earlier frustration over her magic. The weapon's silver tip emitted a buzzing sound and raised the hair on Ingrid's arms.

"It's called a goblin-breaker. We used them to keep the tunnels into Swartalfheim clear before the borders closed. It renders one—helpless," Kelvhan answered. "Pity he's giving up so easily. I'd let you try it."

Ingrid faced Quarn, a dark smile on her face. "There's no harm in testing it. I'd *love* to know how it works."

"I'll talk! Don't use that thing," Quarn cried out, falling to his knees.

Kelvhan handed the goblin-breaker to Ingrid, which she held tentatively in her hands—the energy wafting from it palpable. She stared at him wide-eyed and eager. Did he really mean she could use it?

"Just to hold," Kelvhan said with an arched brow, then leaned toward her. "For now." He whispered with a wink and a grin.

Of those who'd been kind to Ingrid since arriving on Alfheim, the guard just became her favorite.

The hum of the club in her hand reminded her of her power when it flared. She held the safe end and tapped the middle against her other palm while she smirked at Quarn. "You were saying?"

Caelya huffed and turned away, but Ingrid noticed the twitch of her mouth before she did.

"Beril and me . . . we wanted to see the royal city. We overheard some of the guards talking about a celebration, and we wanted to see. That's all."

Ingrid stepped forward.

"And, and . . ." Quarn waved his hands at her. "We are part of the army up in the mountains. We train at the prince's castle."

"You live at Montibeo? I've seen no such army," Caelya said. She glared at the captive with such venom that Ingrid gripped the goblin-breaker harder. If anyone used it, she'd be first.

"We live in the caverns, behind the dragon hive, and we train in the old lava tubes."

"How did you come to be there? You appear elven, yet I don't recognize your kind," Kelvhan said.

"Most everyone is from the smaller towns on the other side of the spirit forest. I was working my farm one day when the guards came through and rounded up all the males. They did that to another couple of communities before we made it to the castle. After we got there, they separated us into groups of ten or so. Then we all had to go through a series of shots. They said it was to ready us for battle. Beril and I haven't finished ours, but he's one treatment ahead of me."

"Tell them who gave you the shots," Kelvhan said.

"It was Prince Jarrick's guards. He was there watching, and sometimes Master Urkon, too."

"This is madness. You have to be lying," Caelya said. She spun and marched out of the light, but Ingrid could hear her breathing hard in the shadows.

Do you believe me now? Ingrid had tried to tell her before that Jarrick didn't share her views on slavery, but even she wouldn't have expected something like this.

A horrendous crash sounded in the tunnel from the direction they'd come, and Ingrid wheeled in that direction. Footfalls, loud and heavy, echoed against the stone walls. She held the goblin-breaker aloft, ready for whoever came for them.

"You'll need a few more of those if you expect to stop him," Quarn said. After how much he'd sniveled and cried about the goblin-breaker, he seemed calm . . . resigned. "He's not himself anymore, and he won't leave any of us alive."

"Who? What are you talking about?" Kelvhan asked, his voice tense but commanding.

"Beril."

At that moment, a figure burst into view. The hallway was at least five paces wide and nearly as tall as two men, yet whoever stood there filled the space. Snarls like a wild animal screeched through the air, and a sulfuric smell, reminiscent of dragon's fire, burned Ingrid's nostrils.

Caelya withdrew a short sword from somewhere within her clothing, causing Ingrid to look twice before focusing her attention at the incoming creature. She spread her feet and readied to launch herself forward, catching the intruder before he could swing at her. Instead, she was swept aside by Kelvhan and had to let herself fall to avoid the silver tip of the weapon she held.

Screams and grunts filled the walkway. Shadows danced like puppets against the walls as the torch lay on the ground. Ingrid scrambled over to pick it up. Holding it high in her left hand, she continued to grip the goblin-breaker in her right.

Both Caelya and Kelvhan attacked the monster. Between the blur of their speed and the low light, it was hard to see all Beril's new features. The only thing Ingrid could tell for sure was that he was huge, and he appeared to have some type of armour that flashed when the light hit it.

Ingrid couldn't rush in without risking the other two. Kelvhan had said the club would render one helpless, but she didn't know what that meant, so she couldn't risk it.

Caelya screamed and flew through the air, crashing against the stone wall. She fell into a heap on the ground and didn't move. Kelvhan did his best, but he was soon on his knees under the weight of one arm.

For the first time, Ingrid could see Beril in full. His features were unrecognizable from what he'd looked like before. His eyes glowed through reptilian slits, sharp teeth protruded from an elongated muzzle when he snarled, and his ears had morphed into lizard-like frills on the side of his head. Ridges of bony spikes replaced his eyebrows, and two tall horns rose from his forehead.

His body was still shaped like a man though he was more than twice as large with a barrel-shaped chest that was as wide as three of Ingrid's arm-spans. Each limb was the size of a tree trunk and covered in scales!

Unable to breathe for several heartbeats, Ingrid finally forced her feet to move. On the ground between herself and the dragon-looking elf, Caelya's short sword lay abandoned. Snatching it on the way by, she used the beast's focus on Kelvhan against him and slammed the sword through Beril's calf. He roared, the sound echoing off the walls as Ingrid yanked the blade free. Throwing the sword, she used two hands to jam the goblin-breaker into the wound.

When the creature roared again, he let go of Kelvhan. The guard threw himself over Ingrid, and they skidded into the far wall.

Dirt rattled from the ceiling as the giant body lurched and fell to his knees, convulsing until there was a loud popping noise. Then the beast lay still.

20

JORG

As the clicking sound in the tunnel grew louder and faster, Jorg slowed his pace. He was in a hurry, but he didn't intend to get caught in some trap before he fought. The ground was softer than before, but it didn't feel muddy. It was spongier.

Whatever it was, it didn't stick to his boots. *What is this?* The clicking sounds mixed with a low hissing. His questions about what he stood upon were long forgotten as the sounds grew louder.

"We have to stay together. Don't let them separate or surround us," Plintze warned.

"I still have this, but I don't know how it works," Bremen said as he held up the goblin breaker.

"Jab it, and wherever the silver tip hits, it'll do the job," Plintze said. Bremen sucked in a deep breath and adjusted his grip on the club.

"Just make sure you aim it at the right body," Jorg said as a shudder rolled over his shoulders at the memory of the breaker's power.

Bremen grunted. "I'll take care of it."

The bead under Jorg's shirt heated and buzzed, creating desperation to move forward. Any moment now, he expected the goblins to charge around the corner while they discussed strategy.

"Let's go," Selby whispered. "I want to get this over with."

"Bremen, you've got the breaker. You go first, next to me. Selby and Plintze, you stick close and guard our backs," Jorg said.

They huddled together and moved forward as one, but Jorg stopped them. "Why is it quiet?" The tunnels were suddenly eerily mute—all hissing and clicking had silenced.

"Stand ready!" Plintze called out as golden eyes glowed in the darkness and shrill hissing returned with a vengeance to pierce the air like daggers.

As the four rushed around the corner, Jorg noticed movement on the walls. Skidding to a stop, he nearly caused Selby and Plintze to run him over. Bremen halted on his own, also aware of the situation.

All along the walls were creatures with segmented black bodies, eight legs, and on each side of their heads were long pinchers—ready to grab and pull in any prey. Several rows of sharp teeth jutted out of their triangular mouth as they made clicking noises. Even in the low light, their eyes glittered with the anticipation of their next meal hurrying into their lair.

"What are they?" Selby asked, the whites of her eyes radiating even in the low light.

"Myrmex," Plintze answered. "They help the goblins."

As the four studied the creatures, they formed a circle. They stood back to back, leaving no blindside as the creatures scuttled closer.

Jorg pulled the dagger he'd hidden in his boot and held it aloft. It was the one he'd given Ingrid and planned to return to her as soon as they found her. As he suspected, he saw Selby with a blade in her hands as well. Where she'd had it hidden, he didn't know, but that didn't matter. As long as she had something to defend herself, he believed she'd be all right. Bremen had the goblin breaker, and Plintze had wrangled his staff back before he'd escaped with Lynheid.

Careful to keep his back rested against Selby and Plintze, Jorg slashed his dagger crossed the abdomen of the first myrmex that charged at him. Blood splashed against his skin, burning, but not enough to stop him.

"Ow! This stuff burns!" Selby cried.

"It won't last. Just don't let them catch you with those teeth," Plintze hollered back.

Every time Bremen used the goblin breaker, the energies simmered through the air. At first, it made Jorg flinch each time he felt it, but the speed at which the creatures attacked soon had him too occupied to notice.

With small steps, the group moved forward, leaving a trail of dead bodies behind them. For a moment, it looked as though they'd made progress. The attacks came slower, and the creatures had backed away with an occasional single myrmex that sprung forward. They no longer seemed intent on destroying the group.

"I think we've got them scared," Jorg said.

"No, they're just reeling us in," Plintze answered.

"That's not what we need to hear, Plintze," Bremen called over his shoulder.

As they moved forward, the tunnel gradually grew wider. When they reached the widest point, they moved to stand shoulder to shoulder. The myrmex had retreated enough for them to view the next repulsive creatures that waited to strike. Across the cavern stood a mass of figures. Jorg could only guess they were the goblins.

Some held torches, some pickaxes, and some held nothing at

all. Sharp, jagged teeth flashed as they hissed. They didn't need weapons.

Hunch-backed, they had slick ash-colored skin covered with splotches of soot. Long, thin pointed ears jutted back along the sides of rounded bald heads. Round eyes, too huge for their face, were solid black. The absence not only of color but of soul.

The goblins were demented, angry beasts. Deprived of sunlight and the simplest necessities, they had no ability to communicate. They existed to survive; live or die, nothing more. To get through the goblins and find the tunnel that would take them to Alfheim, they'd have to kill every single one.

"What do you suggest Plintze?" Jorg asked.

"Too late to turn back now. Alfheim's just on the other side of these monsters."

"What's better? Charge or wait?" Bremen asked

Jorg snorted. "I'm not waiting for anyone."

Selby flashed him a grin, and without another word, the two rushed forward with Plintze and Bremen half a step behind. Their motion triggered the goblins to charge, and the two groups clashed in the middle.

There wasn't any time to help each other. There were too many of them. Two, three, or four goblins at a time slammed against each of them. It was all Jorg could do to keep his feet under him. He slashed his dagger across the throat of one goblin, then jammed it into the spine of another. One landed on his shoulder, raking him with its sharp teeth before he twisted its neck and threw it against the cave wall.

There were so many. *There has to be a weakness we can find. We're too close to lose now.*

Goblin after goblin assaulted them. Most dropped their weapons before they charged, preferring to fight with their teeth and claws. Jorg could feel blood oozing from several wounds he'd gained, but he pushed on.

"Let me get to the front," Bremen called. "This weapon is working."

Plintze dodged to his right, and Jorg felt Bremen against his arm as he moved into place next to him.

"I'll swing this around—stay back!" Bremen yelled.

The growls and shrieks of both man and beast echoed against the cave walls, but Jorg's ears heard Selby growl a little extra at Bremen's implication that he could handle all the goblins himself.

Jorg hesitated, knowing he was faster. Perhaps he should insist on using the weapon himself? There wasn't any time to debate the issue—he had to trust Bremen.

Within moments, Jorg's concern eased. He'd given his brother the benefit of the doubt and relied on him. It paid off. Bremen swung in wide arcs, causing every goblin he struck to fall to the ground in convulsions.

Selby, Jorg, and Plintze handled the stragglers that avoided the weapon. The occasional myrmex would charge in, and they would dispatch that, too, and as the goblins lost ground, the myrmex retreated farther into the darkness.

Jorg's arms tired and his legs shook from staying crouched in a fighting position. He was sure the fight drained the others as well, but no one slowed down.

"There it is. I can see the tunnel. Only a little further!" Plintze called out.

Bremen glanced toward the opening. In that split second, two goblins ducked under the weapon and slammed Bremen to the ground. The club fell from his fingers, and Selby screamed. She surged forward to hold off the goblins, trying to take advantage of the misstep. She kicked the goblin breaker into an oncoming group who squealed and stopped advancing.

Jorg slammed his dagger into the neck of a goblin on top of Bremen, and Plintze used his staff to fling the other off. Grabbing Bremen by the arms, Jorg pulled him to his feet. A large wound bled from his shoulder, and his tunic was wet with blood on his side.

There was no more time; they had to get out of the tunnels. Selby couldn't risk reaching for the weapon, but they were close enough to the opening that they could make it out if they hurried.

"I'll be fine," Bremen said, standing on his own. "Let's get out of here."

Jorg realizing he was so close to Ingrid urged himself forward. Mustering more energy from deep within, he slashed at lightning speed as the others ran for the entrance.

Bremen pushed Selby ahead of him while Plintze took up the lead as they ran down the tunnel. The air grew heavier, and pressure built around them. They kept pushing as it grew even thicker, leaning forward as if into a strong wind.

Plintze halted. "Ach! I can't move."

"What is this? Why can't we move?" Sticking closest to Plintze as they ran, Selby appeared trapped as well. It was as if there was pressure locked around them, binding them in place.

"Try to move backward." Plintze knocked against Selby as he slid his feet away from the opening.

They managed their way to where Bremen and Jorg waited. So far, no goblins had followed them into the passage.

Jorg felt like his lungs were on fire and being squeezed in a vice. Now wedged in the tunnels behind some invisible barrier, he struggled to think straight. "Do you think it's a ward Plintze?" he asked.

"It is. We have to figure out a way through it." Plintze stepped up and ran his hand into the air. It didn't seem like he touched anything, but sometimes he could push farther ahead while other times his hand would bounce backward.

"I think there might be a way we can tear through it," Plintze said. He brought his staff up and tried to pierce the veil, but that didn't work. He lowered it and stared at the barrier once more.

"Plintze we have little time," Bremen called out.

Movement sounded from the tunnels behind them. Jorg could hear the scratching—apparently, Bremen could as well. If he could hear it, that meant whatever made the noise was close enough human ears could pick it up.

Plintze growled and shoved his hand forward as hard as he could. Ripping with his fingernails, he pierced a small hole. A whistling sound erupted through the air, and the relief from the pressure made Jorg's ears pop. Selby grabbed the sides of her head.

"Can you rip more of it, Plintze? It's working!" Jorg yelled.

"Aye, but it's so tough."

Selby tried to help, but as soon as she touched the barrier, her hand bounced back, and she screamed. "It's like it stabbed me. I don't think we can help," she said, holding her fist to her chest.

"Let me try." Jorg squished by Selby in the tight quarters of the tunnel. Dropping to a knee next to Plintze, they both dug into the barrier. There were no painful effects for Jorg like there had been for Selby, so they both clawed as hard as they could. With the extra effort, it was working.

Soon, the wind blew their hair as the hole grew wider. Jorg thought he heard clicking behind them. He didn't know if his imagination toyed with him or if the myrmex had crawled into the passage. He couldn't hear the goblins, but they were quieter.

That was—until they hissed.

Finally, Plintze pushed through and fell onto the other side. Jorg shouldered into the gap and wiggled across, hopping on one foot as he freed his second foot.

"Come on." Jorg motioned Selby forward as she stared at him, terrified.

The wind settled once they crossed through, and there weren't any clicking sounds. In fact, he couldn't hear anything from the other side. He should hear something. The hole they'd made was big enough for him to crawl through. It was certainly big enough for Selby.

Something was wrong. Selby spoke, but Jorg couldn't hear her. A tear slipped down her cheek as she stared at him. If it had been anyone else, he might have thought something was wrong with her voice or his ears.

Jorg reached out to push his hand through the tear, only to find a smooth surface under his palm.

"Plintze, the barrier—it's solid again! Help me."

The dwarf had run ahead and waited farther up the tunnel. They would have to work together, and fast, to get the others free.

Jorg twisted enough to let Plintze claw another opening. As soon as he had worked a finger-sized gap in the invisible covering, the air whooshed Selby's cries into the tunnel. Jorg scurried to help. As soon as he could reach through, he latched onto Selby. Her arm slipped through, but neither of them could coerce her body to follow.

With a kernel of an idea, Jorg pushed Selby's arm back to the other side. He shouldered his way through the barrier once again. Only this time, he stopped halfway, shoving his back against the opening. With one foot on either side, Jorg pushed his arms straight across and held open the barrier. The clicking was louder than before, and he heard the hiss of several goblins. Bremen was three paces away, swinging Selby's dagger, to allow her time to slip through the opening.

There was no more room that Jorg could offer, and Selby had to hold on to Jorg in a tight hug as she maneuvered across the barrier and then hurried out of the way for Bremen.

"Hurry, Bremen. I can't keep it open much longer." Jorg had

to scream over the noise of the beasts gaining ground on his brother.

Without turning around, Bremen backed his way until he was leaning against Jorg's leg.

"Crawl across, under my arms!" Jorg yelled out, even though they stood so close they were touching. The myrmex and the goblins saw they were about to lose their prey and increased their efforts to grab Bremen.

When one foot was through the opening, Jorg wrapped his arm around his brother's waist and dove for the Alfheim side of the border. Both men fell to the ground and rolled. The hissing and clicking went silent.

"Let's not wait and see if they can claw their own way through," Bremen said with a look of relief and gratitude toward Jorg.

Jorg nodded, and as they turned to run up the tunnel behind Plintze and Selby, Bremen squeezed Jorg's shoulder. Although they were running for their lives, warmth bloomed through Jorg's chest.

Light filtered into the tunnel, and the group pushed their legs harder. Plintze led the way at a pace the others struggled to match. They rounded a corner, and a silvery light glowed twenty paces ahead. A surge of relief flooded through Jorg as he watched Plintze dive through the opening without trouble.

One by one, they landed on a soft mound of green grasses and breathed in the fresh air.

21

INGRID

Elves have excellent hearing, so it didn't take long for the dungeon to fill with soldiers. Kelvhan jumped into action and explained the situation. Though Quarn would no longer speak, he sat in his cell with his arms around his bent knees and stared into space. Kelvhan launched an investigation into the claims Quarn had made, ordering extra guards to watch over him. He issued goblin-breakers to each.

After Caelya finally escorted Ingrid back to her rooms, she hurried through a cursory wash before she crawled into bed, too exhausted for anything more. Aguane hadn't come to her rooms, which she realized she'd been looking forward to.

I wonder where she is?

Ingrid lay staring at the brocade fabric gathered above the canopied bed. Sleep eluded her no matter how hard she tried. Images of Beril snarling with his dragon features and mindless brutality haunted her each time she closed her eyes. Then she remembered the book she'd hidden earlier. Some reading might help change her thoughts.

Covered in thick leather, the tome weighed heavy in her hands as she retrieved it from under the mattress. There wasn't much light in the room, and she dragged one of the cushioned chairs to the balcony. She'd read by moonlight, which was abundant that night.

Once settled, she read the cover, and her eyes widened. She stared, unable to move. It was the book she'd nearly chosen from the shelf before dinner. Caelya had noticed, but she couldn't have been the one to bring it into Ingrid's room. They'd been together throughout dinner.

It had to have been Aguane. How she knew about it was a mystery though. Ingrid swallowed hard and forced her fingers to open the cover. Despite the circumstances that brought her the book, something urged her to read it. Perhaps it would take her mind off Urkon, Jarrick, and all the pain they caused. *Perhaps.*

Ingrid handled the pages with care, admiring the illuminations but only skimming the words. Then her skin went cold as a full-page image of a hooded man appeared. He stood in a dark tunnel, a crow on his shoulder and swirling mists all around his feet. It was Odin. Ingrid was positive, but that wasn't what stopped her. It was the words below the picture.

Odin travels the Grimnir Passage between realms.

The hair on Ingrid's arms stood on end. Her stomach rolled as if it were a stormy sea. There was a path accessible to all the realms without a portal? Was it only accessible to Odin? She turned back a page and read. Shaky fingers followed the words to keep her from missing a single one.

It spoke of Odin using the tunnel to pass unseen between each realm. It was how he could travel in disguise to check on the loyalty of his followers, test the hearts of warriors, and even study new forms of knowledge without hindrance. There wasn't any information about how the passage worked. It was dangerous—that was clear—but nothing told where it was or if anyone else could use it.

Ingrid turned another page and continued to read. She

stopped, frozen, her fingers too heavy to lift from the page. At the center of the Grimnir Passage was the Yggdrasil tree. Not only did the tunnels lead between the realms, but they also led to the center of them all.

The Tree of Life where Ingrid had to stand to bind the spell.

There was a pathway to the Yggdrasil tree somewhere in Alfheim. Ingrid had a way to escape and bind the spell. She could defeat both Jarrick and Urkon while she protected Midgard. It was the destiny she'd trained for.

Finding the Grimnir Passage wouldn't be easy. There wasn't an exact location anywhere in the book that she could find. She'd spent the next few hours searching every page. The skies had turned light, and her eyes gritty, but she had no further information.

Ingrid slid the book from her lap and stood. Stretching, she released the kinks in her arms and legs from sitting so long. She rolled her neck and sighed. Was she really going to endure the halls again? And what about Galwain? Could she abandon her to suffer in Montibeo?

Too tired to make a true plan, she wandered out to the balcony. The morning air was crisp against her bare arms. The calm and peace were in direct contrast to the storm raging in her mind.

When Jarrick had hauled her to Alfheim, he'd saved her life because it suited his purpose. He needed her, and that justified allowing his dragon, *Voxx*, to destroy everyone else—including Jorg. If she decided finding the passage was more important than Galwain, how was she any different from Jarrick?

Ingrid stared out at the marketplace with its colorful flags waving in the breeze. It was quiet before the crowds showed up for the day. Beyond that stretched the open grasses, glistening in the dewy morning as the sun peeked over the horizon. If she were to escape—somehow getting through the ever-changing hallways, past the guards, and through the marketplace—she'd be without cover and spotted easily.

Then she looked to the forest. It loomed along both sides of the village, dark and menacing. Did she have the courage to brave it alone? She had to. The image of Odin in the tunnel flashed through her mind. Could the Grimnir Passage be that close? Her hand closed around the runes still secured around her neck. Eir had told her she needed to have her bead. But why? So many thoughts swirled through her mind she couldn't remember the reason.

Well, I don't have it anymore. She huffed a laugh and rested her hands against the smooth stone of the railing. Whatever the purpose, she'd have to forge ahead without the bead. Resolve bloomed in her chest, and she released a long breath. *I have to do this . . . and hope Galwain forgives me.*

With renewed purpose and determination, she returned to her rooms in search of something she could wear besides her night clothes.

After checking every cabinet, Ingrid found her own clothes, laundered and folded neatly at the bottom of a drawer in the bathing chamber.

Interesting.

Finally, able to feel like herself, she opened one door a crack and peeked into the hall. Quiet and lifeless, the path to freedom stood ready.

Instead of charging forward as she'd done before, she studied each direction for a clue to what might have confused her. As she leaned forward to get a better view, she caught sight of the second door she'd left closed. The lines and whorls that appeared as an intricate design drew her attention. She'd noticed them the first time when she entered through the heavy wooden doors.

Ingrid reached out and let her fingers graze over the carvings. Her breath caught, and dizziness threatened to buckle her knees as understanding slammed into her. They were more than a design; they were words-warding the doorway with a spell. It had to be what caused her to become confused and lose her way.

She pressed her hand against the grooves and closed her eyes. Held rapt as the words became clear, her chest heaved from the effort or the excitement, she didn't care. Words took shape and made sense individually, but they seemed jumbled. It was like a puzzle. *How do I release this?*

A memory surfaced from her time with Eir. The first lesson she'd learned. Eir had made her clean the workroom, moving pots, jars, and bottles with her mind. Rearranging everything until it was in order. Could this be similar?

With a deep breath, Ingrid envisioned each word as if someone wrote it on vellum. When she'd found them all, she mentally rearranged them. Deep within her core, her powers rumbled, awakened and watching as if ready to respond. Eager to solve the riddle, she concentrated harder.

Ve a lunte aut-bime a raumo at eccaia, I acsa na- a mysterime— Like a boat tossed by a storm at sea; the path is a mystery.

She'd done it! *I translated the spell. But, how to break it?*

"The storm has passed," she said aloud. Nothing changed, though she didn't know what it would look like when the spell broke. She imagined it had to feel different. "The path is clear."

Still nothing.

Ingrid tried a variety of words and sentences. Calming her mind, she remembered how she'd had to care for each item in the workroom. Find the spot that would make the most sense and keep it safe. It was an uncomplicated solution. Could it be that simple here?

Ar a raumo, i lunte na- at sér-i acsa na- vamme a mysterime —Without a storm, the boat is at rest; the path is not a mystery.

A flash of light blinded Ingrid for a split second. The carving under her palm flared with heat. She yanked her hand to her chest. Ingrid opened one eye and peered at the door. The door was smooth, and the words were gone. Her brows shot up toward her hairline, and she gasped. The polished ebony shined. Intricate carvings decorated the edges but gone were the flecks of gold.

Ingrid sucked her bottom lip between her teeth and focused on the hallway. It appeared no different. There was only one way to find out. Closing the door to her room, she jogged down the hallway to her right.

22

INGRID

A trickle of sweat slipped between Ingrid's shoulder blades as she pressed her back against the cool stone wall. After only three turns, she'd made it within sight of the doors to freedom. The hallway appeared empty, but she waited. She needed to catch her breath and keep her wits. One short corridor was all that stood in her way. Well, that and the guards, the marketplace, and the forest.

Ingrid laughed to herself. Sprinting for the doors, she burst out into the morning light and hurried down the steps. The pebbled path crunched loudly under her feet. She leapt to the grass and continued forward. Then she heard voices ahead.

Skidding to a stop, chest heaving, she measured the closest distance to cover. She rushed to the high stone wall that surrounded the palace grounds. Manicured shrubbery and flowers decorated the base of the wall. As she reached the edge of the grass, she recognized one of the voices. She stumbled as her stomach squeezed tight and her legs wobbled. Ingrid dove headfirst into the bushes.

Urkon walked casually up the path with two guards at his heels. Ingrid sucked in a deep breath and held it until her chest ached. The dark arts master passed by her hiding spot without hesitation.

I made it. He didn't see me.

Not daring to return to the open, she stayed against the wall and crawled along toward the guardhouse. The gate to freedom was in reach. Remembering how relaxed the soldiers had seemed when she arrived gave her a burst of confidence.

She reached the small square room that allowed the guards somewhere to sit during their shift. Ingrid stayed crouched and listened.

The guards chatted together casually. Ingrid peeked around the corner. They had their back to her and the gate. It was the opportunity she needed. Staying low, she hugged the edge of the building and raced around and through the gate. For a heart-stopping second, they'd stopped talking, and she thought they'd heard her, but relief filled her when they'd resumed their conversation.

Ingrid hurried along the outside wall, away from the open path, until she was out of view of the guards. Legs burning from staying in a crouch, she ran as fast as she could across a low-cut field, heading for the first building on the edge of the market-place. It appeared empty, and she hurried around the corner out of sight.

As she rested in the building's shadow, she fought against the idea that perhaps it had been too easy. Was it possible they had allowed her to escape?

No! That makes little sense.

When she'd settled her nerves, she scooted to the edge and peered around. The marketplace was still quiet though some had recently arrived to ready their tents for the crowds to come. Ingrid darted across the grassy gap to the closest tent. Sticking to the shadows, she moved from one to the other, making her way closer to the edge near the forest.

There was a low hedge, and beyond that was an open grassy area to cross between the edge of the market and the nearest trees. She'd be in the open for several seconds. More elves arrived to mill about each minute she waited.

With a deep breath, she set her shoulders and ran. Using a technique she'd learned from Selby, Ingrid launched herself over the hedge as if she were jumping into a swimming hole. Then tucked herself into a ball and rolled to her feet on the other side. Every part of her wanted to whoop and throw her arms in the air at her success, but she kept focused on the trees.

Pumping her legs as hard as she could, she crossed the grass and darted behind the first big tree. Blood pounded through her ears, and sweat rolled down the side of her face. Not wasting any more time in dangerous view, Ingrid hurried farther into the darkness.

The trees grew thicker, and a mist rose above the ground around Ingrid's ankles. Tangles of shrubbery and roots hindered any direct path and slowed her progress. Grateful for her trousers, Ingrid climbed over logs she could wrap her arms around and through rope-like branches. Though she'd plaited her hair down her back, wisps pulled free as she squeezed through the tangles. The strands fluttered around her face like blonde moths.

When she turned back to see how far she'd come, only darkness surrounded her. No sounds from the marketplace penetrated. As she stopped for a rest, she noticed the silence even more. Gooseflesh pricked against the sleeves of her tunic. It was too quiet. There wasn't any rustling of leaves from rodents or buzzing of insects. Not a single bird twittered among the branches.

Suddenly, from a few feet ahead of her, Ingrid heard a clacking sound. Small at first, but it grew louder as whatever it was came closer. It sounded like the rattling of dice in a cup.

Before she could figure it out, more of the same noise rose from all around. She readied herself in a fighting stance and made a slow circle trying to spy what headed her way.

Out from behind a tangle of large roots stepped a deer—or what *used* to be a deer. Gaping cavities of disintegrated flesh exposed sections of skeleton along its jaw, legs, and flank.

Ingrid had heard the ghost stories that were told at night around the hearth fire. Tales to scare the children and entertain the adults. At least, that's what she'd believed.

But all around her, reanimated corpses emerged. It was the work of vetters. Witches who used dead forest creatures to hunt their next meal, and they weren't picky about what they ate.

Ingrid reached near her to a broken branch and yanked it free to use as a weapon. It wasn't a spear or an axe, but it would be better than nothing. She tossed it from hand to hand and sliced it through the air a couple of times to get a feel for it as she again spun a slow circle.

There were several species closing in on her. A few, under normal circumstances, would have been prey for herself. Deer, rabbits, squirrels, and a couple of geese stared at her with life-less eyes. With exposed skulls, their teeth appeared razor sharp and ready.

The first attack came from a squirrel on a shoulder-high branch. It landed on Ingrid's back and sank its teeth deep. She ripped it away and flung it against a nearby tree where the bones scattered into pieces.

The branch batted away each of the next few attackers, but they kept coming. Ingrid didn't have time to wait and see if the bones reformed into the same animal or if new creatures emerged from the trees. She could only dodge, swing her make-shift weapon, and kick away each new threat. Deep within herself, her powers rustled but didn't wake.

Why! I need you. Answer me!

Her arms grew tired, and blood leaked from bites all over her body. Her chest heaved for air as she weakened. When a large hare slammed against her side, she lost her footing and fell. Within seconds, more bodies landed on top of her. She fought to pull them off and strike at them as they clawed and bit.

Tears rolled out the side of her eyes as the pain grew too intense. Wrapping her arms around her face, she waited for death. The bites and claw marks grew more intense.

If only I had my powers. Where is my magic? What has Jarrick done?

As she laid there contemplating how helpless she was, the creatures drug her over the rough ground, her head bouncing along against roots and stones as they pulled her by her feet. She was beyond angry and frustrated she'd allow them to capture her, especially so quickly.

She knew the creatures would drag her to the vetter. If she didn't do something soon, she would be stew. The air got thicker and darker as they plunged deeper into the forest. The cool mist on the ground continued to swirl. It seeped through her clothes, making her cold and powerless.

No! I am not *powerless, even without my magic I* can *do something for myself.*

Ingrid kicked her feet. She reached out with her hands and grabbed the leg of a deer that had a big mouthful of her thigh. Each time she kicked one away, another took its place. She didn't stop fighting—exhaustion warred against adrenaline.

Suddenly, the animals let go. She thought perhaps she'd done something right. Perhaps she'd proved she wasn't going away easily, so they gave up—but she should have known better.

She sat up, rising slightly out of the mist. Standing right before her was the vetter who'd summoned the animals. She was a short woman though Ingrid estimated she was the same height as herself. Long, stringy gray hair poked out from beneath the cloak that covered her head and hung in tatters down her sides. Her shoulders had a hunch, and long claw-like fingers protruded from the sleeves.

A raspy voice rang through the air. "A delicacy," the hag cackled. "I've never feasted on a human before."

"And you won't today either." Ingrid rose on shaky legs and stood her ground.

She'd fight for all she was worth, regardless of the blood oozing from countless cuts and bites. Raising her fist in a gesture that could only look ridiculous, she readied herself to fight the next attacker. If it was her day to die, she'd do it in a way that honored her Viking heritage.

Faster and nimbler than she would have believed, the witch rushed at Ingrid. A vise-like grip wrapped around Ingrid's throat, and claws dug into her skin.

Ingrid stepped closer to the woman whose face she still hadn't seen entirely. There was a long scabby nose that Ingrid could break if she head-butted her. It was one of the sure-fire tactics Selby had taught her to use when fighting off an attacker.

The woman screeched but did not let go. Ingrid wrapped her hand around the woman's wrist, feeling the bony sinewy muscles wrapped around the small skeletal frame. She tried pulling the woman off to no avail. Slipping her foot between the woman's legs, she hooked the back of her heel causing both women to tumble to the ground. There was a slight knoll, and they rolled several feet, tumbling over and under each other.

The woman never loosened her grip on Ingrid's throat. Her vision faded, and bursts of light flickered in the darkness around the edges, but she didn't stop kicking or fighting. There had to be a way to get the woman off of her.

The vetter rolled onto Ingrid's chest. Using her second hand, she pinned Ingrid's shoulder to the ground as her grip tightened. Again, Ingrid tried to call her magic. It rumbled, twisting in her gut, as if it wanted to respond, then sank back quiet.

Just when Ingrid was about to lose consciousness, the woman disappeared. Ingrid tried to suck in a deep breath, coughing and gagging as she rolled to her side. She had to fight the urge not to throw up from the adrenaline mixed with the effects of air loss.

Pushing herself to rise on her elbows and foggy with pain, she saw a shadowy figure hovered over another lump on the ground.

Did the vetter find different prey?

When the figure turned around, through her haze Ingrid gasped and recognized the man stalking toward her. Urkon moved with slow steps, watching Ingrid with a slight curve to his lips.

"No," Ingrid whispered.

23

JORG

No one wanted to move. Jorg, Bremen, Selby, and Plintze lay on their backs, steadying their breathing and staring at the hazy skies overhead. The stars shimmered brightly as if it were night, but the mixture of indigo and purple said it was only twilight.

"Have we made it? Is this Alfheim? The air feels different. It's hard to breathe with all the dirt and soot in my lungs," Selby said.

"This is Alfheim," Plintze said. "It doesn't change too much from day to night. It's like both dawn and dusk last most of the time, with a small portion of fully light or fully dark."

"I can handle that as long as there aren't any more goblins," Bremen said as he pushed himself up and looked around.

They were at the edge of a forest not more than twenty paces from the edge of a city. The buildings were all one story. Some were made of cream-colored stone or wooden slats with reddish-orange tiled rooftops. Others were made in the form of fabric-covered tents.

The bead under Jorg's tunic flared to life, heated his chest, and rumbled an approving hum. "Let's go. Ingrid is here. We need to find her," Jorg said. The anticipation was more than he could bear, and he felt like he could crawl out of his skin.

"Jorg, wait, look!" Selby pulled the sleeve of his tunic and brought his focus to a couple of guards wearing royal blue cloaks. The shimmer of jeweled epaulets at their shoulders signified their importance.

The foursome ducked low and hustled out of sight into the tree line and waited for the guards to continue on their way, out of sight.

"We should head a little further back, where the darkness of the trees will grant us cover while we come up with a plan," Bremen whispered. Plintze and Selby nodded their agreement and inched backward while Jorg stared at the city, unmoving.

"Come on. We'll make a plan, and then we'll find her," Plintze said from behind Jorg.

Jorg rubbed his hand over his face and took several deep breaths to settle his racing heart. *I'm here, Hjarta. It won't be long now.* With a heavy sigh, he backed farther into the darkened forest with the others.

"Are there many cities on Alfheim? How do we know this is the one where my mother and Ingrid will be?" Bremen asked, directing the question to Plintze.

"I only know of one city, but there could be more. The elves aren't too keen on giving out much information about their homeland to the other realms," Plintze answered.

"She's here." Jorg pulled out the bead from under his tunic, and the glow lit up his face. "Eir said it would signal me when she was close. Ingrid is here."

"Ingrid, but we don't know about Galwain," Selby said.

"If the queen isn't here, Ingrid might know where she is. We should follow that," Plintze pointed to the bright amber bead, "to Ingrid and then decide what to do after that."

Selby darted a glance to Jorg and then settled her gaze on

Bremen. "He's right. If we know Ingrid is here, we can't miss our chance to find her."

Before there could be any further discussion, a voice sounded in the distance, farther into the forest. The voice was distant and sounded as if it was calling in distress.

"It's her," Jorg said and ran toward the sound.

"Jorg!" Plintze called out, but Jorg heard no one. The bead glowed, and it vibrated against his chest so he couldn't think of anything but getting to Ingrid.

The small glow of what looked to be a campfire became visible through the trees. Jorg jumped over fallen logs and dodged low branches, slipping only once on the soft moss as he ran. He could hear the mutterings and noise from the other three behind him but paid no attention.

When he reached the sight of a small campfire, perfectly circled by small stones and burning without a spark or char on the wood, he stopped. His chest heaved, and chills broke out on his skin. The only sounds came from the crack of branches as the others caught up to him. They, too, halted and stared in silence at the small clearing encircling the strange fire.

After what seemed like an unnerving amount of time, Jorg was about to turn back when a young woman stepped out of the trees. He thought it looked as though she had been there the whole time, disguised as a tree until she showed her face.

That can't be, can it? That would mean she's a . . .

"Don't look at her," Plintze whispered, but loud enough to make sure the others heard. "She's a spirit folk, a wild-woman of the forest—a skögsra. She'll devour a man's soul and leave him with nothing but a mind full of madness."

While Plintze spoke, a second woman appeared. "Have no fear of us, the dwarf is just trying to frighten you. He's jealous that his kind cannot enjoy our company. Come, sit by our fire and share stories." The women smiled and locked their gazes on

Bremen and Jorg. They stepped closer, and their beauty and songlike voices floated toward the group.

Jorg ignored Plintze's warning and felt himself warm through as he smiled back at the woman staring at him. From the corner of his eye, he saw Selby shake herself and turn away from the women. Then everything other than the fire and the woman disappeared from his view. It was as if nothing else existed or mattered.

Her beauty radiated as if it were the air he needed to breathe, and no other source would keep him alive. When she raised her hand and beckoned him closer, he didn't hesitate—until he found himself face down in the dirt. Sputtering, he knocked the heavyweight laying on his back to the side and jumped to his feet.

The sting of a staff against his stomach caused him to double over. For a split second, he gasped then righted himself, ready to destroy whatever had attacked him. Before he could see who or what it was, someone swept his feet out from under him, and he landed on his back. All his breath left his body. His vision blurred, and a weight landed on his chest.

"Be still, or I'll knock you in the head and drag you out of here," a voice hissed in his ear. He recognized it, but his mind was foggy. As he fought to fill his lungs and breathe, recognition dawned on him. Plintze sat on his chest. The dwarf held him down, but why?

Then he remembered the warning and realized that the woman's snare had caught him. "I'm fine," he said in a wheeze. "Get off."

"Not until you promise not to look at her again. It'll take every bit of strength you have. Hold that bead and think only of Ingrid," Plintze said, his voice harsh.

Jorg only nodded and brought his hand up to grasp the bead that lay to the side of his head, still on the leather string around his neck. As soon as he touched it, his mind cleared. He patted Plintze's shoulder, and the dwarf rolled off him.

"Thank you. I'm better now," he said. "Where's Selby and Bremen?"

"Selby's trying to fight against those two by herself, to retrieve her stupid boy before they have him. If you'll stay here and not move or turn to look, I'll go help her."

"Go! I'll be fine." He clutched the bead harder as he sat upright and closed his eyes for safety, just in case.

Plintze darted off behind him, crashing into what sounded like the trunk of a tree. Now that his head was clear, he could hear Selby's shrieking war cries and the hissing of what sounded like a nest of vipers. With Plintze's added growls, it was an unnerving barrage of battle sounds. The one voice he didn't hear was Bremen's.

Odin if you watch this realm, please keep my brother safe. The prayer surprised him at how intensely he meant it and how much the ache in his chest increased as he listened to the war raging behind him.

A scream rang out from Selby just before a cold breeze blew over Jorg's skin. He was instantly chilled as if exposed to the elements in the middle of winter. He sat still, afraid to breathe. The forest was silent and calm. With the battle finished, but the victor unknown, he didn't dare move.

"Selby, are you all right?"

Jorg sighed and dared a peek over his shoulder at the sound of Plintze's voice. Bremen lay on the ground near where the campfire had once burned but was now only a blackened ring. Plintze hovered over Selby who huddled in a ball, covering her head not far from Jorg. Dizzy, he crawled over to them. "What happened? Is she hurt?"

"I'll be ok. Just let me rest." As Selby spoke, she adjusted the hand she held against her face and blood seeped between her fingers.

"Can you sit up? You're bleeding," Jorg said. The bead still glowed around his neck, but the hum was less. *Ingrid will never forgive me if something happens to you.* The thought of losing Selby when they were so close to Ingrid and her healing powers added a sting to his already aching insides.

"Where's Bremen? Is he safe?" Selby tried to push herself to a sitting position as she asked, her words muffled as she held her hand against her jaw. Plintze supported her against his arm and gestured with his eyes for Jorg to go check on the prone, unmoving figure of his brother.

Still on his hands and knees, Jorg made his way over, dread welling up in his gut. Bremen lay unconscious, but thankfully as Jorg approached, he could see his chest rise and fall to prove he lived. The gash in his leg from the fight with the goblins oozed, but other than that, he didn't appear to have any other wounds. Jorg was about to jostle his brother's shoulders when Bremen launched himself into a sitting position with a loud gasp.

Jorg sat back on his heels and gave Bremen some space. "Where . . . What happened? Is she gone?" He turned his wide eyes to Jorg as he stumbled over his words and regained his senses.

Not knowing how to answer or which question to address, Jorg waited for Bremen to calm down before he responded. If the women they'd seen were truly the skögsra as Plintze thought they were, Bremen may not have his mind anymore. The stories he'd heard said if the forest women allowed a man to live, he went mad and never recovered his sanity, wandering around as a shell for the rest of his life.

"Where's Selby? *Ahh.*" Bremen groaned and clutched his leg as he tried to move. "She fought those women. Where is she?"

Relief washed through Jorg. Bremen was still sane and alive.

Now they needed to get out of the forest and see how bad Selby's injuries were. "She is over by Plintze."

Jorg's head was clearer, and some of his strength had returned, so he stood and moved around to Bremen's other side. He offered his hands so he could help Bremen stand on his good leg. Together, they hobbled over to where the others sat on the ground.

"What happened? How bad is your injury?" Bremen asked when Jorg helped him to the ground in front of Selby.

In the bead's glow, they could see blood glistening on Selby's throat. "We need to get out of the forest, now. Then we can check," Plintze said.

Jorg agreed. They wouldn't survive a second assault, and if the skögsra were watching, they'd know that. "My strength has returned. Let me carry you, Selby, so we can move faster. Bremen, you can use Plintze's shoulder to lean on."

Without waiting for Selby to answer, Jorg scooped her into his arms. Neither Plintze nor Bremen complained about the idea and immediately positioned themselves next to each other. They didn't know exactly how far they'd traveled into the trees, but they set off in the direction they'd come, following the broken branches and churned-up mosses from their hurried pace earlier.

The going was slower than any of them would have liked, but before too long, the air lightened and they reached the edge of the forest. It wasn't fully dark when they entered the clearing between the forest and the city, and they could finally see each other in the twilight.

"Put me down now, Jorg. I can walk." Exhaustion laced the words as Selby spoke, but Jorg let her slide to her feet. "We need to find Ingrid. The bead is still glowing, and I could feel it humming against your chest. Do you think she's close?"

"We need to take care of your injuries first. I'm sorry for

causing this," Jorg said. His chest ached, and a thickness gripped his throat. *How could I have done this to you? I've caused you so much pain.*

"I'll be fine. We all made it through." Selby glanced over at Bremen and then to the ground. "At least, I hope so."

"He's fine. His mind's intact—as much as it was before anyway," Jorg whispered and added the small amount of jest to lighten her concern—he hoped. She tried to chuckle but winced from the effort, using both hands to press on her jaw and chest. "Let's head over to those shadows next to that building. We can rest there."

When they settled against the cool stone of the building, all the males faced Selby. "Well, I'd normally not mind such admiring attention, but I think I'd like all of you to look away for just a minute while I check the damage," Selby said with a crooked smile. Her face had already swollen, and her speech was slurred.

"Let me help," Bremen said with a wink.

Jorg snorted, then he and Plintze turned their backs to give them some privacy.

Selby checked her injuries, and while two cuts were deep enough they still oozed, none were life-threatening. A water barrel sat next to the building where the group rested. Jorg ripped off part of his tunic and hurried over to wet it for her to hold against the cuts on her jaw. There would be scars, and it ate at him that his actions had disfigured her.

While he was at the barrel, the bead flared and felt as though it seared into his skin. He knew Ingrid was near, not only because the bead glowed stronger than a torch, but he thought, for a quick moment, that he'd heard her in his mind. Without concern for anything, Jorg stepped around the side of the building and into the open.

24

INGRID

Ingrid did her best to scramble backward, dragging herself through the mist as Urkon approached. What was he doing there? How had he found her? Part of her felt like she should be grateful since he was obviously the one who'd saved her.

"Come now, Ingrid, you can't be afraid of *me* after all of this?" Urkon spread his hands out, gesturing to the surrounding forest. The scattered bones of the animals finally rested as they should.

The heaped body of the vetter continued to lay motionless as Ingrid gave it a quick glance. "Is she dead?" Her voice squeaked. It was so small in her ears it made disgust rise up her spine. She had once again allowed herself to be captured. When was she going to accept her circumstances and quit trying to change them?

Never; I'll never stop trying. She couldn't, but that didn't mean she had to keep allowing herself to be captured—or worse.

"She is. Now, give me your hand, and I'll help you out of this forsaken place." Urkon stretched out his hand to her. It reminded her of the time that Jarrick had come to her in a dream. He'd reached out and said she had to choose. Though he didn't mean it—he'd tried to trap her. Was this the same? If she took Urkon's hand, would she succumb to his power? His will?

Slowly, Ingrid pushed herself to her knees. The effort was more than she expected, so she rested a moment before standing.

"I do like your tenacity, though I'd prefer you to accept your situation and quit all this nonsense. Take my hand." Urkon pushed his hand closer to Ingrid, his eyes narrowed and impatient.

Weakened from all the bite marks and scratches, Ingrid willed herself to ignore the pain. If she ran, there was no way she'd make it out of the forest before Urkon caught her. Would she even know the way? Whether or not he was trying to trap her, she needed help.

Repulsed by the act, she placed her hand within his palm.

The cold mist rose up and swirled around their bodies. Ingrid's hair whipped in front of her face, and nausea threatened her stomach. A heartbeat later, they stood in the clearing between the forest and the marketplace.

Fresh air and twilight replaced the cold mist and black twisted trees. Ingrid stared at where her hand still joined with Urkon's. He hadn't taken her anywhere other than out of danger. Why? Voices permeated her consciousness, and she pulled her hand to her side.

"We'll discuss what happens next later," Urkon said. Then he turned toward the sound of guards heading in their direction.

Ingrid spun, hoping to see Kelvhan but instead, Dúngarr and six others from Jarrick's guard stomped toward them. If there was a way for her situation to get worse—that was it.

"Where have you been Ingrid?" Dúngarr spat the words as if he'd been searching for quite some time.

Something about the wrinkle of his nose and curl of his lip made Ingrid giggle. It made no sense to her other than she was exhausted. Caught between Urkon and Jarrick's guard, the absurdity of her situation overwhelmed her. Rather than fight it, she gave in and let the laughter bubble over as she slipped to her knees in the grass.

"There is no mirth in this situation. A dangerous event has occurred, and you need to come with me." The guard was so serious it made Ingrid laugh that much harder.

What's wrong with me?

"Ingrid needs rest and possibly a healer if she is going to stubbornly refuse to help herself," Urkon interjected.

"What happened to her?" Dúngarr asked.

It annoyed Ingrid that they talked about her as if she were an object rather than a person. It dampened her giddiness but not completely. She wasn't sure how to answer either of them, so she let them believe she was incoherent.

"I don't know how she managed it, but she was in the forest. Attacked by a vetter. If the event you speak of has to do with the dungeons in the palace, I assure you, she was not near there."

That sobered Ingrid. Could that be why Jarrick sent his guard for her? Did he know she'd killed his beast? She might have laughed again after Urkon vouched for her, except whatever army Jarrick had made was terrifying. Besides, everyone in the palace knew she was involved.

"Jarrick needs to speak with her, and I've been searching everywhere. She can get whatever medical attention she needs later. Come with me, Ingrid." Dúngarr nodded to the other guards who surrounded her as she sat on the ground.

Ingrid was tired of being a pawn for those who felt they were more powerful. She was out of the forest and within sight of the palace. All she had to do was make it through the marketplace to the guard tower. Those were the king's men. They could help her contact Caelya or Kelvhan. Either of them would help her. Possibly. Probably.

While she sat on the ground, ignoring the two males and letting them bicker amongst themselves, she realized that her wounds were not as painful as they had been. Perhaps it was because she was out of the forest. How could that be when she couldn't access her powers? Checking, she confirmed they were still obstinate, like a sleeping cat, ignoring her completely.

Should she risk running? Thoughts of what happened the last time she ran through the marketplace alone tried to dissuade her. That had been a unique situation. She wouldn't let herself dwell on it.

It's not worth it.

Urkon snapped his attention to her. Ingrid checked her barriers and realized she'd let her mental protections drop with her exhaustion. Slapping them back into place, she held Urkon's glare and rose to her feet.

"I'll go with you, Dúngarr. I want to go back to my rooms, anyway." Ingrid strode toward the guard, expecting him to turn toward the palace. "I could use a bath."

Dúngarr grabbed her arm. "Not that way." A smirk played on his lips, and Ingrid held her breath. The touch of his hand on her arm grated like a rasp. "We aren't going to the palace. Jarrick would like to speak to you at Montibeo."

As if she'd fallen off a cliff, Ingrid's stomach lurched. What was the reason for taking her there? It might give her the opportunity to speak with Galwain finally. And, Caelya did come to visit, but . . .

"It's not time," Urkon growled. "Jarrick knows that. Take her to the palace until I speak to him."

"My orders were clear. Because of what happened, he wants her close. He's there now, and I'm sure he'll explain his reasoning to you. We should all go." Dúngarr gripped Ingrid harder. Apparently, if a fight was to break out over her, he was prepared.

"Fine, it will save me from having to speak to Thelonius, anyway."

"How far is it? Will we walk?" Ingrid wasn't sure why, but she had the sensation that she needed to stay. Something was pricking the back of her mind, trying to get her attention, and she wanted to know why. Perhaps it was the idea of being so near the dragons or the beast army. Suddenly, she wanted to stay as far away from that castle as she could.

"We aren't walking," Dúngarr said. Then he looked over her head to his men. "Return through the pass, and I'll meet you there when you arrive."

Mountain pass? There was a passage between the two castles that didn't involve the forest?

"Why aren't we taking the pass?"

Dúngarr rolled his eyes and didn't answer her. The guards immediately marched away, and he said nothing until they were out of sight.

"I assumed you would prefer to travel differently," Dúngarr said to Urkon.

"Of course."

Ingrid was about to ask why the guards went separately when Dúngarr's eyes popped open wide. "How is that possible?" He stared at something behind Ingrid.

Afraid more of the dragon-elf army had escaped, Ingrid peeked over her shoulder, ready to run. Stunned, she twisted and fully gaped at the sight before her.

Next to a building fifty paces away, stood Jorg. At first, she thought she was hallucinating, except it had been Dúngarr who had alerted her. He'd seen him, too. Jorg was alive—and in Alfheim!

25

JORG

There she was. Ingrid stood a short distance in front of him. When she met his gaze, he almost fell to his knees because his heart squeezed so hard. Then he noticed who was with her. Dúngarr had her by the arm. Another, more dangerous looking elf stood close to her as well.

"Ingrid!" he yelled without thinking about the ramifications. He was unworried about his or anyone else's safety at that point. She was the reason he'd risked everything.

Without waiting for an answer, he charged. Ignoring the others, he kept his gaze latched onto her. She stared at him, obviously startled and confused. He urged himself faster, to pull her away from the vile elf attached to her arm, and he cared about nothing else.

Before he could reach her, she vanished. Quicker than the portal he'd witnessed Jarrick use once, she disappeared. They were all gone.

Skidding to a stop, Jorg roared into the sky. Footsteps pounded behind him as he sank to his knees. He could feel the presence of the others but didn't dare speak. His heart pounded, wanting to burst free and follow wherever she went.

Breathless, Selby arrived and slid to the ground next to him. "Was that her? Where did she go? I only caught a glimpse and then nothing."

"There was only a flash of light, not even an opening," Bremen added.

"That was different magic than a portal. Whoever that was, he's stronger than anyone I've ever met." Plintze lumbered over to the spot Ingrid had stood a moment before. Running his hand over the grass, he studied the area.

"Can you tell where they took her?" Jorg asked. It was a stupid question, he knew it when he said it, but he didn't know what to do. How could he have come that far and let her slip through his fingers? What was he supposed to do now?

"There's no way to know," Plintze said.

"Perhaps I could help with that, that is, if you'd like to tell me who you are and how you arrived in our realm?" a male voice said from the left side of the group.

Jumping to his feet, Jorg faced the newcomer. From the look of his armour, he was a member of the elven military or a guard. It was grander than the uniform Dúngarr wore, but Jorg trusted no one who worked for Jarrick.

"How we found our way here is our business. Tell me now if you have information on where Ingrid is." Regardless of the fact he was an intruder to the realm, Jorg only cared about finding Ingrid.

The elf narrowed his eyes as he studied Jorg. Then he glanced at the others as well. "You're an interesting group. I wasn't aware the tunnel to Svartalfheim had re-opened—or that the dwarves helped humans cross their realm."

"Humph." Plintze gave no other response, and Jorg smirked.

"Though, you're not all humans, are you?"

Jorg set his jaw tight and raised his chin, begging for a

comment that would let him take out his aggression in a way he would relish.

Confusion creased a line between the man's brows, and he cocked his head. "How do you know Ingrid?"

"That's none of your concern," Jorg answered.

"We know Galwain, too," Bremen interjected, and Jorg shot him a sidelong glare.

"I think you should all come with me. There's someone I know would like to meet you." The guard stretched his words, and a grin tipped half his mouth. It was as if he found the situation amusing.

Jorg was going nowhere with a stranger. Even if he had information on Ingrid, he wouldn't risk the others—again. "Why would we go with you? Who are you?"

"Pardon my manners. My name is Kelvhan. I'm a member of the king's guard and would like to introduce you to a member of the royal family."

"We've already met the prince, and you must excuse us from any more time with him," Jorg said with a huff, imitating Kelvhan's formality.

"This isn't the prince," Kelvhan said and held Jorg's stare. "It is to your benefit, and *safety*, that you come with me. It won't go well for you if anyone else finds you here."

"Do you know where Galwain is?" Bremen asked too eagerly.

"I do. Please, come with me, and we can talk in a more private setting."

"I think we should go," Selby said, resting her hand on Jorg's arm. She'd risen to her feet to stand between the brothers.

The touch brought an unexpected surge of emotions. Part of Jorg wanted to pull her close and let himself fall apart as if she were his sister. The other part wanted more than ever to find Ingrid and eliminate his emotional turmoil.

"How do we know that you're not leading us into a trap?" Plintze asked.

Jorg reached down and placed his hand on the dwarf's shoulder, grateful for a voice of reason right then.

"To be fair, you don't, but I'm your best bet. Right now, I'm speaking as a friend. If anyone alerts the guard of your presence, protocol will require me to take you before the king. Then everything will become more . . . complicated."

"Why would you do that?" Selby asked.

"Because I know who you are." Kelvhan said the words to everyone but held Jorg's stare.

Selby gripped Jorg's arm tighter. She needed a healer. He felt punched in the gut by the reminder of how Ingrid had been so close. She could have helped Selby, and Bremen, too. Twisting, he looked at his brother. What did *he* want to do? Did he trust this stranger? His own emotions were too volatile at that moment.

Bremen held his gaze for several long seconds before he nodded once, strong and decisive. Jorg exhaled and faced the guard again.

"If you'll provide us with a healer, we'll go with you."

Kelvhan pinched his brow and glanced at each of the group, hovering over Selby and Bremen. He nodded. "Follow me. We'll avoid the main gate."

Kelvhan strode toward the palace on the hill. A tall stone palisade wrapped around the outside, and when they reached it, he followed it around a bend away from what Jorg assumed to be the village. When the guard stopped, he pulled aside the branches of a tall bush and exposed a hidden door cut into the stone. Using a key he pulled from under his belt, he swung it wide and ushered them through while scanning the area.

So far, he'd done nothing but help them, yet Jorg stayed wary and ready as Kelvhan once again took the lead. Bremen was also on edge and stayed near Selby, helping her occasionally, even though he clutched his side as he walked. It was dark, but there was no mistaking the coppery scent of his bloodied tunic. Too brave and stubborn to admit how much pain she was in, the fact that Selby accepted any help spoke volumes.

Plintze appeared the most uncomfortable, yet Jorg was sure it wasn't from physical injury. Knowing the hostility they'd received in his homeland, he probably expected the same treatment for himself in Alfheim. Jorg was nervous for that, too, but had hope the elves weren't as devious as the dwarf council.

"This way," Kelvhan said. He led them up a set of marble stairs and inside a tall door emblazoned with crystals and gold filigree.

Everything was opulent though it *was* a palace. Jorg fought a grin when he checked on Selby and saw her wide-eyed wonder. At that moment, Jorg realized that he had considered nothing about what Alfheim would look or feel like. The air was lighter, and he noticed he breathed easier. If he had to fight, he suspected he'd have more energy and stamina.

I wonder if everyone feels the same, or is this because of who I am?

Dwelling on his elven heritage only brought up thoughts of Jarrick. His mother was somewhere in the realm, too. If he let them, the emotions would overtake him again. He choked them down; what he needed was fortitude, not feelings.

No one spoke as they followed as quietly as possible. That was made easier by all the plush rugs lining the shiny floors. When Kelvhan halted and knocked at a set of double doors, the others stood in positions that would allow them to fight if need be. Kelvhan glanced over his shoulder, and Jorg caught the smirk as Kelvhan returned his gaze to the door.

A woman's voice called for them to enter. Jorg wasn't sure if everyone else had heard it through the thick wooden doors, but he had. Nervous and excited, he let himself wonder for a heartbeat if it was Galwain.

When they entered, however, a she-elf greeted them. She was tall and elegant with the same white blonde hair as Jarrick. Kelvhan had said he was taking them to a member of the royal family. Could this be Jarrick's sister? His aunt? The way she focused on him made it seem as if she was as surprised to see him as he was to meet her.

After they were all inside the room, Kelvhan made introductions. "May I introduce you to Caelya, Princess of Alfheim."

Jorg didn't know what he should do. How did one greet royalty in this realm? When he'd met the king in Jorvik earlier in the year, they'd only nodded to each other. Movement caught his attention at his side. Bremen bowed gracefully from his shoulders and cocked a brow to Jorg as he glanced sideways.

Jorg and Selby followed his example, but Plintze stood still and stoic.

"Though we skipped introductions," Kelvhan spoke again, causing them all to stand upright once more, "I believe this is your nephew and his companions. They've come in search of Ingrid and Galwain."

"Is that true? Are you Jorg?" Caelya asked.

Jorg nodded, his tongue suddenly thick. Silence crept over the room for a long few seconds before he recovered himself. "This is Selby, Bremen, and Plintze."

Caelya followed with her eyes as Jorg gave their names, tipping her chin in greeting as she went. Then settled her gaze on Plintze. "Do we have you to thank for helping everyone find their way into our realm?"

The question could have been an accusation, but she spoke it with a note of gratitude. Jorg watched Plintze out of his peripheral vision, waiting to see what he would say.

"I helped everyone into Svartalfheim. Getting into Alfheim

was a group effort," Plintze said. They all huffed a wry acceptance to his response.

"Well, thank you. We'd heard all of you had perished on Midgard. I'm grateful the reports were false." Caelya then turned her focus on Bremen. "Would you be Galwain's other son, by chance?"

"Yes . . . I wasn't aware anyone would know of me," Bremen answered.

"Both Galwain and Ingrid have spoken of you. I know your mother will be pleased to see you both. And you," she said, turning to Selby with a grin, "must be a friend of Ingrid's. I can see the fierce warrior in your eyes as I've seen in hers."

"Humph." Plintze instantly stared at the ground, having slipped the sound into the air.

Selby smiled, and tension eased around the room, except within Jorg. He continued to stand straight and serious.

"If you'll excuse me, I promised a healer. I'll return shortly," Kelvhan said with a quick dip of his shoulders.

"Pardon me for being blunt, your highness, but can you take us to our mother?" Bremen asked after the guard had left.

"I'm afraid I can't. She's elsewhere at the moment. But I will do what I can to arrange the reunion. I understand you saw Ingrid. Can you give me more details about that?" Caelya focused on Jorg.

No one had said anything out loud to her about what had happened, but Jorg gave her the details. Do they hear each other's thoughts as he did with Ingrid? He'd figure that out later.

"She was with Dúngarr and another male. Before I could reach her, they vanished." He said the words as calmly as he could, giving no hint at how his heart wrenched.

Caelya narrowed her eyes, studying him. Jorg suddenly didn't know what to do with his hands. "What did this other male look like?"

"He was in a dark, hooded cloak. I didn't see his face," Jorg answered.

"Urkon. He's your father's mentor from Vanaheim. That could make things more inconvenient."

Bremen and Jorg exchanged glances, but before either of them could ask what she'd meant, the door to Caelya's chambers opened without notice.

"Apparently, there is a need for my services in here," Eir said as she strode into the room. Several guards followed, Kelvhan among them, while another male stood next to the goddess, wearing a crown.

26

INGRID

Ingrid fell to her backside as soon as her feet met the ground again. Whatever magic Urkon used differed from the portals Jarrick created. None of that mattered—Jorg was alive! He'd found her, and Ingrid was sure she'd seen a flash of Selby's coppery hair before something had sucked all the air out of her lungs.

How had they survived? How had they crossed the realms? Perhaps it was a trick. Could Urkon or Jarrick conjure such a thing? But why? She was already within their grasp.

It had to be real.

Ingrid's arm wrenched as she was pulled to her feet. Wide-eyed, she returned her focus to those surrounding her. Dúngarr dug in his fingers while Urkon stared at her.

"If you'll ensure there's a chamber ready for our guest, Dúngarr, I'd like to speak to Ingrid alone."

The guard said nothing, his jaw muscles popping before releasing her in a huff. He spun and strode away, his boots clunking against the mirrored surface of the black stone floors.

Ingrid recognized the dark marble tiles from the vision Urkon had shown her. She was at Montibeo. They stood in a wide corridor with pillared arches along one side, and more of the same stone lined the wall on the other. Firelight danced from sconces every few feet and cast an orangish-red glow into the darkness.

"Am I a guest like Galwain? Will you be attaching a collar around my neck?"

Urkon narrowed his gaze, and one corner of his mouth tipped upward. "So you understand where you are? Good. Whatever Jarrick does with his wife does not concern me. As long as it doesn't interfere with our plans for you." He stepped closer as he spoke.

Regardless of the unease slithering up her spine, Ingrid stood her ground. She couldn't give in now. However it happened, she needed to make sure the realms stayed safe. Her desire to fulfill her destiny renewed itself with vigor now that she'd seen Jorg.

She'd tried to escape before only to achieve disastrous results. There was only one way she would be free. The thought she'd had before lingered in the back of her mind. Urkon needed to die. They were alone, and she could do it right then—except she had no weapon. Even though her wounds had somehow healed, her powers hadn't resurfaced.

"If you want to use me, do it now. I'm tired of all your talk." She'd end the dark arts master, but until then, she would cause as much trouble as she could. Perhaps she could provoke him into making a mistake.

Urkon gave an oily laugh. "When the time is right. For now, you will tell me how you escaped your rooms at the palace. How did you drop the wards?"

What? Why would he want to know that? Shouldn't the dead dragon-elf in the palace dungeons or the fact that she couldn't fight against the creatures in the forest cause more concern?

"Training," she answered. It was mostly true. He didn't need to know it was also a guess. If he didn't know elves had escaped yet, she wouldn't say anything.

"Your training was in how to use your powers. Are you saying they've returned to you?"

"You know they haven't. Whatever you or Jarrick did is still working." *Believe me, I'd use them right now if I could.* "Why are you making an army?"

Urkon blinked and kept his breathing steady as he stared at Ingrid. She struggled to stand still and not fidget against his scrutiny.

"What are you talking about?"

At first, Ingrid wanted to scream at him, to force him to understand he couldn't treat her as a child and a fool. Then it sank in. She wasn't the fool. *He* was. Jarrick had made an army that Urkon didn't know about. A smile broke across her face.

"Did you really think he'd follow your orders blindly? Jarrick loves power as much as you do." This was perfect. She'd wiggle herself between them like water into a cracked stone and then let the pressure build until they broke.

When Ingrid was young, she hated the way Selby and her sisters fought. It wasn't the normal kind with fists and hair pulling. They would make up lies to manipulate trouble for the others. Selby wasn't good at it and ended up causing herself more punishment than anyone else. But her younger sister, Brigid, was a master.

Hope sprouted when Ingrid remembered many of her tactics. If she destroyed Urkon and Jarrick, she'd be able to tell Selby how she did it because her friend was *alive*. Bolstered, she kept her gaze locked steady with Urkon.

"You're playing with fire, my dear. Jarrick will stop protecting you if he realizes you tried to discredit him." Urkon stepped closer still. His eyes blazed though he kept a calm exterior.

"I'd think you know Jarrick better than me. I found out

about his army while I was in the palace. Perhaps he's made a deal with Thelonius?" It was a lie blended with some truth. That had been Brigid's secret, and now Ingrid knew why. Doubt flickered through Urkon's expression before he righted himself.

"I've been alive a long time, Ingrid. Never bluff when the truth is easy to confirm. Who called for you as we transported? He seemed intent on getting to you." Urkon's mouth quirked in a wicked tilt.

The taste of victory turned sour as Ingrid's breath caught. Had she endangered Jorg and Selby? "I don't know what you mean?"

Her unease sparked a sinister glee from Urkon. "It's a shame you can't access your powers. I wonder if it will be like your sister all over again."

Panic flared and clawed into Ingrid's throat. The sting of tears threatened behind her eyes, and she blinked to keep them at bay. What was she thinking to challenge such a powerful being?

The sound of boots clambered through the corridor as Ingrid clutched the side of her trousers. Urkon moved to stand next to her as calm as if they were strolling through the gardens. Dúngarr approached with Jarrick by his side.

"Ingrid! I'm so glad to see you're well. I heard there was a terrible disturbance at the palace. I can't believe my brother's guards would leave you so vulnerable like that." He pulled Ingrid's hands into his own. "You'll be safer here. I promise."

"I'm sure she's tired from all the excitement. Perhaps she should rest in her room," Urkon said.

"Yes, traveling within the realm must exhaust you. Are you injured?" Jarrick's question came with a squeeze of his hands. When she snapped her eyes to his, there was a knowing look in his eyes.

Ingrid shook her head and tried to extract her hands, but Jarrick squeezed harder. His cinnamon scent cloyed her senses.

"Well, we can be thankful for that. I'll show you to your room." He twisted to her side and slid her hand into the crook of his arm. "If you wouldn't mind meeting me in the council chambers, I won't be long. Then I can give you my full attention," Jarrick said to Urkon. Turning to Dúngarr, he said, "Please be sure the guards are at their stations for Ingrid's protection."

"Yes, they are in position. Would you prefer that *I* show Ingrid to her room?"

Ingrid stiffened, and Jarrick patted her hand. "No, that will be all. I'll show her the way myself."

"Don't be long. We have much to discuss," Urkon said. The irritation in his voice scratched through the air.

Jarrick led Ingrid through one arch and across a large open room. She struggled to imagine what they used the space for because it was too dark to make out any distinguishing features. When they'd reached the other side, they passed under another archway that matched the previous side. Even though an abundance of sconces burned, their light soaked into the obsidian walls. Ingrid couldn't understand how anyone could stand to live in such darkness.

They headed up a set of spiraling stairs, curling up the inside tower as Jarrick ushered Ingrid ahead of him in the enclosed space. The walls were smooth and made of the same stone. Everything was the same—dark, oppressive, and menacing.

"Is it always so dark?" Ingrid couldn't help herself. She needed to know if she'd ever see daylight again.

Jarrick chuckled, low but genuine. "I've put you in a high room that overlooks the mountains. You'll have much more light."

A high room. *So I can't leave, no doubt.* "Is it near Galwain's? I'd like to speak with her."

Silence thickened the darkness. Ingrid held her breath. She'd learned Galwain was there through Urkon and Caelya. Did Jarrick not want her to know?

"No, but I can arrange for a meeting."

The air shifted, and Ingrid shivered. They reached the top of the stairs and headed down the hall once again side by side. There were few doors or decorative touches. The floors were still bare stone and sconces graced the walls, but there were no tables with vases or plush rugs underfoot. It wasn't like Ingrid had grown up in grand style. At least, according to elven standards, but there was a stark difference between the palace and Montibeo.

"Here we are." Jarrick gestured toward a door on Ingrid's left.

Ingrid reached for the handle and hesitated. Twisting to Jarrick, she stared at him and rolled her lip between her teeth. "I saw what you've done—what you've made."

"I know. You're safe here."

"But . . . Why?" Ingrid wanted to scream it. To pummel the answer out of the dark elf. Instead, she sounded weak and hated herself for it.

Once again, the silence echoed off the polished stone. "We'll talk soon, Ingrid. If you need anything, a maid will be by later." Jarrick reached past Ingrid and opened the door.

He had agreed to let her meet with Galwain. It was as good as she would have for the moment. Setting her shoulders, she walked into her new room. A prisoner or a guest, one was the same as the other. Neither made any difference if she could muster the courage to do what she must.

27

JORG

Eir. Jorg grimaced and pursed his lips. From the corner of his eye, he saw the others shrink back. Even his confident brother withered at the goddess's voice. None of them had the fortitude to look her in the face.

"So, you made it. I didn't expect you so soon—well done," Eir said.

Bremen, Selby, and Plintze exchanged looks among themselves. Jorg stared at the ceiling.

"You knew we'd come?" Bremen asked.

"I had an idea," Eir said with a sparkle in her eyes and a glance to Jorg. "Please allow me to introduce Thelonius, King of Alfheim."

They bowed as they had for Caelya, Plintze included. Jorg had to bite his lip at Caelya's light scoff before he rose once again to stand with his shoulders back.

The king stepped closer to Jorg and studied him. "You have your father's features, but your mother's heart, I think. I'm pleased to meet you after all these years." He smiled and gave a slight nod.

Nothing had prepared Jorg for such a warm welcome. All his

life he'd had to hide who he was or suffer the consequences. His father had used his speed and expertise as a warrior to win bets, but otherwise, he held Jorg in contempt. If it hadn't been for his mother, he never would have learned to fit in. She taught him to hone his human skills. The people the king spoke of were as foreign as the realm in which he stood.

"Thank you. I apologize for not knowing the customs and being forward, but we came to find Ingrid and Galwain. Can you help us?" Jorg asked. His brow pinched as his heart warred between loss and new hope. He wanted to soak in this strange acceptance and . . . familiarity? But that would have to come later.

"They are both at Montibeo, Jarrick's castle high in the mountains. Until this evening, I believed his obsession with restoring Vanaheim was a good diversion for his energies. When Galwain arrived, Jarrick told me it was of her own will, and I believed him. I should have investigated further. I ignored the truth for a thin strand of hope. For that, I apologize to you both." Thelonius twisted to acknowledge Bremen, who swallowed visibly.

"Can we go there? Are they safe?" Selby asked, her voice full of emotion. When Jorg glanced at her, he noticed a trickle of sweat down the side of her face, and Eir's hand on her arm. The gash on her face was half what it had been.

"The matter has become more complicated," Thelonius offered, snapping Jorg's attention back. "There are questions that need to be answered before I can send an envoy through the mountains."

"Why can't you just disappear and show up there as Jarrick and those others did?" Bremen spoke this time, irritation rising in his voice. His face was pale as a metallic tang wafted through the air from his blood-soaked tunic. The damage he'd sustained in both attacks was much worse than he'd let on.

"Making a portal is a matter of defense and not a mode of transportation that's condoned regularly," Eir answered. "Keeping one open long enough for a large group would be dangerous."

Jorg stared at her, partly because he absorbed her words, but also for how deftly she worked her healing powers. She'd finished with Selby as she spoke and gestured to Plintze. When he'd seen what she needed, he'd scooted to Selby's side and allowed her to lean against his shoulder. The goddess then shifted her attention to Bremen. Jorg saw his brother flinch at her touch, then squeeze his eyes closed.

"Ingrid told me you taught her how to travel that way. Can she get away on her own?" Jorg asked as he recalled his time with Ingrid in the courtyard. It was during the battle when he'd told her to leave . . . before Jarrick and the dragons.

"Ingrid has not had control of her powers since she's arrived on Alfheim. I wouldn't guess she's able to form a portal," Caelya answered.

Too focused on Bremen, Eir couldn't continue in the conversation. Jorg's insides twisted as he watched the white line of his brother's clamped lips and how his jaw muscles twitched. Whatever injury he'd suffered from the goblins was grave. He'd not complained once. The battle with the skögsra must have made it worse.

A sensation slammed against Jorg. He'd thought the word, *brother*, but for the first time, he felt what it meant.

Help him, please!

Several moans echoed through the room. Thelonius snapped his attention to Jorg, and Caelya slapped her fingers against her forehead.

"Jorg, I need to concentrate. You are on Alfheim now, your elven abilities are stronger here, and everyone can hear you shout," Eir said in a firm, but quiet voice. She sounded as though she grew weary from her efforts. "Thelonius, can you please help him?"

"I'm . . . I'm sorry. I didn't realize," Jorg stammered.

"Why would you? This is a foreign land to you," the king said with gentleness soaking his words. "Your friends need rest. Once we settle everyone in their rooms, you and I can talk. Then I'll show you how to keep your thoughts private."

Kelvhan led the guards from the room, followed by Eir who braced Bremen. Selby stared at Jorg. The remnants of a scar were still visible on her cheek though it wouldn't be disfiguring.

Jorg felt like he'd been kicked in the gut when he saw it—a permanent reminder of his foolishness. Still, it somehow suited her. It added a fierce boldness to her, making her beautiful in a way he'd never noticed. It would never take away the guilt he felt for causing her pain, however. She and Plintze headed after Bremen when Jorg gave an almost imperceptible nod.

The need for air and outdoors slammed against him. He needed to run, to explode with all the emotions trapped inside. When a hand rested on Jorg's shoulder he spun, ready to defend himself. Instead, he saw a kind, yet steadfast expression from Thelonius.

"Justified as your anger may be, there are better ways to handle it. Allow me to help you."

Jorg suddenly felt like a small boy again, searching for the comfort of his mother's arms when someone had teased and taunted him. He'd worked hard to build a thick barrier against such soft emotions. The acceptance that came from the man in front of him threatened his efforts. He felt vulnerable, yet keeping up his facade had grown difficult.

"Let's find your room, and we can talk in private," Thelonius said.

Thank you. Jorg knew Caelya would hear him, too, and he didn't mind. His throat was too thick to choke out words.

EXHAUSTED after his time with Thelonius, Jorg had stretched out on the softly cushioned bench at the foot of the massive bed in his chambers. He couldn't bring himself to settle into the thick mattress. It didn't rustle like the straw he was used to, nor did it feel stuffed with feathers. In the end, he'd decided it wouldn't do for him to relax so completely, anyway. He needed to keep alert. As soon as possible, he intended to find that mountain pass and his way to Ingrid.

A soft knock on the door made him jump to his feet. He reached for his knife. When the ivory hilt fit into his palm, his resolve melted. It was the knife he'd given Ingrid, and she'd lost it in the dirt before she'd slipped away with Jarrick—unarmed and in the arms of the enemy. His gut twisted as he opened the door.

Before him stood a guard. He wasn't dressed in the same style as Kelvhan, but rather in simple black leathers without denotation of rank. Wary, Jorg tightened the grip on the knife.

"If you want to know the way through the mountains to Montibeo, follow me." The elf darted glances over each shoulder and then settled his stare on Jorg. "We need to hurry."

Every impulse inside Jorg screamed to stay. This was not one of the king's guard, and it could be a trap—but it could also be exactly what he needed to get to Ingrid faster than the plan Thelonius and Eir would come up with. He'd move faster alone, and this way, he wouldn't endanger the others.

"Lead the way," Jorg said and closed the door quietly behind him as he stepped into the hall.

With no further words, the guard hustled away with Jorg on his heels.

28

INGRID

Ingrid scanned her new cage. As expected, the walls were dark, but it had three large windows on the far wall that started at waist height and soared to the high ceiling above, curving to a point at the top. There were no curtains or shutters to block the cold, yet no cold entered.

A large but simple raised bed nestled against the wall to her left. It was covered in furs and tempted her to burrow under them, but that wouldn't do. She had a plan to make.

Built into another wall was a hearth. While chilled, Ingrid still wasn't ready for the sight or smell of burning wood. She shuddered. *What's wrong with you? It's not the same as dragon-fire. Besides, Jorg and Selby are alive.* Perhaps she would try to start a fire . . . later.

Then she saw it. Hiding behind a simple woven basket that held extra kindling and slim logs was the handle of a small axe. Whoever's job it was to fill the basket must have left it there.

Ingrid hurried over and picked up the small weapon. The handle fit her palm perfectly, and the axe-head was small but sharp. If it didn't kill someone outright, it would cause severe enough injuries to slow them down. Then she could deal the deathblow. She caressed the smooth handle and ran her finger over the metal. The ironwork, like everything else, was without ornamentation, but it was sharp.

She realized then that she'd never get close enough to either Jarrick or Urkon with an axe strapped to herself. It was too blatant and crude, not clever. What she needed was something small. Something that would fit in her hand. She'd never last in a fight against them. They'd overpower her with magic before she could strike hard enough to kill. Whatever she did would have to be fast and precise.

The basket of wood caught her attention, and a curve tipped her mouth. She'd made many nalbinding needles in her life. Whittling a sapling branch into a small flat piece then shaping a point on one end. This time, it had to be bigger.

Two hard-backed wooden chairs sat near a table holding a bowl and pitcher. Ingrid dragged one over to the hearth and chose a small, sturdy chunk of kindling. Using the sharp axe she scraped. The shavings fell to the floor, and she periodically brushed them into the firebox.

It was awkward going at first, with the handle spinning into her way as she held just the sharp iron. When she forced the axe-head off the handle, the work progressed much faster.

Not long after, she held the first make-shift knife in her palm. It needed refinement, but it was sharp enough to pierce skin and thick enough to do good damage. It was thin, yet sturdy. Once embedded into a jugular or a kidney, she could snap it off, making the fragment irretrievable. That would give her time to get away.

About to start on a second knife, Ingrid heard voices in the hall. Quickly, she threw the axe-head and handle into the basket and swept most of the shavings into the firebox. She'd just sat back down, hiding the finished knife under her, when her door opened.

"Hello, Ingrid," Jarrick said. He'd expected her to be on her bed, and he snapped his eyes around the room before finding her. The momentary flash of concern on his face amused her. Composing himself, he said, "It's time for dinner. I'm here to escort you."

"I'm not hungry."

"We are high in the mountains, and that can cause a loss of appetite. However, it might make a good excuse for you to have company."

"Will Galwain be there?" Ingrid started to stand and caught herself.

Jarrick narrowed his eyes as he snatched a glance at the floor near Ingrid's feet. Several shavings lingered, and she tried to act as though she didn't notice. "No, she takes her meals in her chambers. When she's ready to entertain company, I'll be sure you will be among the first to visit."

Settling against the wooden back of the chair, Ingrid folded her hands in her lap. "Then there's no reason for me to leave my chambers either."

Jarrick wandered near the bed and ran his fingertips through the top fur. "Did I ever tell you how I met Urkon?"

Ingrid sliced a glare in his direction. *I don't care.*

Jarrick grinned and flicked his eyebrows at her reproach. She was sure her mental barriers were intact, but if he heard her, it didn't matter.

"I was on Vanaheim, searching through the ruins. Many Vanir have carved out an existence there. It's meager and simple, yet they survive. It's nothing of the culture it used to be."

Jarrick walked to the windows and stared out at the mountains. While he seemed lost in thought, Ingrid considered leaving the room; then decided against it since she didn't have her knives ready. She slumped in her chair, using her foot to clear away the stray shavings while Jarrick wasn't looking.

It was several minutes before he spoke again. "I spoke with a group of elders, those who remembered the war. Even though they lived among ruins and rubble, they assured me their lives held contentment. They even lied to themselves that they had all they needed. That a simple life had taught them the value of what's truly important. Poor idiots. But what else could they say to keep their sanity?

"As I was walking away, another individual approached me. He wore the same simple robes as everyone else, but it was obvious he was different. For a while, we spoke of the situation. He gave me his insights as the other elders had, but he was testing me. He wanted to know where my heart was, wanted to know if I was strong enough to be the leader he needed. We wandered through the village, conversing for hours. We shared our visions of what the realm once was and could be again."

Jarrick left the window and walked back to the room's center, his hands behind his back as he sauntered slowly across the darkening space. Ingrid rested her hands in her lap as if she didn't have any cares.

"When we spoke of how to accomplish our goals, he told me who he was. Up to that point, I knew his name but not *who* he was. Obviously, he'd been around during the war and knew Njord." Jarrick interrupted himself to turn to Ingrid. "You know of Njord, correct?"

"The ruler of Vanaheim," Ingrid answered with the tone of a bored child.

Jarrick ignored her attitude and continued his story. "When I found out Urkon was the original master of seiðr magic, I was in awe. He'd discovered the secrets of the magic and taught it to a handful of others—including Freya."

Ingrid perked up.

"That much you know though, right?"

She did. Urkon had told her, but if Jarrick had more information, it was worth hearing. With as much casual indifference as she could muster, she shrugged. "Yes, and it seems you have other things to speak about."

Jarrick laughed, but just once. It lashed out more like a whip than mirth. "Do you know why she did what she did? What made her strip Urkon of his powers and link his release to you?"

That wasn't the way Ingrid had thought about it before. She knew the spell protecting Midgard from the other realms also sealed Urkon's powers away from him, though she hadn't connected that it linked him to her. She'd only focused on the rift it had caused between him and Freya. No wonder he wanted her dead. Ingrid shook her head, unable to answer Jarrick's question, but needing to hear the answer.

"In truth, the Vanir won the war—they defeated Asgard. Njord, Freya, and Frey went to secure the surrender from Odin. Instead, they brokered a deal. Freya would teach Odin what she knew of the seiðr, Frey would work with Asgard to protect and provide for the human realm, and Njord would retire in peace to Alfheim."

"Why?" Ingrid couldn't help herself. She'd moved to the edge of her seat and stared raptly at Jarrick. This was new information. Never in any story was there a hint of an Asgardian defeat.

"Because Urkon is stronger than all of them combined."

"And yet, you're working with him. Helping him!" Ingrid slipped her hand to the edge of the chair, her breathing ragged. Should she attack Jarrick right then? He was the one who created an army spliced with magic.

"I made a bargain with Urkon, that day of our first meeting. It was impetuous and stupid. Now, I'm stuck with it. You are the only one that can free everyone, myself included, Ingrid."

The low light that poured in from the open windows bounced off of Jarrick's luminous features. This was the dark elf who'd sent his spirit to her twice through magic. Once in the body of his dragon, Voxx, and the other in a vision where he tried to pull her through, something—a portal most likely.

Now as she stared at him, his eyes implored her to believe him. She was unsure who the true enemy really was. Could Urkon trap Jarrick? Even bound as he was, the seiðr master wielded unnatural power, so it was possible. What capabilities would he have if released? It wasn't an option. Regardless of Jarrick, Urkon could not go free. Not by her; not by anyone.

"I guess the question is, are you going to stab me with that knife you've made, or are you going to help me defeat Urkon?"

29

INGRID

Ingrid's newly carved knife pressed against her thigh where she sat on it. It shouldn't have surprised her that Jarrick knew about it. He always seemed to know more about her than she did.

"I don't think it's fair that I'm unable to defend myself. Since coming here, I've needed a weapon twice." With no reason to deny it, Ingrid pushed as much bravado into her words as she could. Then stood and held the makeshift knife in her hand. Not as a threat, but to display her talents.

Curling his lip into a wry grin, Jarrick reached out and wiggled his fingers for her to hand it over.

Instead, she raised her brows and moved it down to her side.

"I'll give it back. Far be it from me to keep you unarmed," Jarrick teased. "Though I don't know why you need something so primitive when you have abilities more powerful than knives."

Ingrid glared and stepped back. "As if you don't know why I can't access my magic."

An uneasy silence filled the air while Jarrick stared, eyes narrowed and contemplative. "Surely, you don't think I had something to do with it. At first, I believed it was because of the transition between realms or perhaps your human emotions, but this is interesting."

"Interesting? You call locking me up, keeping me helpless, and destroying everyone I love—*interesting*? You are the only one to blame."

Jarrick scoffed. "I believe you experienced some unfortunate circumstances, but you have never been helpless, nor was anyone you love destroyed . . . Were they?" Jarrick inched closer to Ingrid. The chair pressed against the back of her knees as she leaned away.

Has he known all along they were all alive? Of course, he did. "You let me believe they were dead."

Since arriving in Alfheim, Ingrid had been powerless. Jarrick brought her there. Who else could have done anything to her? Urkon perhaps? *How could he have done that? He didn't meet me until the dinner.*

"Has it occurred to you that perhaps the only person in your way, is you?" Jarrick said with a cocked brow.

Ingrid huffed. "It doesn't matter if you tell me. Whatever you did, I'll fight it. Some abilities have already returned. You can't keep me imprisoned forever."

Jarrick looked amused. "Perhaps not, but you're here now. Keep your weapon; it matters not. What's more important here is Urkon and how he's affecting plans to bind the spell for Midgard. We need to stop him."

It was hard for Ingrid to believe that Jarrick had nothing to do with her trapped magic. It was harder to believe that he was on her side instead of Urkon's.

When she didn't speak, Jarrick took her silence for acceptance and her approval.

"If I help, what do you want me to do?" An alliance with Jarrick would help stop Urkon, and that fit into Ingrid's plan. It would also buy her more time to discover what Jarrick was up to. *What else does he want?*

"I don't think we need to discuss all the details right now," Jarrick stepped away from Ingrid and paced to the end of the bed. He ran a finger along the furs again before facing her once more. "I'm relieved he's alive, too, you know. Voxx was careful . . . just like I asked."

Jarrick said nothing more and left Ingrid stunned as he strode through the door.

What did he mean 'like he asked'? He told Voxx to keep Jorg alive? Yet, he had no problem killing all the others.

Plopping into the chair, Ingrid let her hands fall into her lap while still holding the wooden knife. What was she to do now? First thing was to finish her weapons. Since Jarrick knew about them, she didn't need to hide, but she certainly needed more than one.

THE NIGHTS WERE DARKER in the mountains. Though the wards on the windows kept out the cold, Ingrid wrapped herself in a fur blanket. She stared at the swirling snow and pointed peaks. The memory of Jorg's face, surprised and hopeful, filled her heart with joy. Before long, her thoughts would dash against the cold stones of Jarrick's words.

How could she contemplate believing him about Urkon? She knew Urkon was terrible, but she had a hard time accepting that Jarrick could disagree with his mentor. Quarn had said it was the prince who'd overseen the ruvar army, not Urkon. The master hadn't understood what Ingrid spoke of when she told him about it, but deception was what he was good at. That could have been an act. She'd proven herself naïve too many times to think they weren't playing her for a fool again.

The truth was, she couldn't trust either of them. The question remained who should die first. If Urkon had so much influence over Jarrick, perhaps he would be the wisest choice. If someone cuts off a snake's head, the body still writhes, but it can't bite anymore.

How? How could she do it?

Would it be as easy as catching him unaware with one of her newly shaped weapons?

She'd done a good job with scrubbing the wooden knives against the stone fireplace until the tips were sharp and the handles were smooth. She now had four. One under the covers of the bed, another behind the basket of kindling, and two strapped to herself.

She'd torn a hole in the seam of her trousers and tied one to her thigh, letting her long tunic hide the opening. The one along her spine between her shoulder blades was trickier, but she fashioned a simple sheath inside her tunic.

Then there were also the spikes. She wore them in her hair as if they were decoration, like long tapered needles easy to access and plunge into vulnerable areas. Ingrid huffed a laugh. Without access to her magic, she'd become more resourceful than she might have been.

Now—when should I use them?

She sat in the chair near the fireplace again and stared into the dark space, playing absently with the rune pouch around her neck. She shivered from under the fur around her shoulders, even though the wind didn't come through the windows. The chill could have possibly been from planning to kill someone, but she figured it was more than likely the cold. At least, that's what she told herself. It was one thing to kill in the middle of battle when your life was in immediate danger, but it was another to plan someone's death ahead of time.

She didn't like it, but she wouldn't shy away from what

needed to be done either. Thinking of her family gave her courage. They were off to find somewhere new to settle and rebuild their lives. Jorg and Selby were alive, but what about Plintze? She longed to share the good news with Galwain, but then thought about her other son, Bremen. Had he escaped the courtyard inferno?

Ingrid shivered again. Could she handle a fire? She wondered if starting it herself would make a difference. Maybe it would help her put aside the reminder of dragon's fire that came along with the smell and the flash of the flame.

Slipping to her knees, she pulled out some smaller pieces of kindling to lie over the shavings she'd thrown in there earlier. A flint starter sat on the mantle, and she held it in her hand for a few slow breaths before she sucked in deep and struck it. When the thin line of smoke curled from within the pile, she sat back on her heels and watched. Slowly, it grew thicker, and small crackles grumbled with pleasure as the shavings succumbed to the glowing embers. The scent reached Ingrid, and a light whimper escaped her throat.

Determined to watch as the flames popped into existence, she rubbed her temples to relieve the dizziness that made her sway. Before too long, she needed to add larger logs to the awakened firebox. Carefully, she set one and then another within the orange flicker.

Her stomach fluttered but didn't rebel. The dizziness passed, and a single tear slipped down her cheek as she remembered all the men in the courtyard when she left. Men who fought from Bremen's homeland and those who came to destroy them—his grandfather's men. Jorg's grandfather, too. None of them needed to die, and it was possible that not all of them had.

As the flames grew stronger, so did she.

The past was gone. It was time to move forward.

Ingrid released a slow exhale and hugged herself, rubbing

her arms for warmth. The blanket had fallen from her shoulders, but the flames gave off plenty of heat.

Why am I still cold?

The surrounding air chilled further. Ingrid gasped and
sprung to her feet, twisting to face the door. Standing inside her
room was Aguane. The sylph's jewel-like eyes sparkled, and she
held a finger to her lips.

30

JORG

Jorg followed the elf through several corridors and down two different stairways. They finally left the palace from a lower level and headed toward several long buildings. If they didn't have flat rooftops, their size might have allowed them to be mistaken for longhouses. The smell of manure and hay increased as they neared the first set of dwellings.

"It's back here beyond the stables," the elf said.

Jorg didn't answer but kept a wary eye out. Knowing he'd followed a stranger in a foreign land without question weighed heavy on his mind.

What am I doing? Getting to Ingrid while bringing no more harm to the others, that's what. If this leads to a fight, I wouldn't mind that either.

The duo rounded the stables and entered another long building. Inside, there were rows of beds stacked two high along the length of each wall. The center of the room was left open for a walkway.

Jorg had never seen such an arrangement. There wasn't a hearth fire or tables, nor were there any places for lounging as there would be in a longhouse like he'd grown up in. This seemed to be a place meant only for sleeping, albeit for a lot of bodies. Jorg counted the beds; eighteen per side, doubled was seventy-two, yet the room was empty.

"Where is everyone?" he asked, slowing to allow more space between the elf and himself. The closed in space and the possibility of being outnumbered had him questioning his need of a fight.

"This unit is out on patrol. It'll be empty until morning." The elf stopped three bunks ahead at the end of the row and waited for Jorg.

Deciding it was better to hang back, Jorg stopped as well. "So now what? I thought you were showing me how to get to the pass."

"I am, but you need to speak to someone first. It's just through here." The elf pointed with his chin toward a door in the building's side, past where the elf leaned against the bed's frame, waiting.

"I'll follow you," Jorg said.

There had been too many times in Jorg's childhood that groups of bullies had ambushed him after someone had noticed his ears. He recognized the conditions, though this time, he wondered if it was because of his human side. With a deep breath, he prepared himself for what he knew was about to come, hoping it was a manageable number.

The door opened, and Jorg saw just the top of an elf's head as he sauntered into the room followed by others. Jorg counted six before he focused on who came into view. Dúngarr smirked at Jorg.

"Congratulations. I wasn't sure you'd have the smarts to figure it out. Since you followed this far, I expected you to come all the way," Dúngarr said.

"Looks like I'm not the only fool here then."

"Careful. You're outnumbered, and you'll only leave here if I allow it." As Dúngarr spoke, Jorg heard footsteps behind him.

How could I be this stupid? He inhaled and stared at the floor for a heartbeat before squaring his shoulders and meeting Dúngarr's stare. "Whenever you're ready."

"See, now that's why you're here," Dúngarr said and stepped closer. The men behind him followed, and Jorg glanced over his shoulder. The gap front and back closed to two paces each way. "You're a fighter. Ready to jump in and get a job done. That's what I like about you. Because of that, I'm willing to make you a deal."

"I want nothing from you." What was his angle? What did Dúngarr have to gain by making any deals?

"Really?" Dúngarr lifted his brows to a high arch. "I'd have figured a chance to be with Ingrid would be worth more to you after all the effort you've put in to get here."

"Where is she?" *I should have known you'd use her.* "Tell me where she is, and we won't have a problem here." *I can at least make it worth their while.*

Jorg didn't believe they'd kill him. The king knew he was here, and that would cause too many problems for Jarrick. It also seemed unlikely that Dúngarr would make such a move against him if Jarrick knew he was here. *He* might not even know Jorg was alive.

"You can listen to what I have to say or not. Either way, whatever you decide works for me. I win no matter what."

"So, tell me and let's get on with it."

"I see it like this: somehow, you survived after Voxx turned that little hovel you called a fortress into rubble. Anyone who can do that is interesting. More importantly, you might have value to Prince Jarrick and Master Urkon. If you will join their cause and come with me to the castle, then I'd be willing to take you under my wing, teach you what it means to be a real elf."

Jorg smiled with a huff. Apparently, his *father* hadn't been that excited to meet his son. He expected that someone in Dúngarr's position would have known of his relationship to Jarrick. "So, you want to earn favor by bringing me into Jarrick's army?"

"*Prince* Jarrick, halfling," the elf who had lured Jorg in said.

"That's all right, Alof. He doesn't understand our ways yet. You can teach him later," Dúngarr said, and Alof's face split into a wide grin.

Jorg shook his head. "Tsk, tsk, Dúngarr. I would have thought you held a higher position with the *prince*," Jorg exaggerated Jarrick's title with a mock bow. "I wouldn't trust you either. Making a play to earn his confidence—that makes sense for someone like you. A simple henchman, doing all the dirty work, who wants to improve his position—I get it. But you're missing important details."

Dúngarr's attitude made a swift turn. He clenched his fists at his side and curled his lip in a snarl. "Careful. You might be stronger and faster than those little humans in your realm, but you'll find things different here."

"I've been looking forward to a challenge, testing out the way things work. Seems like fun." Jorg relaxed his shoulders and prepared himself. "Don't you even want to find out what I might know that you don't?"

There was a momentary flick of Dúngarr's brows, and hesitation at the prospect of hearing what Jorg might say, but then it disappeared. Which was fine by Jorg. He looked forward to the chance to release his pent-up anger, especially on Dúngarr. It wasn't a time for weapons. This was a test of strength and fortitude.

"What could you possibly think you know that I don't? Nothing happens in this realm without my knowledge." Dúngarr stepped forward out of the crowd to stand in front of

Jorg. "Giants will be here soon—in the next couple days. Prince Jarrick has made a bargain with them for when Midgard opens. You'll want to ally with the right side. Information is what I deal in, as Ingrid knows well. We had a nice chat about it in her room —just the two of us."

Fire scorched through Jorg's veins and turned his vision red. His right fist caught Dúngarr on the jaw and his left to the abdomen. After that, he was a fury of single-minded focus.

The elven guard was strong and ready. The two careened into a bedpost then back to the aisle. Hands shoved them, keeping them in the open area. Strike after strike, Jorg had one purpose. He'd let no one who had hurt Ingrid survive.

Dúngarr stumbled. Jorg leaned forward and released an onslaught of blows. The two fell to the floor, and Jorg pinned the guard's arms under his knees. Then someone grabbed him by the back of his tunic and pulled him to his feet.

Blows came in at different angles, and he roared at the intrusion. He elbowed the nose of a faceless elf and kneed the gut of another as he surged forward at Dúngarr. After the coward had risen to his feet, he stepped behind his men.

An onslaught of fists surrounded Jorg. He spun to deflect and return as fast as he could.

"Is that all you've got?" Dúngarr's voice drifted through the madness.

Adrenaline surged through Jorg. He fought with a speed he'd never experienced. Strength powered through his arms. Three elves crumbled to the floor as he fought his way to his target.

One from behind wrapped an arm around his neck while another pummeled his midsection. Others came in from the sides, from between the beds, to kick at his legs and add to the abuse of his ribcage.

Roaring, he lashed out with his feet as someone bent his arms backward. He landed on the stone floor with a crack to his knees. As he twisted and continued to defend himself, darkness crept in at the edges of his vision.

Whatever extra strength he'd gained now seeped out of his bones. With his arms pinned and his legs useless under him, he was at the mercy of every punch. He tasted blood when he coughed, and if his eyes were open, he couldn't tell.

Suddenly, it all stopped. A new source of shouting rang through the hall, he thought. Perhaps it was only the ringing in his ears. Vaguely, he heard his name as someone rolled him over, just before everything went dark.

31

INGRID

Aguane hadn't been in Ingrid's room at the palace the last time she'd returned. Was the reason because she also spent time in Montibeo? Did she help Jarrick? Could she be a spy?

In the middle of her jumbled and hurried thoughts, Aguane floated closer. Scoffing at Ingrid's fear, she grabbed Ingrid's arm, and peace washed over her. A vision of the large room Ingrid had traversed entered her mind. Yet, her view was distant and darkened, as if she watched from the shadows.

Aguane released her arm. The expression the sylph held as she studied Ingrid's face was hard to decipher. What was it she wanted Ingrid to know?

"Oh! You snuck through the castle. Then you're not working with Jarrick?" The narrowed glare and the flash of light that sparked through Aguane's eyes affirmed how offended she was at the accusation. "Are you here to help me?"

The sylph nodded, then beckoned with her hand for Ingrid to follow to the door. Aguane hesitated and closed her eyes. Ingrid presumed she was listening. The air suddenly turned as frosty as it would be on an autumn morning. Ingrid could see her breath in puffs as it escaped, faster with each exhale. Stumbling backward as a gust rushed against Ingrid's middle, she'd made it halfway across the room when the door opened.

"Now, Now, Aguane. You know better than to come here. Jarrick has made himself clear on the subject," Urkon drawled as he sauntered into the room.

Aguane's skirts billowed and moved as if they floated in water, moving between Ingrid and the seiðr master. How had Urkon known the sylph had arrived?

Thankful she'd finished her weapons, Ingrid reached for the one at her thigh. Before she could remove it, a roar of air surrounded her. She threw her hands over her ears and screamed against the deafening sound. Wisps of hair dislodged from her braid and slapped across her eyes. Helpless to stop herself, she slid across the floor. Her feet scrambled for traction to no avail as the air pressure shoved her into the corner of the room next to the fireplace.

The sound abated as Ingrid turned and pressed her shoulders against the smooth stone walls. The tunnel of air that held her captive was now an arc pinning her in the corner from ceiling to floor. She noticed it wasn't just air, but mist—like Aguane. It swirled and moved as it kept a steady barrier between Ingrid and the rest of the room. It was then she realized that it wasn't only the wind that stopped assaulting her ears but all sound.

Ingrid swallowed hard, and the lack of noise made her own breathing echo. Between the swirls of mists, she saw flashes of bright light and dark shadows. Aguane had formed the barrier as a shield as the sylph and the dark arts master battled.

Though limited in using seiðr, Ingrid knew Urkon still had considerable power. He'd used a form of magic far beyond the level of portal travel training she'd had to bring her to Jarrick's castle. However, that didn't mean much. The training she'd had with Eir focused mainly on how she could bind the spell protecting Midgard, not in how to wield her powers for other matters.

Ingrid shrieked as what appeared to be a dagger made of *shadows* pierced through the air shield. With little room to maneuver, she'd barely avoided the tip of the blade before it retracted. The pressure of the barrier strengthened, and Ingrid had to open and close her mouth, swallowing in between to clear the pressure in her ears.

In a moment of visual clarity between the swirling mist, a chair in her room smashed against the stone just outside her protective wall. Ingrid instinctively raised her hands in front of her face, then pressed her fingers against her mouth. Powerful forces fought over her. Caelya had said Aguane had the strength of two elves and moved even faster. If Urkon could keep up with her, then the strength of the magic he wielded was stronger than Ingrid expected.

What would he be like with full use of seiðr? Reaching out, Ingrid tested the barrier. Her fingers slipped into the mist, but she pulled them back with a yelp. The bite of freezing temperature covered them in frost. Quickly, she stuck them under her arm to warm. She alternated between holding her breath and hyperventilating. The pressure had taken hold of her—or was it a lack of air?

She wasn't as cold anymore. That's when she felt the heat slipping into her space. Fire blazed on the other side of her protective wall, and the heat infiltrated her space, making her dizzy.

The mist slowed and offered her a better glimpse into her room. Aguane glowed and hovered in the air, her features unrecognizable. She was nearly transparent as Urkon pushed a wall of fire toward her and Ingrid at the same time. Black smoke billowed from the flames like living shadows.

Suddenly, Aguane grew so bright Ingrid had to shield her eyes. Ice crystals bloomed on Ingrid's temples where sweat had formed seconds earlier. The mist wall thickened once again. Frigid temperatures made Ingrid hug herself tightly and slip into a ball on the floor.

Tears stung her eyes at the helpless feeling of being trapped while someone else fought for her. Urkon might hurt the sylph, and then what would happen? How would the princess ever forgive Ingrid if something happened to someone so important to her?

While Ingrid huddled on the floor, another shard of darkness pierced the icy wall. The sword-like shape sliced in a downward arc, ripping a hole in the protections before it left. It would have cut through her body if she'd been standing. Sound finally entered, and Ingrid's blood went cold. A horrid keening rang through the air.

Jumping to her feet, Ingrid pushed her hand through the ripped barrier and opened it wide enough to view the room. Aguane's light gauzy body bent close to the floor as both fire and shadow assaulted her.

Ingrid screamed and pushed herself through into the room, causing the wall to dissipate. "Leave her alone!"

Urkon darted a glance to Ingrid, and the distraction gave Aguane a momentary reprieve. "Stay back, Ingrid. I'll deal with you in a moment," Urkon rasped in a voice so evil it seemed to come from the depths of Helheim itself.

"No! Leave her alone. Whatever you want from me, I'll do it. Just stop!"

Urkon tilted a glance at Ingrid, then a smile slowly curled his lips. The pressure seemed to lessen against Aguane, and she stared at Ingrid shaking her head.

Ingrid turned to Urkon, ignoring the pleading sylph. "What do you want?"

"Agree to come with me to the Yggdrasil tree on the morning of the king's birthday celebration. Bind the spell as I instruct without fail and tell no one you've made this bargain."

Ingrid's stomach turned in on itself. Her magic shifted and rolled, taunting her as it stayed out of reach. She knew what Urkon's request meant. He would sacrifice her and free himself. The power of the seiðr would be back in his full control, and he'd use it to fight against Asgard and enslave humanity. The king's birthday was less than two days away, but maybe she could find a way to the tree before then.

"I agree."

The fire and shadows disappeared as Urkon's smile grew. Aguane stayed on the floor, drained and defeated.

"To protect our bargain from further disruption," Urkon flicked a glance toward Aguane, "you will stay in more appropriate quarters."

Ingrid stared at Aguane, but the sylph did not return the gaze. She kept her focus on the floor in front of her.

"I'm sorry. I couldn't let him hurt you like that," Ingrid whispered.

"Enough. She isn't worth your pity," Urkon said. He snatched Ingrid's arm and squeezed. "It's about time all this nonsense ended."

Ingrid heard the door latch, but she paid no attention. Her focus stayed with Aguane as she faded, slowly growing lighter until, like a field of spent dandelions, she fluttered into the breeze—then disappeared.

"It's the way of the sylph. She becomes the air itself to heal. Once she does, all will be well with her as it was before," Jarrick said from where he stood by the door. "I suspect that might not be a comfort to know if you've done something foolish thinking you could save her."

"I would say she's finally come to her senses," Urkon cooed.

"Perhaps it would be best to speak further someplace else?" Jarrick asked in a tone of reverence to Urkon.

What had she done? Aguane didn't need her help. Ingrid should have realized that. She stared dumbfounded at the empty space Aguane used to occupy. Something caught her attention, a glint of metal. *What is that?* It appeared to be a necklace.

Ingrid casually checked that her runes still hung around her neck. It couldn't have been them because both the string and the pouch were made of leather. There wasn't any way to get closer without drawing attention to what the sylph had left behind.

"I have just the place," Urkon answered to Jarrick.

This time, it didn't shock Ingrid when the air escaped her lungs, and everything turned dark. Nor did she stumble when her feet suddenly landed somewhere new.

But she gasped when she saw where.

32

JORG

Excruciating pain was the first sensation to rouse Jorg. The second was the voices. A moan escaped before he could stop it, and the litter he laid on came to a halt. Hair clung to his face from sweat. He tried to open his eyes but could only see through slits. Blurry images of faces peered down at him.

Blood mixed with the saliva in his mouth, causing him to choke when he tried to speak. Someone rolled him to his side as he coughed, the movement nearly making him lose consciousness again.

When he'd finished retching, he willed himself to take small shallow breaths, then waved his hand to signal he was better. Gentle hands moved him once again to his back. They raised the litter to an angle where he wouldn't choke.

"Jorg, we're moving you to a safer area, and then we can help you better. For now, Bakkan will help you so you can breathe easier. Can you hear me?"

Vaguely, Jorg thought he recognized the voice, but he didn't care. He moaned and hoped he nodded. The stabbing behind his eyes told him he had. If anyone could help, give him some relief, he was up for it. Even if it was Dúngarr at that point.

Fingers touched his face on either side of his head. Bursts of light like shooting stars flashed behind his lids. He held his breath, then the pressure in his eyes faded some, and he could exhale with lesser pain. He was considerably better, though not healed.

Jorg knew what a healing felt like. Ingrid had helped him more than once. This was different but effective. He tested one eye and then the other, able to see those around him clearly. Only one face was familiar—Kelvhan—the king's guard who'd taken him to his aunt.

"Where are we?" he rasped.

"Along the pass to Montibeo. The others are waiting near the top for us to meet them. For speed and safety, it would be best if you stayed on the litter until we reach them," Kelvhan answered.

"Thank you," Jorg said. He held Kelvhan's gaze.

The guard smiled. "Any time." Kelvhan gestured to the others. They picked up the litter again, and the group started forward.

Jorg gritted his teeth and did his best to keep his breathing steady. He refused to groan. The guards had saved his life. There was no way he would act like a coward over a few bruises, though he knew it was worse than that.

He'd been rash, and because of that, he'd jeopardized more lives when his goal had been the opposite. He hadn't helped Ingrid, and he wouldn't if he didn't make better decisions. As if in answer to thinking of her, the bead around his neck warmed. He had another chance to find her. He wouldn't waste it.

As they hurried forward, Jorg noticed that his breathing had evened out. His ribs still sent a stabbing pain when he tried to move, but he was healing. Maybe whatever Bakkan did would continue to work on its own.

"Jorg!" Selby screamed from somewhere up ahead on the trail.

He smiled at the sound. They were in the mountains, surrounded by snow and high peaks. They had laid a blanket over him, but he warmed through knowing he'd made it back to his friends.

"What happened?" Selby asked when she stood by his side. Her eyes were wide enough he could see white all around the chestnut color.

"Shh. You'll cause an avalanche," Jorg joked and then paid for it with a spasm of coughs.

"If you didn't look like trolls had trampled you, I'd smack you myself. Where did you go?"

"Let's get settled and let Bakkan work. Then he can tell us how he fought an entire guard unit," Kelvhan said, hustling the guards holding the litter forward.

Not long after, Jorg's pain was manageable as he lay near a fire. He sat up and stopped Bakkan from any more ministrations. The guard was the largest of the group with bright red hair and sparkling blue eyes. His shoulders were wide, and muscles bulged from under his tunic, but the elf appeared drained.

Jorg didn't need to add more guilt to the pile he already carried with him. "Thank you, but you need to rest. I can live with a few bruises," Jorg said to Bakkan.

"It's my pleasure. You did a fair amount of helping yourself, but if you will allow me a short time to rejuvenate, I can work again," Bakkan said.

"I'm fine. There'll be no more need." *What did he mean? I did nothing.*

Bakkan stood and gave a slight bow to Jorg before he moved

to a spot in the shadows and laid down. Almost immediately, snores emanated from the robust figure.

Kelvhan chuckled as he settled near the fire. "He can fall asleep faster than anyone I've ever met. Oh, and he snores the loudest, but you'll not find a kinder-hearted soul."

"Plintze, are you tired? We can take bets and see who really snores the loudest," Selby teased.

"Humph. You'll need to join the competition," Plintze answered.

The guards stared at the duo, seemingly unsure how to respond. A heartbeat later Bremen and Jorg chuckled.

"Ah, stop. Bakkan did a great job, but don't make me laugh," Jorg said.

Selby gave a toothy grin, and Plintze's eyes crinkled in a tell-tale sign of the smile hiding under all his facial hair.

"So," Bremen pierced Jorg with a direct gaze, "tell us what happened?"

Suddenly, the space seemed too small, and Jorg could feel the stares of everyone on him. There was no hiding. He had to face up to his mistake and move forward. "A guard came to my door and told me he could show me the way to the pass. I knew I shouldn't trust him, but I thought if it was true . . . I could go by myself and not risk the rest of you."

"Oh, because that's why we came here? To sit around and wait for you to risk your life while we do nothing?" The irritation and hurt were louder than the sarcasm as Selby chastised him.

"After the tunnels and the forest . . ." Jorg let his words trail off.

"We knew this would be dangerous. We all came for our own reasons, and you didn't have a right to leave without telling us or giving us the chance to go along," Bremen said.

"I know."

"It was stupid. Don't do it again," Plintze added.

Of everyone, his disapproval pierced Jorg the most. He realized more than ever how much he valued Plintze's guidance and respect. "I'm sorry."

Plintze grunted and nodded. "That's the end of it then." Turning to Kelvhan, he added, "Tell him the plan."

The guard raised his brows at the command.

Caelya answered before Kelvhan could respond. "I will speak with my brother and keep him occupied while the four of you, along with Kelvhan, sneak into the palace to rescue Galwain and Ingrid. The rest of the guards will wait at the perimeter to keep watch and help if necessary."

Jorg stared at her, unaware until that moment she was present and part of the group. She'd stood off to the side, out of his view. The princess' attendance had stunned him. He hadn't judged her as one who would take such a risk.

"Sounds like a good plan. How will we know where Ingrid and Galwain are?" Jorg asked.

"A dear friend of mine is already at the castle helping them. She'll lead you to where she has hidden them. Ingrid already knows her, and I gave her the medallion Bremen wears so Galwain will know to trust her."

Bremen wears a medallion? There was still so much he didn't know about his brother.

"We don't know where Urkon will be, however. So, we must be careful to get in and out as quickly as possible. I've been to the castle frequently and can navigate the corridors," Kelvhan added.

"There's something else. When we were in Svartalfheim, we learned of a deal the dwarves made with the giants. It turns out they've made a deal with Jarrick, too. They will invade Midgard as soon as the spell falls. A delegation will arrive in Alfheim to meet with Jarrick at Montibeo in the next day or two. I didn't get an exact time," Jorg offered.

"Where did you hear about this?" Caelya asked.

"It came out when I was *chatting* with Dúngarr."

"Giants entering our realm without Thelonius' permission would be an act of war. What is Jarrick trying to accomplish? We must stop them. Kelvhan, send the guards to the border gate nearest here." There wasn't any room for debate in Caelya's command.

"Send me. I'll say I have a message from the dwarf council to postpone the meeting. Give them a reason to wait."

"That would be too dangerous, Plintze. Why would they believe you were meeting them in this realm rather than the gate from Svartalfheim? You'd be taken hostage . . . or worse," Bremen said. "Since Jorg and I didn't arrive at that gate as planned, they'll be too suspicious."

"You need the guards to make sure Ingrid and Galwain get safely away. I can do this while you find them." Plintze stood tall and resolute. He'd decided and wouldn't change his mind.

"Perhaps if we let the giants come, it would cause enough of a distraction to help keep both Jarrick and Urkon occupied," Kelvhan said, though he seemed to speak his thoughts out loud more to himself than toward anyone else.

"No, we can't risk starting a war if we can prevent it," Caelya said. "Plintze, if you fully understand the risk you're taking, I think it's the best option."

"I do."

"Let me at least send a couple of guards with you," Kelvhan offered. "If we do our job in the castle, we won't need them, anyway."

Plintze nodded. Selby sniffled, and Jorg peered sidelong at her. Tears glistened on her cheeks as she focused on their friend.

It mirrored the wrenching he felt in his own heart. What the dwarf offered was likely a one-way mission.

A loud grumble sounded from where Bakkan rested. "I'll go. It's been a long time since I've had the opportunity to tangle with one of those behemoths."

"Take two others with you, my friend, and see that you all return," Kelvhan commanded.

Without a further word, two elves stepped forward and the small group turned to leave.

"Plintze! Don't you dare leave like that," Selby called, then hurried over to him. She wrapped him in a tight hug. At first, he seemed shocked or irritated by the gesture, but then his hand settled on her back. After a couple of pats, he pulled away and hurried off with the others.

33

INGRID

Sulfur in the air squeezed Ingrid's lungs closed, and tears streamed down her cheeks. Her skin prickled with heat as she clutched at her throat.

Then in an instant, the air cleared, and the scent vanished.

"I've warded the opening. You won't have any further harmful effects," Jarrick said. He stood over Ingrid's left shoulder as she wiped her face and allowed herself to accept her surroundings.

They stood at the center of a large cave, open on the end. She recognized it from her vision. It was the dragon hive. Cautiously, she peeked over her shoulder. Behind her appeared to be a tunnel that led into the darkness.

At least there isn't a nest. There wasn't a threat of a mother trying to return to her eggs—or younglings needing a meal.

When she'd straightened herself and had her bearings, Ingrid twisted her neck toward Jarrick but didn't look at him. "Did *you* bring me here?"

"This was not my doing, but Master Urkon always has good reasons for the lessons he chooses. Perhaps now would be a good time to explain? I'm not sure how long Ingrid's human form can remain in such conditions," Jarrick said. The last comment was directed over Ingrid's head to her right where she assumed Urkon stood.

Ingrid could see clearly with the ward in place, and while the air was stuffy, it was breathable. Across from the opening, dozens of similar caves covered the far wall of the hollow interior of the mountain. Orange and black shadows flickered against the walls belying the swirling molten lake far below.

Movement from one cave drew Ingrid's attention, and she stared dumbfounded as a dragon lumbered to the edge, stretched its large wings, and heaved into the air. She followed its flight path as it twisted and turned, then dove straight back to the ledge. Holding its wings wide, it landed with a grace Ingrid would not have expected.

The dragon was at least half the size of those Ingrid had seen before. It had a light yellow-green hide that darkened into a deeper pine color on the wings. Even from that distance, she could see the amber-colored eyes that winked closed as the beast yawned and stretched its front legs far in front of its arched back. It reminded her of a cat getting ready to take a nap.

Ingrid shook her head. The view didn't match the confrontations she'd experienced. The creature she watched was . . . cute.

"Marvelous, aren't they? The young ones are entertaining as they learn to fly and hone their skills." Urkon stepped closer to the edge, enthralled with the same youngling that Ingrid studied.

There was no way she'd admit to admiring the beasts, though she couldn't help herself. Before the dragon ambled back to what she could only guess was its nest, it had rolled to its back and wiggled. Then flipped quickly to its feet and shook a cloud of black dust from its body while it hopped in a circle. It looked as though it were playing.

"Why have you brought me here?" A tingle of fear skittered

over her skin. When she'd struck her deal with Urkon, he'd said she needed to stay somewhere more appropriate. Was this where he meant? *Oh please, gods no.*

"I won't make you stay here—if that's what concerns you. But it makes a wonderful place for private discussions," Urkon said. He tilted his head as he watched other dragons take flight or land on various outcroppings.

"Is this where Voxx lives? Will she be joining us?" Ingrid directed her question to Jarrick, peering at him with a side glance.

He, too, seemed enamored with the activity of the busy hive, but he shook his head slightly. "This is the nursery. The younglings stay here until they are strong enough to survive on their own. Grown females without a nest to warm come and go, bringing nourishment. When these little ones are ready to live in the caves of the weyr, they will fight the female for her offering rather than wait for it. If it survives, it will leave and establish its own nest and order within the flight."

"Jarrick is being modest. Voxx is the queen, and every member of the flight must earn her respect, or they do not survive." Urkon faced Ingrid. A glint of excitement sparked in his eyes as he spoke.

"Earlier, you thought I didn't know about the army you became privy to in the marketplace. Not only do I know of it, but I also designed it. No detail is without my knowledge. We'd created those you met from one of the higher-ranking dragons. We found that the stronger the dragon—the closer to Voxx in rank—the stronger the warrior. Unfortunately, they are harder to command as well. An alpha dragon's independence is unequaled. It was a small detail but easily corrected.

"Once you perform your duty, as agreed, I will control not only the ruvars, but the entire weyr. No realm will dare oppose me. If they do, their rebellion won't last long."

"There is a slight miscalculation in your assessment, I'm afraid," Jarrick said. He stepped closer to Urkon, and his cinnamon scent spiked through the air. Ingrid brushed her finger under her nose at the sensation.

"I've missed nothing, my friend. No one will rival my power or control. Have no fear."

"That's where you're wrong. When you proposed creating the ruvar army, I understood the necessity. I also knew that such a force would need a strong leader. One who would win every challenge to thwart any attempt at a coup of leadership. It's the way of the dragons, as you know. None have challenged Voxx in centuries, but occasionally, a young buck gets the notion in its head. It's short-lived—the notion and the beast."

"That's why we never used Voxx's blood," Urkon answered.

The two elves faced each other, and while they spoke in civil tones, Ingrid slid backward. Something didn't feel right. She pressed herself into an indentation of the cave wall and watched in silence.

"We didn't use Voxx's blood because neither she nor I allowed it. You have taught me well. When you explained the process of mixing dragon blood with that of an elf, I recognized it was exactly what we needed. Not only would it establish an army of loyal soldiers, but they would be controllable only by whoever connected to them. Unfortunately, this is where you made your mistake." Jarrick advanced closer to Urkon.

"I've made no mistakes. You are treading dangerously near the edge of my patience. Even limited, my powers surpass yours, and I will not tolerate such insubordination," Urkon said. He sounded as strong and oily as ever, but Ingrid noticed the small shift of his weight. If Jarrick moved any closer, Urkon would step backward.

What is happening?

"The last piece of the plan needed the human healer. When

you discovered Ingrid, I rejoiced, but I also wondered—what all that power would be like? I concluded it would be glorious." Jarrick stepped closer, and as Ingrid predicted, the master scooted backward.

Urkon's back was toward the cave opening, but the ward would keep him from falling off the edge. At least, Ingrid thought it would, but as her heart raced at Jarrick's behavior, she realized there were no guarantees.

"I also wondered why I should deny myself. You've made a deal with Ingrid to bind the spell during my brother's celebration, and she'll keep that bargain. Though it will be for me," Jarrick said. "Each time you used the seiðr to create another batch of serum, some of your essence soaked into it. You never paid attention when I connected to each elf before injecting them. As the serum coursed through their veins, their connection to *my* will solidified. They sought to please me, connect with me once more. When they did, the seiðr essence you'd given away, flowed to me. The ruvars listen to me. The victory belongs to me."

"That's not possible! Even if you've stolen some of my power, it is minuscule. Unbound, no one will have more power than me," Urkon boomed. Even from the shadows, Ingrid could see the red blossom over his cheeks. Rage overtook his demeanor, and suddenly, the cave grew warmer.

At first, Ingrid thought the ward had dropped from the cave, but the sulfur smell hadn't returned. Then she watched as Urkon's hands formed balls of fire. A glowing aura of bright yellow blended to orange then red and surrounded him as it flickered against the walls. Movement near Urkon's feet drew Ingrid's attention. Shadows slithered up his legs and branched out from all around him.

It was the same magic he'd used against Aguane. Ingrid searched for a better place to hide.

"Stay where you are, Ingrid," Jarrick warned. "You'll be unharmed."

How had he known what she would do? Her body trembled, and she pressed her back harder into the uneven rocky wall. *He's so calm. I'd almost believed Urkon was more dangerous.*

Ingrid closed her eyes for several heartbeats to force herself to breathe evenly. When she opened them, she straightened herself and stood tall. Whatever the outcome, fate tied her to the winner of the battle shaping up in front of her. She'd face whoever it was with strength, not cowardice.

Jarrick cut a glance in her direction and smiled before concentrating on Urkon. The two stood five steps apart. Urkon's magic crackled, echoing off the chamber walls. Flinging his hands, the balls of flames sailed at Jarrick.

Rather than duck out of the way, Jarrick stretched his arms out wide. When the magic hit him, he sucked in a deep gasp. Instead of flying backward or bursting into flame as Ingrid expected, the magic absorbed. Where flaming spheres had been, a bright green fog appeared. It encircled Jarrick in a cloud then soaked into him.

"What have you done?" Urkon screamed.

"I tried to warn you, my friend. Do you understand now why I can't allow you to control the seiðr. It has been so long since you've controlled it that you've lost the ability to adapt. The leadership Vanaheim needs, that *all* the realms need, is one of proactive planning. I'm afraid your time to rule has passed you by."

Urkon charged at Jarrick, a steady stream of fire flowing from his hands. As soon as it hit the dark elf, it again turned to green mist and absorbed.

"Stop!" Ingrid cried out. Not because she didn't want to see anyone injured, but because she realized the more Urkon used his magic, the more powerful Jarrick became.

It was too late. Urkon was nothing but fury. When the two

collided, sparks and blinding light forced Ingrid to cover her head. In a flash, the cave was dark again. A sizzle, like a dying campfire, hissed through the air.

Ingrid stared at Jarrick. His face tipped to the ceiling, arms spread wide, as the last of the green mist disappeared into his body. Urkon shuddered in a heap near Jarrick's feet as a light moan emanated from him. He was still alive.

With a deep breath, Jarrick rolled his neck and seemed to swell taller and broader. He flicked his hands toward the front of the cave. The wards fell, allowing the blazing heat and sulfur scent to waft back inside.

Covering her nose, Ingrid squinted as she watched what would happen. Jarrick crouched down and spoke something to his mentor she couldn't hear before rising to his full height again. A shadow crossed in front of the cavern, momentarily blocking the view. Then, rising from below, Voxx appeared. Her eyes latched onto Urkon as she hovered in front of the opening.

With a natural, unhurried stride, Jarrick reached Ingrid and held out his hand to her. "Come, Ingrid. Let's leave Voxx to her prize."

Wide-eyed, Ingrid snapped her attention to the front of the cave in time to see the dragon strike. The spikes surrounding her face scraped on the sides of the cave as she seized Urkon in her jaws.

A thunderous boom from her wings drowned out the screams of the seiðr master as Voxx flew away.

34

JORG

An hour after Plintze left, the others were still in the process of breaking camp and preparing to finish the trek to Montibeo when two guards came rushing into camp.

"What is it?" Kelvhan asked with Caelya at his side.

"We were watching the pass behind us as commanded. There is a large contingent marching this way—led by the king," one guard said.

Caelya grumbled and shared a look with Kelvhan. "How much longer until they reach us?"

"Thirty, forty minutes at most," the second guard answered.

"We can hurry and leave before he arrives," Jorg said as he strolled closer.

"That would only cause him to send a party after us. They'd make more trouble than it's worth," Caelya said. "It's best if we wait and explain our plans."

"He will not be happy that you're here," Kelvhan said to Caelya, ignoring the others.

"I know."

"We should be ready to leave at least. So, once we explain,

we can be on our way," Jorg added. Selby and Bremen had joined the group and nodded in agreement.

READY TO GO but being forced to stay had Jorg irritable. He paced the edge of camp, making the occasional growl under his breath. Distracted by his own behavior, he spun, ready to fight as Thelonius and Eir burst into camp. Two units of guardsmen stopped along the trail behind them, waiting.

"How did we not hear them coming?" Selby asked to no one in particular. Several of Kelvhan's guards glanced her direction, seemingly confused by the question.

"I think they travel differently here than we're used to," Bremen responded. "Just be happy they're allies."

"Brother," Caelya greeted Thelonius and gave a shallow bow. Everyone else in camp bowed deeply to the king. "What brings you up the pass?"

"Last we spoke, Eir and I were negotiating a plan to solve this situation. I am not the one who needs to explain their presence."

Eir cocked her brow and stared at Caelya, contributing her mutual annoyance at their decision. She leveled the same look at Jorg, Bremen, and Selby, then her brows pinched. "Where is the dwarf?"

Jorg stepped forward to stand next to Caelya. "There is a situation on the Jötunheim border. He's gone to masquerade as a dwarven ambassador to delay an invasion."

"What? By himself?" Eir demanded.

Thelonius rubbed his hand over his face and clamped his lips into a tight line. "How are the giants involved?"

"Apparently, Jarrick has made a deal with them," Caelya said. "And the dwarf isn't alone. Three others went with Plintze to help."

"If a dwarf is the best hope to stop a horde of giants, we're all in trouble. When did he leave?" Thelonius asked.

"An hour, maybe more," Jorg answered.

"I'll try to catch them before they reach the border. But before I go, what happened to you?" Eir asked Jorg.

How do you know anything happened? "Just a disagreement, and I'm fine now."

The goddess stepped close enough to touch the side of Jorg's face. A far-off look clouded her eyes for a few heartbeats, and then she smiled. "Your elven blood grows stronger. Though you obviously received help, you have finished the job well enough yourself."

How? I felt nothing? Jorg kept his thoughts to himself and let Eir turn away without creating more of a spectacle. Bremen and Selby stared at him, and it made him fidgety.

"I'll be back as soon as I can," Eir said to Thelonius before hurrying away in the direction Plintze had gone.

"Why doesn't she portal ahead?" Bremen asked. "You all have these abilities, but you pick and choose when to use them."

"There are reasons, but it's not a discussion for now. I presume you have a plan that brought you here without informing me," Thelonius said, directing the question to Caelya with a glance to Kelvhan as well.

"Of course." She smirked at the king without continuing.

"I have always admired your spunk, Caelya, but don't try my patience just now."

She rolled her eyes and sighed. Selby turned her face away and tried to muffle a giggle.

I think those two might be more alike than is a good thing. Jorg bit the inside of his cheek slightly to keep his own expression neutral.

"I will speak to Jarrick, convince him it would be best to release Ingrid and Galwain. There is a low likelihood he'll agree, but while we're discussing the matter, Kelvhan, Jorg, Bremen, and Selby will infiltrate the castle with the help of Aguane and remove the two women. The rest of the guard will stand by to charge in if necessary."

"When will you know that Aguane has secured them?"

"We have designated a meeting place. That's where the others will head when we arrive."

"So, you won't know until you arrive if the first part of the plan has succeeded? This is a poor idea," Thelonius said. "You're endangering yourself and the others unnecessarily. Wait here until I return. I will take my men to the border, and then we will speak with Jarrick together."

"We don't have time to wait. Once Aguane has Galwain and Ingrid, they will need to be removed quickly. Why have you come if you didn't know about the giants?"

"Jarrick cannot unleash his ruvar army. I've come to stop him and release the others in the process."

Jorg's gut twisted. *What is a ruvar army?* He glanced at Bremen and could tell the king's words bothered him also. So, focused on getting to Ingrid, he'd let nothing else matter. Most likely, Bremen realized he'd succumbed to the same tunnel vision regarding their mother.

"If we succeed, no one will know we've been there. We can remove Ingrid and Galwain from danger. Then when you arrive, regardless of how Jarrick behaves, they'll be secure," Jorg said. He knew it was a thin plan, and Thelonius was right. But, like Caelya had said, they couldn't wait. Once Aguane moved them, they had to be there to get them out of the castle.

"The border issue is now our priority. You need to take your men and go there. While I'm speaking with Jarrick," Caelya held up her hand as Thelonius made to interrupt, "he won't release his army. That will buy not only Kelvhan and the others the time they need, but it will buy you time with the giants as well. This is the best way to proceed, Thelonius."

"Unfortunately, I don't believe I have an alternative but to agree at this point. There are many places where your plan can fall through. Exercise caution. I know that you have always been close to Jarrick. Understand he is no longer the same brother we have loved. Don't take unnecessary risks, and if it looks as though you are in danger, leave to regroup and wait for me."

"I understand, and I will be careful," Caelya said with a soft smile.

Jorg didn't know what he'd expected, but it certainly hadn't been such love and tenderness. He'd fought for acceptance so much during his childhood—within his own family as much as elsewhere—and their relationship stabbed at his heart.

"And Kelvhan," Thelonius addressed the guard with a hard stare, "we will discuss your dereliction of duties in keeping my sister safe."

Kelvhan bowed to the king. "Sire."

Caelya scoffed. "We need to hurry, Thelonius. Pester the poor guard another time."

The king inhaled and stared at the skies for a moment before turning to his men stationed down the trail. With only a gesture of his arm, the army unit was in formation and moved to march through camp.

Wasting no more time, Jorg followed Kelvhan and Caelya toward Ingrid—finally.

35

INGRID

Ingrid followed Jarrick out of the cave in a daze. She shuffled her feet behind him, stumbling occasionally as she snagged a toe on the uneven ground of the tunnel. Urkon was dead, defeated by Jarrick and *eaten* by Voxx. Ingrid's stomach rolled, and she had to swallow the bile that rose to her throat.

"Don't be so melancholy, Ingrid. We're much closer to our goals now." Jarrick broke the silence as they reached the end of the tunnel.

Our goals? She ignored him. Outside the tunnel, wind blew snow in lazy circles, and Ingrid shivered. "Where are we?"

"Between the mountain peaks, where the dragons have their weyr. I thought fresh air would do you good before we headed back to the castle."

It was true. The brighter light after the dark tunnel and crisp temperature helped soothe her nerves. Something Jarrick had said came back to her. "Why did you say that I'd still bind the spell with you on the morning of Thelonius' birthday? The deal I made with Urkon died with him, didn't it?"

"Since I have assumed Urkon's essence, I've gained his debts

—and his assets. Your bargain now rests with me. Only satisfying the agreement will release you, or you will suffer the consequences as before. The solution is clear—bind the spell in a way that benefits me. It'll all work out for the best now that the deal is between us." Jarrick faced her with his hands folded in front of him. "Earlier you asked to see Galwain. Is that still your desire?"

Jarrick was as calm as if what happened to Urkon was as natural as the sun rising in the sky.

"Did you plan for it to happen that way? Why did you tell me we needed to work together to defeat Urkon?"

"First, let me establish this. Once we leave this tunnel, we'll speak of this situation no more, understand?" Jarrick stared at Ingrid, waiting for her response. His always piercing eyes had a deeper glow to them. Ingrid nodded. "There is no need to concern ourselves with *might have been* or *previous* plans. Everything has worked out for the best. You and I are the only ones now who need to worry about the fate of the realms. What's done is done. How one gains power is never as important as how one wields it."

The ends justified the means. She shook her head. It was a sentiment her father had vehemently denied while Ingrid grew up. He had believed that a man's word and his honor were the only items of true power and wealth. Ingrid agreed with him.

"Do you have further questions? You are cold, and we should get you out of the elements."

Ingrid shook her head. There wasn't anything more to ask. Nothing mattered except binding the spell now. She had to protect humanity and keep Asgard in control before everyone's lives belonged to the dark elf. "I'd like to see Galwain."

"Good. That will save Jorg from having to run through all my halls to find you separately."

"What?" Ingrid grabbed Jarrick's sleeve as he turned away. "Jorg is here?"

"Dúngarr told me he saw him before he and Urkon brought you to my home. Did you think if he made it that far, he wouldn't find his way here? My son is resourceful. Though my guard might try to dissuade him from remaining in our realm, he'll find his way to you. It's that tenacity which will serve both of you well as you establish your kingdom on Vanaheim."

"You still want to make me queen? Why?"

"Because I will be busy bringing all the other realms into proper form. I must set up those I trust in key positions. Who better than my son and the savior of the human race to manage the reconstruction of the ruling realm?"

"And if that's not what we want?"

Jarrick smiled and placed his hand on Ingrid's cheek. "Then I'll find others more suitable."

INGRID DIDN'T REALIZE how nervous she was to see Galwain until she'd stood outside the queen's door. The vision Urkon had given her was of a tortured woman at the end of a chain. Yet, Caelya had visited with her and didn't mention such conditions. Jorg was alive, but she didn't know if Bremen had survived. Everything swirled within her as the door swung open.

Jarrick placed his hands between Ingrid's shoulder blades and pushed her into the room before closing the door behind her. He said nothing nor stepped foot into the room. Set up exactly as the chambers Ingrid had, Galwain stood near the tall windows with her back to the door. She wore a fine gown of purple velvet with her nut-brown hair in loose waves about her shoulders. She didn't turn around, and Ingrid didn't know what to say.

"Whatever you need, please just do it and be quick," Galwain said.

She must think I'm a servant. "I'm here to see you." Though she tried to sound confident, Ingrid's words came out in a squeaky whisper.

Galwain turned slowly around, her eyes wide. "Ingrid!"

A smile crept across the queen's face, and tears instantly sprung into Ingrid's eyes. For the first time since arriving in the new realm, she wasn't alone. They hurried toward each other and embraced.

"I'm so happy you're safe," Ingrid said, her words muffled against Galwain's shoulder.

"As I am for you." Galwain pushed Ingrid to an arm's length without letting her go. "Let me look at you. Are you truly well? He didn't hurt you?"

There was too much involved with an answer to that question, so Ingrid only smiled wider. "I'm much better now."

"Come, sit with me and tell me what's happened." A hint of apprehension flashed over the queen's face, but she maintained her smile and composure.

Even in her current circumstances, Galwain was the epitome of grace and elegance. Ingrid sat on one of the hard, wooden chairs, scooting it so they faced each other.

Galwain waited while Ingrid tried to find her voice. She didn't know where to begin or how much to say. *Better to just tell her everything.* "Jarrick brought me to Alfheim alone. The others stayed behind." Ingrid hesitated.

"I see. But you have more information, I can read it all over your face. Nothing you can say will be worse than what I've imagined these past weeks. Please help me put aside the suspicions and accept the reality."

Ingrid smiled weakly. "There was a battle before I left. Your father attacked. It was chaos, and then Jarrick showed up. At first, he seemed to fight with us. Then he called his dragons. I still had my powers then, and I killed one of them—but not the one I should have."

The queen exhaled, her eyes narrowed and her shoulders rigid. "So, you've been here a while if you know who Voxx is. She enjoys flying close to my windows at least once a day. Mocking my captivity while she flies free."

At that moment, Ingrid decided not to give all the details of the courtyard. Perhaps Bremen had survived, and Jorg could tell her so when he arrived.

"Please continue. I'm sorry to interrupt," Galwain said.

"I made the choice to go with Jarrick to save the others. At least, I hope that's what happened. We stepped through a portal and arrived on a hilltop outside of Lyallona. I have spent most of my time at the palace until recently."

Ingrid explained about meeting Caelya, Thelonius, and Vimala. Then she spoke of the ruvar army and her time in the forest. The queen listened intently, growing pale as the story continued.

"But I have good news, too. As I was coming here, to Montibeo, I saw Jorg and Selby. They're here and coming for us."

Galwain covered her mouth with her hand. "Just the two of them?"

"It was so fast. They were the only ones I saw." It wasn't a lie.

"I hope they don't come here. It's too dangerous. They should speak with Thelonius and get his help."

That was the wiser course to take, but Ingrid knew they wouldn't. No one praised Jorg or Selby for their patience. If they planned to come to Montibeo, as Jarrick believed and Ingrid couldn't deny, Galwain needed the rest of the story.

"There's one more thing." Ingrid fidgeted with her fingers in her lap. "Aguane was here. Have you met her?"

Galwain nodded. "She's special to Caelya."

"Well, she wanted me to follow her out of my room, but before we could leave, Urkon arrived. They fought, and I guess she's now in the air. She needed to heal her wounds. Jarrick came to my room, and he and Urkon took me to the dragon hive."

Galwain gasped and took hold of Ingrid's hands. Her brows pinched together as she listened.

"Jarrick challenged him. They battled, and Urkon used his magic on Jarrick. But . . . Jarrick pulled it into himself somehow. Whatever Urkon threw at Jarrick, it became part of him until he'd overpowered the master. Jarrick said something to him at the end, but then he must have called to Voxx. She showed up and . . ." Ingrid let her words trail off, not able to voice the rest. She kept her eyes focused on her lap but could hear Galwain quietly crying.

"So he has all the power for himself now?"

"Yes."

"What does he want? I've been expecting him to come and speak with me. He hasn't."

"He wants everything. To restore Vanaheim, overthrow Asgard, and rule all the realms. Stopping him is the only hope we have. I know how—even where I need to go—but not how to get there."

"Oh, Ingrid, you can't take such responsibility onto yourself. What could you do against someone as powerful as Jarrick?"

"Freya's blood runs through my body. No one else can do this but me. I have to bind the protections provided to the human realm. Jarrick will force me to change the spell to allow him to establish his rule. He says he'll protect Midgard, even though it will allow him to defeat Asgard. It isn't true, and I know it. I need to do this on my own before the king's birthday celebration."

"You say you know where it is you need to go?"

"The Yggdrasil tree. The goddess Eir taught me what I need

to do—though I need a bead she gave me. Unfortunately, I lost that in the courtyard before coming here. Even so, I have to try."

"What about calling out to Vimala? You said the two of you spoke. Don't let her beauty fool you. Unicorns are warriors and will do whatever necessary to protect their loved ones. If she protects Thelonius by aiding you, nothing will stop her."

"I have barriers in my mind that keep my thoughts private. If I drop them, any of the elves could hear me, including Jarrick."

"I see."

Both women sat in silence, still holding hands. Finally, Galwain pulled her hands free and slapped her legs before she stood. Ingrid followed, confused but ready to hear what made the queen have the wide smile on her face.

"If you call to Vimala from here, perhaps Jarrick *will* hear you. If he arrives in my room before the unicorn, then he must speak with me. I'll keep him busy while you get away."

"Are you sure? What if he won't stay to talk with you?"

Galwain narrowed her eyes with a mischievous gleam. "I can be very persuasive."

Ingrid bit her lip to keep from a chuckle. "Are you sure?"

"Yes, call to her."

Ingrid closed her eyes to concentrate and dropped her mental barriers. *Vimala, if you can hear me—I need your help. I'm at Montibeo.*

She opened her eyes and nodded to the queen. It was a short message, but all she dared. Now they had to hope it was only the unicorn that heard her.

36

JORG

Kelvhan raised his fist, calling everyone to a halt. They were at the edge of a stand of trees, and a black stone castle towered in the distance. Before they could attempt infiltration, they'd have to traverse the open field. Not only that, but the knee-high snow that covered the landscape stood in their way as well. They had woolen cloaks, but the wind pierced through any opening.

Jorg glanced at Selby. Even with lips that were tinged blue, she stared straight ahead, ready for battle. Bremen stood on her other side, tall and confident, composed just as a warrior should be. Galwain and Ingrid were too close to bother with the elements. Jorg turned to Kelvhan. "How do we cross without alerting the entire castle we're coming?"

"I'll take care of that," Caelya answered. "I've learned a thing or two about magic through the years. A glamour will hide us, but we must stay close."

Jorg remembered the glamour that had hidden the witch's cottage when he and the others traveled to find Eir. That had been effective until they knew what to look for. Hopefully, no one would expect them and wouldn't notice the slight shimmer in the air. He also hoped Caelya was as skilled as she claimed at creating the spell.

No one spoke as the princess closed her eyes and whispered words in a language Jorg didn't understand. When she finished, she nodded to Kelvhan. "It's ready."

By appearances, nothing had changed. Jorg didn't even see the telltale waver in the air as he'd found before. "Are you sure? How do we know it's working?" he asked.

"If you see arrows coming at us, run the other way," Caelya said with a grin.

"Comforting," Bremen mumbled.

As they'd planned earlier, the guards stayed hidden in the trees as the five trekked toward the castle. There were no arrows, nor were there any bells or signals that someone had spotted them. But Jorg breathed a heavy sigh when they reached the stone walls.

"You know where to meet Aguane?" Caelya asked Kelvhan.

"Yes, we will be in and out as fast as possible. I'll let you know when we leave. Stay no longer than necessary," Kelvhan said in a way that sounded more like a plea than a command. "Stay safe."

Caelya tilted her head up, and Kelvhan met her lips with a gentle, yet passionate kiss. Selby snorted from behind Jorg's shoulder. When the two parted, Caelya stared at him with a cocked brow. He immediately raised his hands in surrender and said nothing. It wasn't like he hadn't suspected their relationship already. Who was he to judge his aunt for being in love with a guard? He loved Ingrid, and she was a goddess compared to him.

The princess turned from the group and hurried along the wall toward the front of the castle. She'd pretend she'd taken a portal to the front door while they snuck in through a scullery door.

"We no longer have the glamour, so stay alert," Kelvhan commanded as they hustled around a corner.

The scullery was empty when they entered. No maids scurried about washing dishes or laundry. It was unnerving, but Jorg pushed it aside. He didn't know the elve's customs. Perhaps they didn't need as much time to prepare meals as Norse women.

He only wanted to get to the meeting place and hold Ingrid. The bead around his neck hummed so loudly he expected the others to hear it, but it wasn't noticeable to them. The heat grew against his flesh as they traversed the dark corridors. It didn't burn this time, but it spurred him to move faster.

The group huddled together at the bottom of a set of stairs. "There's a room midway down the hall past this tower. Stay here while I go to check if Aguane has moved the women yet," Kelvhan whispered. Both Jorg and Bremen protested, but he stopped them. "We have to get them out of here as fast as possible. Reunions can wait for a more secure area."

Neither of them liked what he said, but they waited with Selby as Kelvhan moved forward alone.

Seconds passed like hours as the three stared at the door Kelvhan disappeared behind. Finally, they heard muffled sounds, disturbing sounds as if there was trouble. Waiting no longer, the three raced ahead.

Kelvhan appeared, disheveled and wide-eyed. "Get out of here! They aren't here—save yourselves. Now!"

At that moment, a large body crashed against Kelvhan, and several others poured out the door. Selby screamed, and all of them scrambled backward, slipping on the polished black tiles under their feet as they tried to help each other.

It was no use. The beasts slammed into them before they could gain their footing. Snarls echoed off the walls. Gigantic creatures with dragon snouts, horns, and forked tongues seized each of them. Elven bodies that were twice as large as they should have been held them in place with arms the size of logs and covered in shimmering scales.

Those must be ruvars.

Even though all three fought nonstop, they could not free themselves. The creatures scurried hastily to a set of stairs spiraling into a dark abyss. When they reached the bottom, the beasts tossed them to the floor in the middle of a dark room, but Kelvhan was not among them.

The brutes lit sconces along the walls, exposing many deadly weapons, a large stone table, and other various items for torture. There was only a single prison cell with open bars across the front. It faced the room, allowing whoever occupied it to witness whatever horrors might unfold.

Someone approached from behind, clicking their tongue as if scolding a child. "Such a predictable rescue attempt. I had hoped you'd provide more of a challenge," Jarrick said with casual boredom lacing his words.

The creatures slunk into the darkness along the edges of the room as the dark elf approached the trio. All three rose to their feet and stood tall. "Where's Kelvhan?"

"Who? Oh, that bumbling guard my sister is in love with. He's elsewhere. Hello again, Selby." Jarrick leered at her, making Bremen place his arm protectively in front of her. "How charming, but at the moment, I only want to speak with my son. The two of you will be useful later."

Jarrick motioned to the beasts, and two of them snatched Bremen and Selby before anyone could respond. A third one held Jorg's arms behind his back as they dragged the others away down a dark tunnel.

"Where are you taking them?" Jorg snarled.

"Into other cells, where they can wait until I need them. Don't concern yourself with trivial matters. We have more important matters to discuss. Like how we will get to know each other better. Father and son, together at last."

"I have no intention of joining you."

"No—" Jarrick twisted suddenly as if listening to the air behind him.

The bead flared under Jorg's tunic, and he gasped. Faintly, in the back of his mind, he heard Ingrid's voice.

"Our conversation will have to wait." Jarrick rushed into Jorg shoving him backward until he tripped and landed on his backside within the empty cell. The bars slid closed. Jarrick touched them, and the doorway blended away so there were only bars without an exit.

Without speaking further, Jarrick strode out of the room while Jorg grabbed the bars, trying to free himself.

37

INGRID

I ngrid paced the length of Galwain's room while the queen sat patiently, staring at the fire they'd started. It had been hours since she'd called for Vimala, and yet there'd been no sign of the fylgia.

She probably can't help me. Why would she risk coming here?

"At least, Jarrick hasn't come either," Ingrid said, though mostly to herself.

"I was thinking the same thing," Galwain said.

A booming sound like thunder rattled through the wards on the windows. Cold air blew in and caused the flames in the hearth to dance and sputter. A dark shadow streaked across the outside of the openings. Galwain rose from her chair so suddenly it fell with a clatter to the floor.

The women rushed to the farthest corner of the room and ducked behind the bed. They held their breath and huddled together as the door opened.

When Jarrick sauntered in, Ingrid's heart sank. It was a ridiculous thought, but she'd hoped it was Jorg. He stared straight ahead and sighed.

"I had hoped you would accept working with me, Ingrid. Once again, I see my wife has led someone away from me."

"I've done nothing." Galwain stood and kept Ingrid behind her. When Jarrick refused to turn toward her, she marched up to him. "It's about time you came to see me. We need to talk."

Jarrick spun and stared down at her. "I'm not here to speak with you."

"When you brought me here, you appeared to want to restore our marriage. Why can't we discuss that?"

"I brought you here for two reasons. One was to keep you from returning to another man while you are still *my* wife. Two was to draw out our son. He never had the chance to know who he is, and I want to correct that. Once you are no longer of use, you will not be here."

"Send her home now. You have me, and Jorg is coming. You said so yourself." Ingrid rushed to stand by Galwain's side.

"Is that what you thought? I mean to send her home? Ingrid, you know me better than that by now. Elves mate for life. Since Galwain no longer wishes to be at my side, there is only one option for her."

"Jarrick, you can't mean that!" Ingrid cried. "I won't help you if you harm Galwain."

"You will. The bargain you struck is stronger than a marriage vow. Though the penalty for violating it is the same. Come with me, Ingrid. And Galwain, *darling*, Voxx will guard the skies. I've cleared the windows of the wards so she can hear if anyone enters. I suggest you hope no one does."

Jarrick grabbed Ingrid by the arm and dragged her toward the door. Galwain wrapped her arms around Ingrid's waist to stop him.

"Leave her alone. Let her stay with me. No one is coming, or they would have by now. We'll both do as you say, just leave

Ingrid here." Galwain pleaded and pulled, her feet slipping along the floorboards as Jarrick paid no attention.

When they'd reached the door, Jarrick turned. With one hand, he knocked Galwain to the floor before he shoved Ingrid into the hall and closed the door behind him.

Guards lined the corridor. "No one goes in or comes out!" Jarrick called as he strode away, hauling Ingrid by her arm once again.

"Where are we going?" Ingrid clawed at Jarrick's hand squeezing her arm. She even stooped to bite his fingers.

The dark elf paid no attention. He continued to drag her along as if she were casually strolling behind him instead of fighting like a shadow cat. "Since you don't want to behave, you've forced me to restrain you."

Jarrick descended the circular stairwell with Ingrid stumbling behind. Twice she fell, once cracking her knees against the stones, and another time her skull. She'd become dizzy and hadn't been able to right herself. She could only throw her arm around her head as she tumbled on her back. Her arm wrenched as it stayed firmly in Jarrick's grip.

When they reached the main floor, Jarrick turned and skirted the large open room between the arches. Instead, they went through a door at the end of a long hall and descended yet more stairs.

By the time they arrived at their destination, bruises welled on too many places for Ingrid to count. Jarrick finally dropped her hand, and she fell onto all fours, not bothering to look at her surroundings.

"Ingrid!"

She heard her name. *Jorg?* Roars from a crazed and trapped man drowned out her own inner voice. Lifting her head, tears blurred her vision. There he was, reaching for her through the bars of his cell.

Scrambling to her feet, Ingrid raced to Jorg. Despite her battered back and the cold bars between them, they held each other tight. Tears she'd held in since she'd arrived in the elven realm released like a flood, and she didn't care. All that mattered was that Jorg held her. He'd come for her, and whatever it took, they'd make it. Any other alternative fled from her thoughts.

"I need to hear you," Jorg whispered into her ear.

She knew what he meant, but she hesitated. Anything she said was public to all the elves. Jarrick was obviously behind her, but she heard other bodies shuffling around as well. Ingrid pulled back enough to gaze into Jorg's eyes. Tears stained his cheeks as he smiled at her.

I've missed you. She no longer cared who heard.

Relief flooded over Jorg. He rested his forehead against hers. Ingrid felt his bunched and strained muscles soften. At the same time, she collapsed into him, her insides turning to liquid. The tension she'd carried melted away.

Thank you, Jorg's voice said—but not out loud.

Startled, Ingrid flinched and stared into Jorg's face. He pinched his brows as they both realized what happened.

Can you hear me? she heard him say again though his lips didn't move.

Ingrid nodded.

How?

I don't know, and I don't care. Within her middle, sparks like a hundred logs popping in a fire surged through Ingrid. Her breath turned ragged, and she slumped against the bars. Knowing Jorg had survived, that he'd come for her, suddenly relaxed the tension she'd carried. Her magic released and surged through her body.

What is it? Tell me! What's happening?

"Finally! I've been wondering what it would take to force you to awaken your powers," Jarrick said from across the room. "Now we need to make sure you know what to do with them."

Ingrid placed her hand against Jorg's face, a soft smile on her face as she ignored everything else. Jorg turned his lips to her palm, and she closed her eyes. It was all she needed—*he* was all she needed. There wasn't anything more important. Let Jarrick win as long as they were together.

A whimper came from somewhere down a corridor to her right. Before she processed the sound, a large arm wrapped around her waist and ripped her away from Jorg.

Ingrid kicked and fought while Jorg screamed. He yanked at the bars that kept him away from her to no avail. Whoever held her was too large for an elf. Her feet dangled off the ground and sharp armour jabbed against her shoulder blades. A slight sulfur aroma reached her nose, and she glanced down. With a sharp inhale, she froze. Shimmering scales covered the arm around her waist.

All thought halted. It wasn't *armour* she felt. It was the body of a ruvar. At that moment, Ingrid finally noticed the room.

A stone table the size of a single bed stood in the center. It was fitted with leather straps hanging limply from each corner. On the far wall was a device like a loom, only it had shackles attached to the top and bottom of the frame. Along the same wall, another table held knives of every variety. Curved ones, straight ones, some with short blades, and some with long needle-like tips. Maces, mallets, and axes hung on the wall like gruesome decorations.

This was a room someone only entered alive once. Horrid images flashed in Ingrid's mind. She grabbed the sides of her head as the assault continued. From somewhere outside, she heard her name. It wasn't Jorg . . . it was female. Ingrid snapped her eyes open to watch two ruvars hold Selby down as Jarrick gagged her and strapped her to the center table.

When he finished, he faced Ingrid. One of the ruvars reached for a curved blade and held it against Selby's stomach.

"Now, shall we discuss our plans for binding the spell? Or do you need more motivation?"

38

INGRID

Ingrid's best friend was a welcome sight though that relief was momentary since a beast was about to spill her guts like a deer. Rather than panic, something else took root inside Ingrid. The barriers locking away her magic completely disappeared. Emerging like a bear in spring, it flowed throughout her body with a roar.

It was a heady experience. Ingrid closed her eyes for a moment to relish the familiarity. Perhaps Jarrick had been right, and she'd blocked her powers with her own fears. That didn't matter anymore. When she opened them, she focused on her friend.

Selby's eyes sparkled behind her gag. She gave a slight nod, and Ingrid knew she'd get her friend off that table before anything happened to her. There was no way she'd allow Jarrick to hurt those she loved any longer. She broke her connection with Selby and faced the dark elf. A slight grin cracked the corner of her mouth.

"It's stunning, the way your eyes become like gemstones. Remarkable. Ingrid, we will make the realms take notice. No longer will we cower to those lesser. You and I are unstoppable."

Jarrick stepped closer, ignoring Selby as he focused on Ingrid and how her magic manifested physically.

Ingrid held his gaze. Over his shoulder, she kept track of the leather straps around Selby's hands as they released and silently dropped away. The ruvar waited for his next order and didn't pay attention.

"I will not help you, Jarrick. You only want destruction. What you consider helpful denies the realms of their own choices. Everyone deserves to live in a way they choose, not under the controlling thumb of a dictator."

The last strap slipped away from Selby's foot.

"You don't understand it yet, but you will once you see Vana-heim and experience the beauty and power there. Don't make me force you." Jarrick closed the gap between them. Towering over Ingrid and within reach.

"Caging and torturing those I love isn't the way to convince me."

Jarrick narrowed his eyes though he kept his grin. "Maybe not, but it is a way to test you."

Test me? The air thickened in the underground chambers. "What do you want?"

"What is she going to do with all that freedom? Can she overpower the ruvar before he slides that blade into her belly? Can you? I admire your friend. She's a fine warrior, but she's human. Do you really think she can stand against either of us if we don't allow it?"

He'd known the whole time what Ingrid did behind his back. Ingrid shook her head at herself. No matter, she wasn't afraid anymore. Jarrick had stolen Urkon's powers, and he might do that to her as well, but she'd make him earn it and see her friends go free.

Power surged into Ingrid's palms, and she slammed them against Jarrick's chest. The dark elf flew backward into the table, startling the ruvar into lifting his blade. It was all Selby needed to roll her legs sideways and kick both feet into the creature's chest. It stumbled, and she flipped herself off the table, throwing the gag to the ground.

While Jarrick and the ruvar righted themselves, Ingrid sprinted to Jorg. "Step back," she said as she grabbed a bar in each hand. The metal warmed in her palms, glowing as if the bars had been placed in a forge. Ingrid felt the spell used to remove the door flicker then fade with a fizzing sound. Pulling on the bars, the latch popped open, and Jorg rushed out.

Rather than the embrace she'd have preferred at their reunion, Ingrid spun away. She raised her hands, letting her magic surge through her. The potency coursing through her veins created a euphoric sensation. Like a parched land finally receiving rain, she soaked in the nourishing succor.

"It's intoxicating, isn't it? The raw force that bends to your will. You are capable of so much more, things you haven't yet experienced. Join me and let me teach you." Wild and wide, Jarrick's eyes shone brightly. The power in the room sizzled into the air.

Selby and Jorg grabbed weapons and kept the ruvar busy. Ingrid needed to get them out of the castle. The room had only two exit points; the stairs she'd tumbled down earlier, and a dark corridor leading the other direction. The likelihood of that being a dead end was too great a risk. She slid her foot sideways and encouraged Jarrick to circle with her.

"You can't escape from this room," Jarrick jeered.

"We'll see, but right now I'm wondering something about your plan,"

"Yes?" Jarrick's smile widened. His excitement over her interest obvious.

"When you realized you were stronger than Urkon, it made

you want his position. Perhaps I'll do that to you," Ingrid said. She narrowed her eyes and let her magic build.

"I suppose you could try, but that's years away. You have far too much to learn to overthrow me."

Ingrid twisted her mouth as if to weigh his words, then shrugged. "Do either of us *truly* know how much power I have? Freya's blood runs in my veins. Could you beat her in a battle?"

The taunting made Jarrick's expression grow cold. His sardonic smile replaced by a thin white line as he pressed his lips tight.

War cries and roars echoed through the chamber. Her friends held their own against the large beast, but Ingrid knew how hard they were to kill. "Go for the joints and heels. It's where they're weakest," she called out.

"Thanks for the tip," Selby grunted out as she swung a club with spikes on the end.

Ingrid flicked a glance their direction in time to see Jorg spin with blurring speed and jam his blade into the ruvar's neck. The beast roared and sputtered, falling to his knees. Selby slashed his throat. The duo raced closer to where Jarrick and Ingrid stood locked in a standoff.

"Father, I'm hurt. You give Ingrid all this attention, and you barely notice me. I thought we would be close," Jorg taunted.

Ingrid rolled her lip between her teeth. The influence of his time spent with Selby gave a spark of joy, despite the madness surrounding them.

With the room silenced, Jarrick sighed and tilted his chin to the ceiling for a heartbeat. "I had high hopes for us, son. It's possible you have too much of your mother's stubbornness, which is unfortunate."

A faint scream came from the corridor. Ingrid saw Jorg glance that direction and knew he'd heard it, too. Would more ruvars come for them? It had only sounded like one voice.

Ingrid toyed with dropping her mental barriers, but Jarrick would hear whatever she'd say to Jorg, anyway. No use in keeping only Selby in the dark.

"Who is that?" She directed the question to Jarrick, but Jorg seemed to have the answer as well.

"Ah, the other human. Let's not forget about his safety. I think that may make poor Selby distraught," Jarrick sneered.

Ingrid met Selby's gaze. "Bremen?"

Selby nodded as she narrowed her eyes at Jarrick—fierce determination oozing from her disposition. It meant they couldn't escape just yet. Ingrid would need to release the wards from his bars as she'd done with Jorg's.

Only Ingrid could free him. She flashed a grin at Jorg and bolted from the room.

39

JORG

Every fiber of Jorg's body wanted to follow Ingrid down that dark hallway. But she'd been glorious as she'd unlocked the bars of his cage. Her turquoise eyes glowed, and her skin radiated. Even her wildflower scent overpowered the stuffy odor of the chamber. The bead hummed constantly now, purring against his chest like a content kitten. She could free Bremen on her own.

Keeping Jarrick busy was his job. Selby was a great warrior, but the journey had shown them her vulnerabilities well enough. He needed to keep his *father's* focus directed at himself. Knowing he shared the same blood as the monster in front of him churned in his gut.

"Tell me, does it ever bother you? Do you have any remorse for the pain you cause others?"

"I do. It pains me that so many refuse to listen to the message I present. They'd rather wallow in their diseased beliefs than change their ways. I'm not without compassion, son. If I were, you would not be standing here. I wouldn't care so well for your mother and keep her tucked safely away in a comfortable room."

"Do you still hear her? The space and the silence clawed at my mind, nearly driving me crazy when Ingrid left. The relief from that pain is as sweet as honey. Don't you agree?"

If Jorg could get his father to reveal where Galwain was, they could still get her out of the castle with them. Selby fidgeted by his side. She wouldn't stand for the inaction much longer. They needed to get the information so they could run as soon as Ingrid returned with Bremen.

"The intensity of a pain like that is unequaled. And solitary. Your mother never realized the effect because of her humanity. Never again will she hold any control over me. The reminder of her betrayal serves me well."

"You keep yourself in pain, even though you stole her to be with you? That's just foolish," Selby said.

Jarrick flicked his hand toward her, and she slammed against the far wall. Rather than slide down when her body went slack, she stuck there as her head hung limp. As if suspended, her contorted shape adorned the wall like a painting.

"What have you done?" Jorg's jaw clenched. His chest rumbled from his animal-like growl. Everyone he cared about suffered because of this vile menace.

"We have more important details to discuss than a nonessential human, son." Jarrick sauntered across the room. "If Ingrid chooses the wise path, I'll make her queen of Vanaheim once I settle everything. You can become her king or become as unnecessary as your mother. The choice is yours, but I hope you join us."

"Is my mother alive?"

"Does that matter?"

"If you want to make a deal with me, then I need something in return. Assure me she is alive, release her, and I'll consider your offer."

Jarrick laughed. "So, the question becomes, 'what's in it for you?' That's the closest you've acted like my son, yet, I can't nego-tiate regarding Galwain." The dark elf grimaced as if saying her name tasted foul in his mouth.

Jorg still held the sword he'd grabbed off the wall earlier. He was faster, lighter on his feet, and stronger since he'd arrived in the elven realm. Was he fast enough to reach Jarrick before he flicked his wrist as he'd done with Selby?

A smirk played on Jarrick's lips. He stood calm, his hands folded in front of himself, waiting.

"You're right about something, you know. It is a shame I didn't grow up here, understanding the strength this realm gives me," Jorg said. He let his shoulders relax though he stayed on the balls of his feet. "Instead, I grew up scorned. Taunted and teased because I was different. Facing bully after bully who thought he could beat up the pointy-eared demon. The thing is, it forced me to hone my skills at fighting."

"You think you can beat me? I have more power than anyone. When that spell falls and I gain the last of Urkon's magic, not even Odin will resist me. Don't challenge me, son."

"I don't think I will." Jorg dropped the sword to his side in what appeared to be surrender. The bead under his tunic pulsed with energy he'd never felt. "One of the best lessons I learned from all those battles growing up—when someone is stronger than you, step aside and fight another day."

Jarrick tilted his head. The suspicion over Jorg's intentions clear on his face. The dark elf had been so focused on his son he hadn't noticed Ingrid and Bremen arrive. They waited at the edge of the corridor, their backs pressed against the wall out of view of Jarrick.

"Did you think I meant you?" Jorg smiled and flicked his eyebrows. Though he dared not glance in her direction—or drop the mental protections Thelonius had shown him to speak to Ingrid—he knew she understood.

As fast as lightning, she jumped into the room and slammed into Jarrick with her power. He stumbled backward, tripping over the body of the dead ruvar.

Jorg and Bremen charged to Selby. They tried to pull her down, but something kept her tight against the stone. Jorg glanced over his shoulder to see Ingrid advancing on Jarrick. His body jerked as if he'd had been hit by the goblin-breaker club.

The air in the chamber was still and stuffy, yet Ingrid's hair swirled as if she stood in the wind. Her skin glowed, and his face tingled from the power radiating from her. Whatever she did, it caused the spell against Selby to fall, and she slumped into Bremen's waiting arms. As soon as she was secure, Jorg called to Ingrid.

We need to go now, Hjarta. Come with me. She didn't respond, and he worried she couldn't hear him. *Ingrid, it's time to go.*

Slowly, she twisted her neck and met his gaze. Her eyes were so bright he had to squint, but he held steady. Stretching out his hand to her, he nodded.

With a gasp, her eyes dimmed, and she hurried to slip her hand into his. Together, they ran for the stairs with Bremen carrying Selby in ahead of them.

40

INGRID

Ingrid squeezed Jorg's hand. Solid and secure, she hurried up the stairs after him. Her mind a swirl of images.

The bars on Bremen's cell had been easy to break. There wasn't even a ward on them, but he'd been so far down the hallway it had taken them too long to return. Whatever Jarrick did to Selby sickened Ingrid, and it was all she could do to keep Bremen from charging into the room when he'd seen her.

Instead, they waited out of view and listened. She'd been so impressed by Jorg. Instead of fighting his father with strength, he'd used cunning and prowess. Then, he'd stepped aside for her. He believed in her, and it had strengthened her.

When the first surge of magic released from her hands, it had made her dizzy. As it slammed into Jarrick, she worried that she'd fall right after him. Instead, she'd settled into it, letting it flow through her like the blood in her veins. It became euphoric the longer she attacked.

It had been a struggle to stop. Only with the help of Jorg's voice was she able to reel back her power. What would have happened if he hadn't stopped her? She shuddered and returned her focus to the climb. After all the time her magic had been locked away, she wouldn't question its return. There would be time to figure it all out later, after she'd saved everyone.

At the top of the stairs, Selby groaned against Bremen's shoulder. They ducked around a corner and hid in the shadows.

"Let me closer," Ingrid whispered. Jorg twisted to let her by but didn't release his hold. Despite the worry she held for her friend, she smiled. She didn't want to let go either.

Laying her free hand on Selby's arm, Ingrid closed her eyes. The healing energies swirled in her middle, and for a heartbeat, she let them soothe her own soul. She pushed a thread through her fingers into her friend, watching as it traveled through her body. Bruises healed on her kidneys, and her lungs inflated to full strength, but something was still wrong.

Pinching her brows together, Ingrid kept her eyes closed as she searched for what kept Selby in pain. When she reached her spine, she saw it. A crack ran through one bone and fluid leaked around it. Sounds from the castle distracted Ingrid for a moment, but she heard Jorg's soothing voice.

Don't worry. Help Selby. Everything is fine.

Hearing his voice in her mind gave her a rush of adrenaline. She focused on Selby once more. Releasing a thin, steady stream, Ingrid watched the golden thread shimmer and spark as it mended the wound and sealed the cracked bone.

Selby gasped and sprang into a sitting position. Ingrid sat back and leaned into Jorg. He snuggled her close to him. Short-lived as it was, in that moment, life was perfect.

The clang of metal on metal and the shrieks of battle cries grew louder. Whoever fought was headed in their direction. Before they rose from the floor, Selby snatched Ingrid from Jorg in a crushing hug. Tears sprung to her eyes as she embraced her friend.

"Let's get out of here. I have so much to tell you," Selby said.

"I can't wait to hear every word," Ingrid replied and had never meant it more.

"Ingrid, do you know where my mother is?" Bremen asked.

The stairs leading up the tower to the upper floor were halfway down the hall. Ingrid pointed, and they all scrambled to their feet. "This way."

Two steps up the tower, Ingrid stumbled as a gentle voice sang into her mind. *Ingrid, I'm here for you. Come now, and I'll get you through the passage to the Yggdrasil tree, but you must hurry. Meet me outside.*

Vimala! She'd arrived to help Ingrid. The fighting grew louder as the group continued to lead the way up the stairs. At the top of the stairs, they found Kelvhan's guards fighting Jarrick's.

"Her door is there," Ingrid pointed to a spot in the middle of the melee, then tugged Jorg to the side. Bremen and Selby charged forward.

"I have to go," Ingrid said as she lay her hand next to Jorg's cheek, gazing into his eyes. The sounds of battle faded as she soaked in the moment. "I can bind the spell and stop Jarrick."

"You will, and then you'll come back," Jorg said. He slipped the bead out of his tunic and over his head.

Ingrid gasped. "My bead! How did you find it?"

"It was in the courtyard, buried in the ash. Eir used it to form a connection between us. It's how I knew where to find you." He lifted Ingrid's hair, so the bead rested around her neck. "You are so strong, and I felt it. I hate that you have to go, but whatever happens, know that I love you."

"I love you, too." Ingrid wanted to assure him that she'd be back, and they'd have more time together, but she couldn't form the words. It wasn't a promise she could make. Whatever the spell needed, she had to give. All the realms would crumble into chaos if she didn't.

Allowing themselves another moment, they kissed softly. Every ounce of their emotions—enough to last a lifetime— flowed between them. A tear slid down each side of Ingrid's face as she broke away.

There wasn't anything left to say, and they both knew it. Jorg nodded, trying to smile but failing.

Ingrid spun and ran for the stairs. If she stayed with Jorg any longer, she might not leave. The magic, which was so distant before, flared at the ready. She couldn't let anything or anyone stop her from putting an end to Jarrick's plans.

The bead bounced against her chest, knocking against the rune pouch already there. She had everything she needed.

Vimala, I'm coming.

41

JORG

When Ingrid disappeared down the tower steps, Jorg turned his focus to the fight taking place in the hallway. Bremen and Selby had already joined the fray. They held their own, but the two were no match for the elven warriors.

Jorg let himself feel the power within that had presented itself as soon as he'd entered Alfheim. His elven blood tingled with energy. Charging forward, he added his battle cry with the others.

Still holding the sickle blade he'd snatched from the torture chamber, Jorg pulled his dagger for his other hand. These men weren't ruvars but Jarrick's standard guard, like those who had ambushed him in the barracks. Even though these were not the same elves, Jorg found the situation redemptive.

A flash of red caught his attention. Jorg glanced to his left to see Bakkan, the king's guard who had helped him recover. He'd gone with Plintze to the border. The dwarf wasn't in the hallway, and Jorg could only hope he was fighting somewhere else. The alternative was not an option.

"Bremen, she's behind that door," Jorg called to his brother and gestured to the door only steps away from where he stood. The other king's guard surged forward at the information and helped to clear the way.

Selby was the first to reach the handle, and she darted into the room. Bremen followed with Jorg at his heels. Huddled in a corner, Galwain crouched with her arms over her head. Shrieks rattled the walls from the large obsidian dragon hovering outside the windows.

Jorg's grip tightened on the weapons at his side. It was the dragon from the courtyard, but it wasn't the time for revenge.

They needed to get Galwain out of the castle.

"Mother!" Bremen yelled and dodged for the queen.

She either didn't hear him over the dragon, or she was too frightened to move. Jorg and Selby moved to stand guard over the two as Bremen knelt beside Galwain.

Jorg heard a gasp and peeked over his shoulder. Galwain clutched Bremen in a tight hug. Relieved she seemed uninjured, Jorg returned his focus to the threat outside. Without warning, the dragon flew toward the windows, and its gigantic head crashed through the stone arches.

Thankfully, it did not spew its deadly fire. Jorg and Selby twisted away from the burst of stones spraying into the room.

"We have to leave," Jorg said urgently. Galwain had tears streaming down her cheeks as she nodded to him with a smile.

Bremen pulled their mother to her feet and held her next to him as Jorg grabbed hold of Selby's wrist. She was fierce enough to handle herself, but he needed to know she was safe.

When the dragon pulled back from the rubble, they ran for the door. They'd just made it through when the hallway shook from another impact by the dragon.

There were only a handful of warriors battling down the hall. Bakkan and four other guards joined Jorg and those helping to get the queen to safety.

"Did Plintze make it back with you?" Jorg asked Bakkan as they ran.

Selby skidded to a stop, dragging Jorg with her. She slammed her hand into the large elf's chest. "Did he? Why isn't he here?"

Bakkan stopped running, stunned, then shook his head. "He made it. He's with Eir and the king. We should keep going." He directed them toward the stairs with a hint of a smile directed at Selby's fervor.

"He'd better be all right," Selby mumbled as they continued forward.

Jorg hurried down the steps after Bremen. He and Galwain hadn't stopped when the others did, so they were out of sight though they could hear Bremen's boots as they thudded against the stone.

"This way." Bakkan gestured to a wall of arches when they'd all reached the bottom of the tower.

Following his red hair into the large darkened area, their pace slowed. Ten steps later, sconces flared to life around the space. Firelight bathed the grand room in an orange glow and revealed a dais along the front wall. High above the floor, sitting in a lavishly carved throne, was Jarrick.

The group halted. The warriors formed a semicircle with Galwain at their backs. Weapons at the ready, they faced the dark elf.

"Hello again," Jarrick said. His voice carried through the room and echoed off the smooth black tiles glittering with flame. "Bakkan, can I assume you are not escorting my prisoners back? Has my brother chosen an ill-advised attempt to involve himself in my affairs?"

Bakkan bowed at the shoulders without releasing his stare. "He is outside, Your Highness. If you'll allow me, I'll finish my duties here and ask him to join you."

Jorg let his eyes flutter in a slow, exasperated blink at the chivalrous behavior. Jarrick didn't deserve such respect. His grip tightened on the carved handle of the dagger, and the ivy design sank into his palm.

"That won't be necessary. No one is leaving," Jarrick said as he rose to his feet. With slow, measured steps he descended the dais and sauntered toward them. His posture was tall and strong as always, but there was a hint of something else.

Agitation and wariness etched his face. Jorg watched as he scanned the group in a heartbeat and clamped his mouth tight.

"Where is she?" Jarrick directed the question to Jorg.

"Gone." Jorg saw no reason to give any details. He knew his father meant Ingrid, and Jarrick knew why she'd have left.

With a deep inhale, Jarrick closed his eyes with what appeared to be an attempt to calm himself. When he returned his stare to the group, his eyes glinted as black as the stone encasing the room.

"She knew the consequences. I wouldn't have guessed her to show such disregard."

Jarrick stretched his fingers, and the crackle of magic sizzled into the air.

42

INGRID

Ingrid rushed out the main doors to the castle and stumbled as she jerked to a stop. Chaos had erupted. Guards in Thelonius's colors fought against massive ruvars. Growls and snarls, from both elf and beast, tore through the air. As she stood frozen, absorbing the scene, part of her relished the awe. It was a battle unlike any she'd witnessed.

In her world, there was a uniqueness in Jorg's speed and grace, but in this realm, bodies blurred into a mass of living tissue—one being, breathing and killing. It was music and poetry come alive in a fabulously terrifying way.

When she remembered to breathe, the other reality in front of her settled. Despite the speed and skill of the elven warriors, the ruvars had the upper hand. They would win. Their size and mindless vengeance powered forward without mercy.

Could she help? She'd accidentally slammed a dragon out of the skies once. Would she be able to send the ruvars into the trees of the forest that surrounded the castle?

Before she could decide, another sight tore all thought from her mind. A single combatant withdrew from the others and loped in her direction. Plintze! She hadn't known he'd come with the others. Something inside her cracked.

The sight of the dwarf who'd once saved her from a dragon, rushing forward to save her again made tears flow down her cheeks. She did nothing to stop them as she hurried down the steps to meet him.

As they neared each other, Ingrid stretched out her hand, intending to wrap it around Plintze, but instead he grabbed it. He twisted mid-stride and rushed them away from the battle. They headed for the trees, and the dwarf surprised her once more with his agility as she fought to keep her feet under her.

Standing between two overlapping pine branches, Ingrid saw Vimala. Her glowing white body a beacon against the darkness of the forest. She tapped the ground with her front hoof and shook her mane. The silver horn sparking an echo of light as it moved.

"Hurry, that dragon is here," Plintze said, his chest heaving from exertion.

"Thank you." The words came out in a squeak as Ingrid's throat clogged with emotion.

Plintze squeezed her hand between both of his, eyes glistening with emotions. Then he released her and disappeared back to the fighting.

Come, Ingrid, we must go!

Snapped back to the present, she hurried to the unicorn. As a shriek boomed through the skies like thunder. Ingrid pumped her legs harder and threw her arms over her head, for all the good that would do. Voxx's shadow blanketed the sky overhead.

Drop to the ground, Ingrid! Vimala's words rang into Ingrid's mind.

She didn't hesitate and let herself drop into the snow. The dragon's claws ruffled the back of her tunic, barely missing her.

When the shadow passed, Ingrid jumped to her feet and sprinted once more for Vimala.

She peeked into the skies and watched as Voxx curled around like a snake, ready for another strike. The dragon had eyes only for Ingrid. She was not out to stop the battle, but to destroy Ingrid.

Within five strides of Vimala, sulfur and blistering heat crackled into the air. Ingrid screamed as she slipped on the icy surface, stumbling and costing precious time.

I won't make it!

Vimala left the cover of the trees to meet Ingrid just as a gale of wind whipped the snow into a fury. The unicorn arrived an instant before the visibility became impossible. Grabbing mane, Ingrid hoisted herself atop Vimala, and they bolted at breakneck speed into the forest.

Twisting to see over her shoulder, Ingrid saw Aguane hovering in the air, eyes a blinding silver. Voxx's fire beat against a thick wall of ice held in place by the sylph. A sigh of relief escaped her chest, both because she'd made it into the cover of the dark forest and because Aguane appeared to be whole again.

The feeling immediately turned cold when she realized she should have known Urkon couldn't destroy the sylph. She'd made a poor decision. That was something she could no longer afford to do.

Gliding over the forest floor, trees blurred by like a crowd of shadowed onlookers lined up to bid her farewell. Her battle wouldn't be for gold or gems; it would be for realms and redemption.

Will you take me through the Grimnir? The thought occurred to her that, even though she trusted the unicorn implicitly, she didn't know where they headed.

No, dear one. I must leave you at the entrance. You must face the passage alone to prove yourself strong enough to cross the realms.

What? The book had told her no such thing. How would she prove herself? What did that even mean? Before she could voice her questions and concerns, Vimala slowed to walk, then stopped.

Ingrid felt her eyes grow wide. The page she'd seen in the book came alive in front of her. An arch of black branches, crusted and old with ragged thorns and twisted limbs, loomed. Only the opening was clearly visible, and beyond the first few feet, a mist shrouded the pathway. It was eerie and dense and cloaked in secrets.

Ingrid wasn't ready. Entering such a place alone and unarmed, made her resolve drain down her body and leak out the bottom of her feet. One roughly carved dagger still clung under her tunic at the base of her neck, but it would be no better than a child's toy pitted against the monstrous task before her.

You are stronger than you understand. Within yourself is all the power you need to face any fear. Stay focused on what you must accomplish. It will guide you to your destination.

With shaking limbs, Ingrid slid from Vimala's back. Her veins felt like they'd turned to tunnels of ants racing under her skin as every part of her shuddered. Rooted to the ground, she stared.

Vimala must have moved, but Ingrid hadn't noticed. A soft muzzle nudged her in the back, and hot breath like a kiss of confidence tickled her neck. Before she realized it, she'd stepped closer. With a start, she realized she hadn't thanked the unicorn or said goodbye. Twisting around, she glimpsed a sparkling white feathered tail as it disappeared into the darkness of the forest.

Alone, Ingrid turned back to the archway. Dim light emanated a slight glow in the mist from some far-off place just enough to see the path. She set her shoulders, swallowed hard, and strode forward.

43

INGRID

The forest had been damp and cold. The kind that could seep into bones and no fire could thaw. As soon as Ingrid stepped under the arched branches, the misty swirls encircled her. She shivered so deep in her core she thought she'd turned to ice. Two steps onto the path, she peeked behind her and only saw a wall of white. In front of her, the mist parted to view the next few steps as she moved forward, but no farther.

Gingerly, she crept, one step after another. The surrounding branches rustled. Not from wind, but as if giant raven's wings had created the path rather than twigs and thorns. Then, somewhere in the distance, Ingrid heard a voice. Small and tentative, it called to her. She drew in a breath and held it, listening, waiting, but there was nothing.

Two more shaky steps, another held breath. Had she imagined the sound? Chiding herself, she clenched and unclenched her fists. There wasn't any time to waste. Her friends, the king, everyone battled while she dawdled. The Yggdrasil tree and the fate of the realms were at the end of this path.

Then she heard it again. This time, she recognized the voice.

Even though she knew it couldn't be real, her heart skipped a beat. Her mother's voice seeped through her resolve, and she gasped. Her name echoed around her, razor sharp, and it sliced her heart.

A figure stepped out onto the path ahead of her. Ingrid peered through the mist. Golden hair flowed in a breeze that didn't exist as her mother smiled at her. The air was still, stagnate, and it confused her as she looked on—but none of that mattered. Her lungs turned to mud and her feet to stone. She wanted to run, to fold herself into her mother's arms. Willing herself to move, she closed the gap, inch by inch.

The woman smiled such a warm, inviting smile with the same turquoise eyes as her own. Perhaps it *was* her mother? She was also a descendant of Freya. Had she come to help? Ingrid reached out, her fingers splayed open. Her mother's smile suddenly grew cruel, and her eyes darkened to black pits. A vetter cackled in her place.

A scream stuck in Ingrid's throat and choked her as she jerked her hand back to her chest. Stumbling backward, Ingrid tripped over a raised tree root. The branches closed in to trap her as the vetter edged closer. The witch's mouth open in a twisted, wicked grin, showing pointed teeth as if they'd been sharpened with a file.

Twigs slapped at Ingrid's arms. Her tunic tore where thorns sliced at her skin. She fought to free herself and run, but she tangled within the vines. Stuck in a vice-like grip, Ingrid's feet rose into the air, and warm breath scraped against her neck. Sulfur mixed with body odor shrouded her senses. Not a branch, but a muscled arm covered in scales locked her in place.

Ingrid froze like a deer in the woods waiting for the arrow. She forced herself to concentrate. Beyond the mist, through the passage, she had a purpose.

Face my fears. This isn't real.

How could she do that? Ingrid's chest heaved as she stared ahead into the unknown. Fear gripped her by the throat. Had she truly ever helped anyone?

Like specters rising from the grave to reach out for her, images assaulted her mind—her unconscious brother on the moors, Jorg's side impaled by a spike, Lazuli's severed wings fluttering to the ground, Selby hanging limply on a dungeon wall.

She'd caused pain to so many. When would it stop? Every time she charged forward to prove herself, someone she loved paid the price. When she'd chosen to come with Jarrick, she'd left those in the courtyard to burn in dragon's fire. Was that what she'd done again? Would the ruvars kill the king and allow Jarrick to rise in his place? Did her friends travel through the realms only to die after all?

No! Imagined fears were worse than real fears. Creating scenarios in which she failed only paralyzed her from moving forward. There wasn't any way to know for sure what would happen. The risks to herself, her loved ones, and the realms were real, but doing nothing only insured success for her enemy.

Ingrid slid her foot forward. The arm locked around her fell away. She couldn't control the actions of others. Another heavy step. Pain was part of life. Her shoulders lightened, and she moved ahead another stride. One foot, then the other, she kept moving forward.

Hope swelled inside her like a beacon. It wasn't skill or cunning or chance that would keep her safe. She was the healer born of Freya. It was the confidence to believe in the truth of her task that would bring her success whether or not she could envision the outcome.

Ingrid inhaled. Acceptance bolstered her resolve, and she strode forward. No longer hesitant, her destiny lay at the end of the passage. Whatever happened next, she'd face it and know she'd given everything she could.

The tunnel illuminated, the mist giving way to a shock of blinding light. Ingrid shielded her eyes but didn't stop. The outline of something shone ahead. What was it?

The end of the tunnel!

She sprinted and fell to her knees in delight when the path spilled her out into an expanse of green grass.

Water bubbled as it flowed over rocks into a deep pool on her left. A stag, majestic and proud, watched from her right. But ahead, reaching higher than she could see, and larger around than a hundred arm spans, was the Yggdrasil tree. She'd made it.

Ingrid rose to her feet. Peace embraced her and soothed her heart like chamomile and honey. With a smile, soft and sure, she glided forward and placed her hand on the smooth bark. Vitality pulsed under her palm. With her other hand, she lifted the runes and the bead over her head. She slid to her knees, sitting on her heels.

Spilling the smooth gray stones onto the ground, the etched lines facing up, she read them out loud. "Othala and Thurisaz. Home and protection." They represented everything that mattered.

The bead hummed and grew brighter. The amber light swelled until it encompassed Ingrid within its glow. She reached out and pressed it against the tree, covering one hand over the other. With her eyes closed, she watched the golden thread of her magic sway as if in a dance.

Returning to its life-giving sap from within the tree, the amber mixed with the gold, boundaries forgotten as each swirled together. Then other threads appeared; brighter and stronger. The loose ends of the spell created by Freya and Odin.

Her power swelled. Ingrid embraced the ebb and flow as the threads blended with the power of the Yggdrasil. The spell held the power of protection, and the tree held the power of life. Ingrid floated in the space between.

She took hold of one frayed cord, gently wrapping her fingers around the magic. Then she reached for the other. A jolt shocked her body, painful yet gratifying. As she held the golden ribbons, they pulsed like a heartbeat. When she brought the two close, power surged through her.

Light flashed, her body melted. She gasped but did not let go. The threads of the spell stretched and extended into Ingrid's chest, twisting over her magic and weaving together in an unbreakable cord that was no longer distinguishable separately.

Like bringing an anchor up from the bottom of the river, Ingrid's thread rolled out from her body and restored the circle between the others. Lightning crackled, sizzling through Ingrid, then cooled. When the bond completed, she let go and floated in the amber sea—at peace. Her destiny complete.

The realms would survive. As if to offer proof, a vision opened before her. Children laughed and played along the shores of a river. Hammers thrummed with steady beats as buildings grew. Two men helped hoist a beam high into the air and set it in place, forming a section of the roof on a new longhouse.

It was Klaus and Hagen, Ingrid's father and brother, smiling and slapping each other on the back as they built their new lives. A new village would grow and thrive. They would continue their lives in freedom.

When the vision ended, Ingrid rested.

44

JORG

Jorg stared at Jarrick, watching the magic rise from his fingers and roll between them like an eel swimming in the shallows. He looked to his right, then to his left. There were eight of them, but he knew they were no match for Jarrick and his magic.

"You're bothered that Ingrid didn't stay? She's defied you, I understand that, but it's more. You thought she wanted the same things as you." He'd said he wanted a relationship with Jorg, to build that father-son bond. Perhaps, in his twisted way, he'd tried to replace that sentiment with Ingrid. "Father . . . I can call you that right?" Jorg asked.

"At one point, nothing would have made me happier," Jarrick said with a sigh.

"I'm willing to try if you are." Jorg shifted on his feet and peeked over his shoulder at Galwain. Was it worth it to let *her* know what kind of family had raised him? Besides, was it that bad? It wasn't, not really. Right then, however, it was about saving lives and nothing more.

"A father and son relationship is special," Jarrick said, stepping closer to the group. The elves on either side of Jorg raised their weapons and prepared to attack.

Jorg hurried forward and met Jarrick face to face. He wanted to diffuse the situation before things went too far if that was possible. "I had a good family. They loved me, mostly." Jorg flicked his eyebrows and shrugged. "I had to hide who I was, which I didn't understand when I was small. When you're different from everyone else, you learn pretty quickly that other kids can be cruel—adults can be worse."

"You should have grown up here."

"Perhaps," Jorg rubbed his hand over his jaw. "There's still so much I don't know, and I'm here now." It was only partly an act. Since he'd arrived in Alfheim, he'd recognized changes within himself. He breathed easier, felt lighter, and more agile. And . . . accepted. Did he dare open himself up that much to the dark elf?

Jorg heard the warriors behind him shuffle their feet. They grew restless. How long could he keep Jarrick talking?

"If only . . . Dangerous words. I can't tell you how many times I said them when I contemplated how I could have kept your mother from betraying me. They lead down a sad path." Jarrick leaned in as if he would share a secret. "A weak path."

"You think me weak?"

Jarrick slipped a sly grin across his face. "No. I see the strength in you. Whatever may have happened to you as a child, it didn't break you."

"You're right. It strengthened me. If I stay here now, among our people, and you train me, just think about what we could do. You said you wanted to rebuild Vanaheim. It's not too late, Father. Let me help you." There was churning in Jorg's gut.

The words were too easy to say, and he realized they might not be a ploy. A father who wanted him, who he could learn from, sparked a fire within him. Memories of watching Ingrid's father and brother and wishing he had the same relationship came boiling to the surface.

"Oh, that we could stand together and make the realms what they need to be—what they should have always been." Jarrick's eyes sizzled with the same thrill that burned within Jorg. The others faded away, and they stood eye to eye, forging a path to replace what each had lost.

"My father never had time for me. I was the second son after all. Thelonius was busy with his lessons, Father was busy running the realm, and they left me to wander. It wasn't a bad life—do whatever you want, lay in the fields, gaze at the stars, swim in the heated springs, and explore the realms. I did all that and more, yet I was restless. Until I visited Vanaheim.

"Such a beautiful place that had been left to rot. I tried to convince Father and Thelonious that we needed to do something about it. I went to Frey and tried to persuade him to stand up and lead his people once more, but he'd have nothing to do with me. It's a sad day when a man won't step up for what's right."

Jarrick's held Jorg's gaze and leaned forward. "Together, we can do what those others wouldn't. We will restore the glory and beauty of Vanaheim. We'll bring back the full extent of our culture and our heritage."

Jorg's mouth was dry. He had to force himself to breathe. The chance to build something great, to feel not only accomplishment but acceptance—it was everything he'd ever wanted. He nodded. It felt right and *wrong* at the same time. What was he doing? Taking hold of what was his, that's what.

The possibilities flashed through him. They'd need to assess the damage, make a plan, and find materials. Did Vanaheim have enough resources, or would they need to bring in supplies? Questions flew through Jorg's mind. The most important one of all he voiced out loud. "When can we get started?"

Jarrick's face split wide with a smile. He reached out with both hands and squeezed Jorg's shoulders.

From behind him, Jorg heard his name. Someone had gasped and called to him in an anguished voice laced in fear. He ignored them as he soaked in his father's pride. A new purpose took shape inside his chest. He shifted his weight onto the balls of his feet, barely able to stand still. With his hand clasped onto his father's forearm, the future seemed bright, and he wanted it.

Then, a wave of nausea rolled through him. Jorg stumbled backward and clutched his head. He peered through eyes, slitted against the pain and realized he wasn't the only one struggling.

Jarrick had a grimace on his face and braced himself against his thighs to keep from falling. The entire room seemed to shift. The flames in the sconces sputtered along the wall.

Just as quickly as the shift occurred, calm returned.

Breathless, Jorg swallowed hard and scanned the room. When his eyes returned to his father, he found rage covering his features.

Jarrick tipped his chin to the ceiling and roared so loud, Jorg felt it vibrate through the tiles and into his body.

Whatever had just happened, changed everything.

45

JORG

Jorg had witnessed hatred in the eyes of an attacker before. The intensity blazing in his father's stare was a new level.

He let out a long exhale. Whatever small bond they'd experienced, whatever hope it had kindled, died. Jorg's heart pinched.

What did you expect? But that means . . .

Ingrid made it—she'd bound the spell. Jorg's desire to have her safely back at his side flared and overpowered all other emotion. Despite everything, he smiled.

"You will pay for this," Jarrick sneered. The air rumbled with his rage. Gone was the eager father, ready to build a future. Magic sparked into an aura like lightening around Jarrick.

Jorg spun and raced for Galwain. He tackled her to the ground, and they rolled as they landed. Pain lanced the back of his shoulder, and he grimaced. The ground vibrated, from Jarrick, but also from thundering footsteps spilling into the room.

Ruvars flooded through the arches and blocked the exits.

"Jorg." Galwain pushed against his chest. "You need to help

the others. I can fight for myself." She touched his cheek, and a brief smile crossed her lips.

There wasn't anywhere for her to hide, and she was right. He needed to join the battle. He jumped to his feet and pulled her with him. Before he could ask, his mother produced two small daggers. He raised his brows and nodded with a grin.

All the women in his life were strong. He wouldn't hinder her. Jorg turned his attention to the others.

Two guards lay motionless in the room's center. Bremen and Selby fought back to back near the far wall, closest to freedom. Bakkan and the two remaining guards attacked from the near side. Galwain rushed toward Selby in time to cut down a ruvar charging at her.

An enraged Dúngarr stormed through the arches and immediately engaged with Bremen. Before Jorg could decide which threat to tackle first, Selby shrieked and dodged at Dúngarr. The two clashed, and with a speed and accuracy Jorg hadn't seen from her before, she sliced her short-sword across his calf. Twisting as the guard exposed his chest, she drove her blade through his middle.

There was only one other threat unaccounted for, and Jorg spun to face it—his father. Sliding the curved blade, he'd gathered before from his belt, he also pulled the ivory-handled knife from his boot. He had no defense against Jarrick's magic.

"I didn't lie," he called, bringing Jarrick's attention solely on himself. "We would have made a good team."

Jarrick chuffed. "I believe we would have. You can still surrender and join me."

Squaring his shoulders, Jorg sauntered three paces and stopped. "You know I can't do that. You've got more power than I do, I concede. How about we make it fair and see how matched we are without the magic?"

With a flourish of his fingers, Jarrick's aura faded, and

swords appeared in each of his hands. He cocked a brow and waited.

Jorg twirled the curved blade as he felt the weight, though it was more to buy time to settle his mind. The other sounds faded around him except for the occasional female grunt or shriek he couldn't block out. He trusted both women, but it didn't stop his concern.

Jarrick stood still, watching as Jorg closed the gap between them. Neither dropped their focus—Jorg's blade up and ready, Jarrick's held relaxed at his side.

From the corner of his eye, Jorg leaned back in time to avoid a ruvar that charged him from the side. He sliced the beast's neck and plunged the dagger through its eye.

Another one tried to attack, but Jarrick slit its throat and dropped it out of the way. Apparently, Jarrick wanted the privilege of killing his son for himself.

Jorg swung his sword in a wide arc that Jarrick blocked. They stayed locked together, gauging each other's strength. To Jorg's surprise and delight, his force was equal to his father's, maybe even more.

Finally breaking apart, Jorg swung again. To the left. Across to the right. Straight down the middle.

Each time, Jarrick blocked or spun away. Then he came slashing, chopping, and thrusting. Jorg spun to jab Jarrick's kidney, but his father matched the move and knocked the dagger from Jorg's hand. The ivory clattered along the smooth tiles and rested at the base of the dais.

Using two hands, Jorg came at Jarrick. He feigned right and swung left, knocking one of Jarrick's swords through the air. Jorg dropped low and swept Jarrick's leg, causing him to fall.

The dark elf sprang back to his feet, determination set over his features. He didn't expect such a worthy opponent, and Jorg wondered when he'd last faced one.

Before Jarrick could reset, Jorg swung again. The blow came too close to Jarrick's hand to block properly, so he grabbed the blade with his palm. Jorg pushed harder, feeling the sharp edge slice into flesh. He hesitated for a split second.

It was all Jarrick needed to twist his shoulder and ram Jorg backward. Blood dripped from the dark elf's palm, but Jarrick gave it no notice. Jumping into the air, he spun into a kick aimed for Jorg's head, but Jorg caught the elf's foot in midair.

Using his momentum against him, Jorg twisted Jarrick's leg, feeling the knee pop as he did. The Dark elf landed on his stomach but only for a second. With just his arms, he propelled himself into the air and landed gracefully onto one foot. The other leg he gingerly balanced against the floor.

Out of respect for his opponent, Jorg waited before he charged forth again.

"Wait long enough, and I'll heal. Are you sure that's what you want to do?"

The talk fueled Jorg's rage. He charged forward but raised his fist instead of his sword. Jarrick grabbed him by the front of his tunic and threw him five feet into the nearest pillar. Jorg landed against his back. He fell to his knees and had to gather his breath, but Jarrick was there too fast. Grabbing him by the back of the head, he slammed Jorg once more into the pillar.

He tried for another, and Jorg elbowed Jarrick's side, finishing with a punch to his jaw. Using the hilt of the sword as they wrestled, Jorg slammed it into Jarrick's stomach. Then he clasped both fists together driving them into Jarrick's face.

Jarrick fell to his knees dazed. Jorg raised his sword. He only needed to bring it down, and Jarrick would lose his head.

But he couldn't do it.

Jarrick lurched forward, thrusting his shoulder into Jorg's stomach and shoving until Jorg's back slammed against the side of the dais.

Jarrick squeezed his hand around Jorg's throat, and Jorg clawed at Jarrick's eyes. They grappled, and Jorg pushed Jarrick off him. He caught sight of the dagger down by his feet, but, Jarrick followed his eyes and dove for the dagger first. Jumping to his feet, his knee either healed or ignored, he roared and slammed the dagger into Jorg's chest.

Jorg's eyes popped wide. He gasped and stumbled backward. Jarrick let go of the handle and stared at his son. Jorg slid to the ground, coming to rest with his back against the platform and his legs straight out. Jarrick crouched down and stared at what he'd done.

The dark elf's brows pinched together. His head shook side to side as if he were confused. He reached out and touched two fingers to Jorg's cheek, appearing stunned. Jorg saw the regret in his eyes. The life they could have shared, gone.

Ingrid—I hope you hear me. I love you.

Jorg didn't have the strength to keep his mental barriers in place. His eyes fluttered, and he fought to keep them open.

A shrill scream rang above all other sounds. Jarrick spun on his heels staying low as Galwain sprinted toward him. He stood and shoved her backward with both hands. Flying off her feet, she landed on her backside. Jarrick watched her scramble to get her feet under her and try to make another charge, but he didn't notice Bremen.

Jorg saw him though. The brothers met each other's gaze; Jorg's tired and fading, Bremen's desperate and pleading.

I think I would have liked having a brother.

Bremen didn't scream. He didn't shriek. He charged forward like an enraged bull. He pierced Jarrick's chest with his sword and kept going until it went all the way through.

He pulled the sword out. Jarrick swayed on his feet, and Bremen slid the sword through him one more time. The dark elf slumped to the ground. Bremen turned to Jorg and saw that he'd watched it all.

Behind Bremen, the ruvars stopped fighting. It seemed to Jorg that they'd become confused, then shuddered and fell. He swallowed and tipped his chin with a smile.

It took more and more effort for Jorg to catch a breath. He could feel his heart racing like a confused squirrel. Sounds muffled as if he was underwater, but he knew he wasn't. He wanted to rest. He closed his eyes and let himself lean further and further till his cheek met the cool tile. Then silence and peace enveloped him.

46

INGRID

Ingrid didn't know where her body ended and the sweet amber that surrounded her began. Since the magic threads had snapped into place, she'd floated free. Vaguely, she knew that she used to be different. It didn't bother her. She had no worries, yet something tugged at her occasionally as if trying to draw her away from the peaceful bliss.

It had been easy to ignore at first, but it had grown more insistent. In the distance of her mind, she recognized that she'd known another life once. Thinking about that made her feel cold, and she'd shove the thoughts away. Nothing could be better than where she was.

There was that buzzing again. Like a persistent fly in summer. Ingrid furrowed her brow. She remembered flies . . . maybe. Were they important? She didn't think so. The more she thought, the more she remembered that they weren't. They were pests. Why would she bother thinking about pests when she floated in bliss?

Then the buzz turned to a hum. A soft song that made a ripple in the amber, and she liked it. She let herself sway. When the hum grew louder, she listened on purpose, trying to determine the source. Ingrid's eyes were open, her heart was beating, and she could move if she wanted. When she looked around, everything was amber and without form.

I think that's odd. There should be shapes.

For the first time, she wondered if she'd forgotten too much. Perhaps she should be somewhere else? The hum grew louder and turned into muffled words. Ingrid reached out and waved her hand through the thickness. A voice carried through to her as a woman called her name.

Who is out there? Would you like to join me?

The thought occurred to her that she was alone. It would be nice to have company as she enjoyed the peaceful space. When she didn't hear the voice again, she grew worried. The amber crowded her. It didn't feel restful anymore. She wasn't floating; it trapped her. Like a fly! The substance grew thicker. If she didn't get out right away, she never would.

Help! Please help me!

She hoped the singing woman had heard her. It was harder to move her arms, and she wasn't sure if her eyes were open any longer.

"Can you hear me?"

Yes!

The woman's voice was clear that time, so Ingrid replied quickly. *Here I am. I can't move. Can you come to me?*

"Do you remember who you are?"

That was an odd question. She knew who she was. Didn't she? She was . . . her mind was blank. There were no memories to draw upon. She knew she had a name and a different life once. Yes, she remembered that, but what was it? Why didn't she know? An ache grew in her temples.

"Search your heart. Allow yourself to feel what your mind doesn't remember."

Wiggling and uncomfortable within the amber liquid, she

tried to do as the woman said. It was hard to concentrate as her surroundings grew more restrictive.

Suddenly, her heart squeezed, and her memories flooded back. Faces flashed into her mind; Jorg, Selby, Plintze, Bremen, her parents, her brother, and Selby's sister. Then she recognized the voice, too.

"Eir, please help me," she called.

"I'm here, child, but you must help yourself. When you bound the spell, you released your own essence as well. You need to draw from the amber and allow the Yggdrasil to restore you."

"How? It's becoming harder to move."

"Ingrid, concentrate. There isn't much time."

Ingrid heard the urgency in Eir's voice. Something wasn't right, and she couldn't figure out what. She had to bring the amber into her body, even though it no longer flowed like liquid. When she'd first touched the tree, there had been light. Then she remembered how the thread of her magic and the spell had shown with a brilliant golden shimmer. Though her eyes were closed, she searched.

There . . . just out of reach . . . a speck of gold. She willed it to come closer, and it grew larger as it did. By the time it brushed the tips of her fingers, it was large enough to fill her palm. She squeezed it, and light flared through her body.

A moment of excruciating pain coursed through her, and then she lay on the ground gasping for air. Grass tickled her cheek, and a gentle hand rubbed her shoulder. Turning, she met Eir's gaze. The goddess smiled at her, and Ingrid sighed.

She rolled to her back, then sat up. They were at the base of the Yggdrasil tree. Everything was at once familiar. Not because she'd been there before, but because she felt connected to it. Invigorated, she rose to her feet and looked around.

"The spell is bound," she said.

"Yes, you did well."

"I feel . . ." she let her voice trail off. How did she feel? Stronger, more aware, powerful. Then realization hit her. She'd not been floating, and the amber hadn't hardened. It had been her own essence seeping away. "How?"

Eir smiled and understood what she asked. "It was what the spell required. To bind the spell, you had to give up your magic, and with that, your life. I couldn't tell you that because it had to be of your own will that you made the choice."

She'd known, though. It was the way it would always happen. Regardless if she made the choice herself, the spell required the thread of her magic. The only way to release it was to release herself. But how was she alive?

"The Yggdrasil restored you. I could only call to you and hope you found your way back.

Ingrid looked down at her hands. They seemed the same. She touched her arms, her legs, her face, and she could tell no difference. But inside, everything was new. No longer did she have a thread of magic that coiled in her belly, it flowed through her veins. A thought struck her, and she reached down and touched a blade of grass. Instantly, a stem grew, and a large purple flower blossomed. Ingrid smiled, then snapped her eyes to Eir.

"Can I go home?"

"You can go anywhere you want. You are no longer bound by the laws of a human body."

"What am I now?"

"Partly the same as you've always been—Freya's descendant, only now you are as she is, a goddess immortal."

How can that be? "Immortal? Like her—like you?"

"Yes, like us."

"What happens now? Do I have to live here? I want to go home." Panic filled her, and she laughed because she didn't struggle to breathe or become nauseous as she'd always done before. She worried, but it didn't affect her physically. Her heart beat normally, and her hands didn't shake.

"You can live wherever you'd like, with whoever you like," Eir answered.

Jorg! With all the changes, she'd not asked about the battle. "Is everyone alright? Did Jarrick surrender when I bound the spell?"

"Jarrick was a stubborn fool, but the battle is over."

"I want to go back. Jorg and I can start a life now. We can deal with whatever changes have happened together. Will you take me?"

Eir sighed and hesitated before she spoke. "You can take yourself anywhere you want to go now. But are you sure that a life pretending to be a mortal is what you want?"

"I won't pretend. Jorg will understand, and we can decide what to do together."

Eir held her gaze and nodded. She took hold of Ingrid's hand. "All you need to do is think about where you want to go. Be as specific as possible, then go there. I'll take you this time— until you've had time to practice."

There was a sadness in her tone and in her eyes that Ingrid didn't understand. Perhaps because Ingrid wouldn't be her pupil any longer. She'd give it more thought later. All she wanted was to hurry and get to Jorg and her friends. She wanted him to wrap her in his arms and celebrate with her that the task was complete. They were free and could start their lives together.

Eir squeezed her hands. "You'll need to be strong. Are you ready?"

Ingrid flinched. Cocking her head to the side, she held her breath. Eir knew something she didn't.

47

INGRID

Ingrid and Eir arrived in the room's center with everyone's backs to them like a wall.

It had been dark before when she'd walked through with Jarrick, but Ingrid recognized the arched walls and the expansive space well enough to know where she was. Last time she was there, however, the room hadn't had dead ruvars scattered about.

She sensed various injuries in those still living, but she couldn't sort them between individuals. It was a new sensation.

Ingrid heard a muffled gasp and met Selby's stare. Instead of running to her as Ingrid expected, her friend stayed rooted where she was. Tears glistened on her cheeks, and Ingrid creased her brow.

Because of Selby's reaction, everyone else noticed her as well. Ingrid saw they all held the same sad expressions as they spun and stared at her. Even Bremen had glistening lines etched down his face. Off to the side, she saw the prone form of Jarrick. Unmoving and alone, she could tell that he was dead.

What bothered her as she scanned the room, was that she saw everyone—Plintze, Galwain, Caelya, the king—everyone except Jorg. Where was he? While she'd remained calm when she stood next to the Yggdrasil tree, her heart now raced, and a realization she refused to accept tried to rip through her resolve.

"Where is Jorg?" her voice was commanding and solid.

Everyone but Selby looked to the ground. Galwain's breath hitched, and tears streamed harder down her face. Why would they act like this? She trembled. Something was wrong. Horribly, terribly wrong.

Ingrid's eyes settled on the dwarf. "Plintze?"

He had his hat in his hands and wrung the edge between his fingers. When she'd said his name, he closed his eyes and sank his chin deeper into his chest. It was when the sconce light sparkled on a tear dropping into his beard that Ingrid panicked.

Her chest heaved, and she couldn't get enough air. A scream wanted to rip through her throat, but she forced it back. Her knees wobbled, and she swayed. Bremen rushed forward to steady her. In the process, he opened enough of a gap that she saw him. Lying on the floor. Still. Lifeless.

All the air sucked out of the room. Sound didn't exist, and Ingrid's vision caved in on itself until only Jorg was before her. With slow steps she dragged her feet forward, aware of Bremen's arm around her shoulders that kept her upright. The crowd parted and let her pass.

Her eyes homed in on the ivy and leaf pattern of the bone-handled dagger protruding from his chest, sunk deep into his heart. It was the one he'd given to her before the other battle they'd fought. The battle Jarrick allowed her to believe he'd died in but hadn't. He'd come for her, so they could be together. It wasn't right.

When they were close enough, she flung herself forward, letting her knees crack against the stone as she slumped over Jorg's unmoving form.

NO! I will not accept this. We have plans. Everything is in place now, and it's time for us. You will not leave me!

A hand brushed her shoulder, and she yanked herself away from it. Leaning over Jorg's chest, she lay her fingers on the side of his face. Sinking lower and lower until her forehead rested against his.

Ingrid didn't have to call upon her magic. It was always aware, always available. Her fingers crackled with it as she let the ridges and valleys of the dagger etch into her palm before she yanked it out and threw it to the side. Her other hand covered the wound.

There wasn't much blood. It had pooled under him on the ground. Jorg must have been lying like that for some time, long enough that only a trickle of crimson seeped between Ingrid's fingers. She ignored everyone and let the world fade away.

The other times Ingrid had healed Jorg, the images she saw inside his body were hazy and distant. This time, she found the view accessible, yet faded. She didn't see the bright reds and yellows of blood and muscle, but everything was light pink and ashen gray. His heart still pulsed, but barely. Far too much time stretched between each beat.

Ingrid concentrated on closing the puncture that ran deep into his heart. Then, she willed her anxiety to settle and her own heart to beat at a steady rhythm. When she had a regular cadence, she let it seep into Jorg's, willing it to match.

Nothing happened.

So consumed with watching his heart, she almost missed the flash of light that sparked at the corner of her vision. A golden glow that hadn't come from her flashed throughout his body, reforming shriveled veins and restoring lifeless organs. Not restoring—rebuilding. Elves could heal from most wounds, but even they had limits.

He was only half-elf. Did he have enough elven blood to heal himself? Ingrid added her own energy to help it, using a gentle push to blend it with his own.

She watched the sparks move through his body. Organs stretched and grew healthy, except for small sections in each one. It was the human part. As the elven blood revived, it replaced what had been in his dying human veins. The threads of gray absorbed into vibrant hues awash in life. Under her palm, she felt the thump of a beat, then another until Jorg's heart kept time with hers.

Her eyes fluttered open, and she stared at his face. He didn't move or look different from when she'd fallen next to him, but then his skin brightened. A luminescence spread across his face.

Ingrid gasped, and her excitement grew. Jorg's skin glowed with the vitality of life. She cupped his face as tears blurred her vision. A movement under her fingers made her brush Jorg's hair away from his ears. They were growing, extending longer with the same pronounced points that the other elves had.

"Wake up, my love. Come back to me," she whispered.

48

JORG

Jarrick was dead. Ingrid would be safe. That's all he'd wanted. Well, not all, but it was most important. He was tired, so tired. If he could rest, then he'd be better.

Why couldn't he sleep? It was as if the battle continued, only it had moved inside of his body. His chest felt split open and seared with fire. Pain flared then ebbed through his back, his arms, and his legs.

In the part of his mind that still paid attention, he knew he was dying. He wanted to wait for Ingrid, but he didn't think he could. It was like his insides were two armies in a melee, and both sides were losing.

Then, slowly, he felt the shift. The tide turned, and he knew he'd never see her sweet face again. All his strength drained until his mind fell silent.

The skies glowed in aubergine hues. A butterfly swirled through the air on a lazy wave, and in the distance, birds chirped in the trees. The scent of wildflowers and honey filled the air in a heady mixture that made his mind giddy.

Ingrid lay next to him, tucked under his arm with her head on his shoulder. He tipped his chin and kissed the top of her head. Inhaling, he realized it was her heavenly fragrance that filled his senses. He sighed, content to stay just like they were forever.

"Jorg."

"Yes, Hjarta?" He waited for Ingrid to answer, but then he realized she hadn't said anything. In fact, they'd been laying together for hours, and she hadn't even moved. Perhaps she was asleep. But, how did he hear her?

He tipped his chin to look at her, but her hair was in the way to see her face. Should he disturb her? No, he'd let her rest.

"Please don't leave me."

Jorg pinched his brow at Ingrid's words. Again, they didn't come from her, yet it was her voice. She sounded different that time, too. Something in her tone, but he couldn't place it. Sad? No, it was more . . . anguish. She was in pain!

Jorg sat up, and the surrounding scenery changed. Ingrid was no longer beside him, and the sky and peaceful meadow were gone. A murky gray fog pressed in on him.

What is happening?

Rising to his feet, Jorg peered around, trying to pierce the veil and understand where he was. Then he watched as everything changed again. He was a boy winning a foot race while his father collected bets. There was another shift, and he stood inside a circle of older boys who jumped him and left him huddled in the dirt. He chuffed at that memory. It was the last time he'd let anyone win a fight—he'd been twelve. His family had moved after that, and he'd met Hagen.

The world around him shifted several more times. Jorg watched as memories from his life surrounded him. It occurred to him that such changes should be disorienting, but they weren't. Like a spectator, he witnessed events that had shaped him into the man he'd become.

The last few though, the times he'd shared with Ingrid, they made him ache. He'd wanted to reach out and touch her, but he couldn't move. Suddenly, he stood over her as she cried against *his* chest.

That wasn't a memory he could place.

"Wake up, my love. Come back to me," she whispered.

I'm here, Hjarta. I won't leave you.

Once again, Jorg was among the hazy grayness. It swirled around him, creating a roar of wind in his ears. He covered them and fell to his knees. Pain radiated in his chest, then throughout his body as the pressure built. Then, as if grabbed by an unseen force, he was plunged into the fog.

Golden light pulsed behind his closed eyelids. The pain subsided and so did the noise. He lay on his back, and something soft and warm rested on his chest.

With more effort than he knew it should take, he forced his eyes to open. He blinked, trying to get his bearings, but something caught in his lashes. It was blonde hair.

He swallowed, and she must have felt it because Ingrid sat up with a start. Her bright turquoise eyes, sparkling with tears as she gazed down on him.

She flung herself onto him, and he moaned, but when she tried to pull away, he wrapped his arms around her. Without letting go, he sat up and slid her into his lap. When he finally relaxed enough to lean back and look at her face again, she was glorious.

"You look different," he said. His voice scratched against his throat.

"So, do you," she answered with a smile.

Other sounds assaulted his hearing, but he ignored them for

the moment. "You came back." He ran his hand through her hair. While he couldn't pinpoint it, she'd changed somehow. She was stronger. Vitality and power thrummed under his fingertips as he caressed her cheek.

He loved her so much it overpowered all his other senses. When she lay her hand against his face, he stopped breathing for a moment. Then her fingers trailed to his ear, and he felt her soft touch as she followed the outline. Her eyes never left his, as if she were watching, waiting, for his reaction.

Jorg gasped, and then he knew. Everything became clear. He'd not awoken from sleep—but from death. Somehow, he'd transformed. His human body changed, and he'd become a full elf. It bothered him a little, but he'd think about it later. At that moment, all he cared about was how Ingrid watched him.

He leaned forward and pressed his lips to hers. *I love you.*

I love you, too.

Jorg felt her smile against his mouth. *I want to marry you and never leave each other's sides again.*

It's about time you figured that out.

He nudged her playfully, and she giggled. When she rolled her bottom lip between her teeth like she always did, he thought his heart would explode.

Jorg finally allowed himself to pay attention to the muffled noises around him. He peeked out the side of his eye, to see a crowd of legs pointed toward him, just out of reach.

Will they go away if we keep ignoring them? he asked Ingrid and relished the ability to speak with her through his mind.

"No, especially when you leave your thoughts open for all to hear," a voice from the crowd responded.

Both Jorg and Ingrid turned their faces toward everyone. Tears and smiles beamed from them. When Jorg moved to stand, he noticed the stickiness of his tunic and the surrounding tiles.

A large hand reached into view, offering to help him out of the muck. Bremen grinned as Jorg took hold. He pulled Jorg upright then wrapped him in a tight hug. It only lasted a moment before others interrupted for their own greeting.

Selby practically knocked him off his feet again. Plintze tried for a wordless handshake, but Jorg knelt and brought him close. When Galwain approached with red, puffy eyes, he pulled her tight into his arms. Even the king and the princess hugged him.

His family, those who mattered, had survived. Peace flowed through Jorg in a way he'd never known.

There was only one more matter to finish.

49

INGRID

Ingrid stretched against the soft down of the mattress. She was in her rooms of the palace once more. It felt good to relax without fear of what the day would bring. She let her mind wander to everything that had happened over the last two days. After Jorg had revived, and they'd faced the carnage at Montibeo.

Thelonius performed a small funeral ceremony for Jarrick. They'd all attended and watched as the pyre flames rose into the sky. He'd been a prince of Alfheim with noble dreams once. It was the right thing to do, but none of them would ever forget who he'd become and what he'd done.

There was another combined funeral for the fallen elven soldiers. That didn't include Kelvhan. When he'd been found alive, Caelya had broken her stoic resolve and ran through the snow to him. She and Aguane had taken him right away to the palace to heal.

When Jarrick fell, so did Voxx. The other dragons carried her body away. Thelonius said they'd choose a new queen, and he'd negotiate a peace with them. Without Jarrick or Voxx, the connection that bound the ruvars also severed, and they'd fallen where they stood.

The giants had tried to force the king to honor Jarrick's deal and let them cross through Alfheim into Midgard. They'd captured Plintze and used him for ransom, but faced with Eir's power and Thelonius' army, they'd surrendered and slunk back home, leaving the dwarf as a concession. They'd stopped an impending war, but the increased tension between the realms would continue.

It had been a long emotional experience. When they arrived back at the palace, everyone was tired and in need of rest. Despite protests, Bremen and Kelvhan had insisted that Jorg join them for some male only, pre-mating rituals. They'd each had a gleam in their eyes when they'd drug him off. Jorg grumbled and complained, but he had a grin on his face when he'd winked at Ingrid before disappearing around a corner.

The door to her room slammed open against the wall, startling Ingrid to jump to her feet atop the mattress. Selby bounded over and bounced onto the bed with her. Ingrid fell backward and giggled with her friend.

"You're getting married today!"

"I know," Ingrid bit her lip but couldn't keep the smile from splitting her face. "I tried to wait another day and not interrupt the king's birthday festival, but he insisted he'd rather not have the attention, anyway."

"This place is amazing. Do your rooms have a bathing chamber like mine?" Selby asked.

"It does." The backs of Ingrid's eyes stung, but she fought the tears. She'd shed too many sad ones recently and didn't want to taint her wedding day. Still, she couldn't help thinking of everything Selby had suffered to find her. Ingrid reached over and gently touched the scar on her friend's cheek. "I can help with this, you know."

Selby slapped Ingrid's hand away and let her own fingers trail over the ragged line. "I know, but I kind of like it. Besides, Bremen says it makes me look more like a warrior." She wiggled her brows with a grin. "His people will give me more respect because of it, too, I guess."

After the wedding, Selby, Bremen, and Galwain would return to Midgard. They would go to Ireland and marry according to Celtic tradition. Selby would be a princess. It made Ingrid smile and wonder how that would work. It would be an adventure and one her friend deserved after all she'd been through.

"Are you two going to lounge around all day? I thought Ingrid was eager to get to the village?" Caelya asked as she and Galwain entered the room.

Ingrid scooted off the bed, dragging Selby with her. Her strength still surprised her. It would take time to adjust to her new status as an immortal.

A cool breeze wafted into the room. Selby shivered and moved slightly behind Ingrid's shoulder. Aguane entered, carrying a gown over her arms.

"Let's start with a bath," Galwain said, and all the women headed off to ready Ingrid for her big day.

50

INGRID

A large platform had been erected in the center of the village. It was meant for Thelonius to preside over the festivities and revel with the crowds. Instead, it had pillars wrapped in ivy at each corner, flowers and plants growing from pots set in groups along the edges, and too many candles to count.

It was early evening, and the brightest light of the day had given way to the purple hues of twilight. In the distance, Vimala stood shining on a grassy hilltop as Thelonius and Eir waited in the center of the platform, facing the stairs where Ingrid approached. Caelya and Selby were to the right, Bremen and Plintze to the left. Ingrid, however, only had eyes for Jorg, who stood waiting for her at the top of the stairs.

Aguane had dressed her in a light teal gown made from a fabric that shimmered in the low light. Her hair cascaded in curls down her back, and a small silver diadem encircled her forehead. She epitomized her new status as a goddess.

Jorg wore a deep blue tunic over black trousers. A sword hung from his waist with a golden hilt encrusted with rubies and sapphires. His hair was pulled away from his face, and his ears stood tall and proud. It made him even more handsome, and Ingrid held her breath as he took her hand. She giggled as the dimple in his cheek burrowed deeply as he smiled.

A crown of silver in the same leaf and ivy pattern as Thelonius and Caelya's sat on Jorg's brow. He'd accepted his position as a prince of Alfheim, somewhat begrudgingly, but it suited him.

They stood together as Thelonius and Eir took turns saying words, wound a cloth around their entwined hands, and made them repeat their vows. Ingrid hoped she'd remember it all later, but at that moment, she was too happy to think about anything other than Jorg.

When he bent to kiss her, a shock wave jolted through them both. It was the bond locking into place. More than a simple agreement to love each other, their souls connected and wove together—inseparable for eternity. They smiled at each other and kissed once more to the cheers of the crowd.

Music and laughter filled the village. A constant stream of well-wishers approached Ingrid and Jorg. Others bowing to them took them a while to accept.

They'd danced when they could, ate from platters spilling over with food, and soaked in the joy. Several times, someone asked them about where they'd live or what they planned for the future. Ingrid didn't care about any of that. She knew there were details to work out, and they had responsibilities to fulfill, but they'd think about it later.

In a rare moment, when the couple had only a few others around them, Plintze caught Ingrid's attention. He stood off to the side and nodded to her. He held his staff and appeared to be going somewhere.

Ingrid squeezed Jorg's hand, and he followed her gaze. Together, they strode over to the dwarf.

"You aren't thinking of leaving?" Jorg asked.

"Ach, it's time," Plintze said. "I need to go."

"Why? Where will you go? Can't you stay with us?" Ingrid heard the desperation in her voice, but she couldn't help it. The thought of Plintze going away pained her. Since the moment the cranky dwarf had sauntered into her life back on the moors, he'd grown into one of her dearest friends.

Plintze stared at the ground, shifting his weight from one foot to the other.

Don't push him to stay, Hjarta. If he wants to leave, we need to respect that.

I'll miss him too much.

Jorg pulled Ingrid close and kissed the top of her head. She huffed a wry laugh to herself. With all her new power and abilities, she had grown no taller.

She reached out and took hold of Plintze's hand. "Wherever you go, will you send word, so I know you're safe?"

"Humph." Plintze eyed her sidelong with a grin.

Ingrid's cheeks pushed into her eyes as she smiled back. "How am I supposed to live without you?"

"Lazuli is alive. Eir told me, and I need to find her."

"What?" Ingrid and Jorg said together.

"How is that possible?" Jorg asked. "You searched for her before we left and never found her."

"She hid from me," Plintze said. "Eir found her and healed the injuries on her shoulders where the wings used to be. Now she's living alone, embarrassed to show herself to anyone."

The thought of the mischievous sprite as a recluse broke Ingrid's heart. "Will you go back to the home where you lived when we met?" Ingrid asked, hoping it was true. Then she'd know where she could visit them.

"Aye."

"I can't imagine anyone better to care for her," Jorg said and squeezed Plintze's shoulder.

Ingrid wrapped herself around the dwarf in a strong hug. It hurt to let him go, but he deserved happiness—even though thoughts of he and Lazuli bickering and pestering each other made her wonder if happiness was what he'd have. Then she realized they'd care for each other, and in their own way, it would be more than happiness. It would be love.

They watched him walk away through watery eyes. Eir tipped her chin to them as she took his hand, and they disappeared.

When they turned back to the revelry, Ingrid tugged at Jorg's sleeve. He stopped and gazed at her, a question creasing his brow.

In the distance, Selby's laughter rang out. She and Bremen danced happily. It seemed so long ago she and her friend had sat on a barrel, watching the other girls practice while hoping to become shieldmaidens. They'd wanted grand adventures and glory.

Ingrid shook her head with a grin and focused on Jorg. "I think we deserve time alone now, don't you?" she asked.

"It's all I've wanted for hours." His voice rasped as he stepped closer. "For years, actually," he whispered against her ear as he kissed her neck.

Ingrid leaned into him, and Jorg fell backward, landing on a soft mound of grass. She'd opened a portal behind him and taken them to a hidden valley Caelya had told her about.

"I like your new talents," Jorg said with a laugh as he sat up.

She snuggled herself onto his lap as they scanned the area. Just as Caelya had described, a small cottage sat in the distance, nestled among the trees. Nearby, a waterfall created a private swimming hole. Bushes laden with blue and red berries sweetened the air. It was a private hide-away all to themselves.

"How long do you think it will take the others to notice we left?" Ingrid asked.

Jorg brushed his fingers through her hair and held her gaze. "I don't care, but they won't be seeing us for a long time." He kissed her, and she melted into his arms.

They had forever, and she'd treasure every minute.

ACKNOWLEDGMENTS

I have to say thank you, to you—my reader—first and foremost, because when you bought my book, you changed my life. When I started this writing journey I had no idea where it would take me. It was a crazy idea that began years ago and needled me until I finally decided to give it a try.

Creating a character and developing a life for them is a personal experience. There's a reason authors call their books, babies. Just like in real life, sending our babies out into the world on their own, is terrifying. We hope they make friends, fit in—yet stand out as special, and succeed. The only way we know, as authors, if that dream comes to fruition, is when we hear that others enjoyed our work.

I absolutely love what I do, and I have you to thank for it. I get up every morning excited to create more adventures and develop more worlds to enchant and entertain. It gives me purpose that I can share it with you. So thank you, truly with all my heart, thank you.

Without a support system, however, I'd be lost. I'm somewhat of a work-a-holic, and I wouldn't eat or go outside some days if it weren't for my family. They keep me grounded (and fed) and help me enjoy real life. Craig, thank you for having real discussions with me that start like: Would an elf be able to . . . or how would a dragon. . . . Wearing blanket capes to draw a sword, blocking out fight scenes, and watching research videos instead of movies fills my love-tank! Sydney & Audrey, knowing that you are proud of me never fails to bring tears to my eyes. I love you both so much! How could I function if I didn't have you with me every minute, Libby and Bear?

To my parents, brother, aunts, uncles, and cousins: no one has a better family than I do! Your encouragement means the world!

There's a saying in Proverbs that goes: As iron sharpens iron, so one man sharpens another. Well, that is the perfect definition of my critique partner, Ashley McLeo. You set a worthy pace and I'm happy to have you as a friend on this journey.

To my "Novelistas", I also give my gratitude. The advice you give me is invaluable and necessary—as you all know! Thank you for reading my early ugly drafts.

I thank the Lord everyday for His strength to keep me sane in this crazy mind of mine.

ALSO BY KELLY N. JANE

The Viking Maiden Complete Series

Ingrid, The Viking Maiden

Amber Magic

Realm of Fate

Enchanted Shadows

Rune of Secrets

Rune of Thorns

Rune of Oaths

Rune of Blades

Rune of Crowns

The Royal Quest Complete Series

Dragon Prince

Dragon Magic

Dragon Mates

Dragon Betrayal

Dragon Crown

Dragon War

ABOUT THE AUTHOR

Kelly is a USA Today bestselling author who writes heroic epic fantasy immersed in elaborate worlds rich with myth, magic, slow burn romance, and fast-paced action.

In her office, there's a chihuahua on her lap and a cat nearby. Coffee always flows and she believes that dessert goes with every meal. When she's not in front of her keyboard, she's probably reading, playing with yarn, or on a wild rabbit chase down an interesting research trail!

www.kellynjane.com